[illegible]2076-1-8

Love and gratitude to the friends and family who supported me.

Special thanks go to Kate McEwan who gave me the inspiration to start and Adam Crowther who gave me the confidence to finish.

The Second Envelope

By Suzy D Harris

CHAPTER ONE

It was a disgusting sight. Well, it disgusted me. I was getting out of the shower and I noticed them. My feet. It wasn't my feet themselves, really, I mean, I'd had them for fifty years. It was the state of them. There were a few chips of polish left, the nails were ragged and the skin looked old and dry. Neglected. Forgotten. I picked at a little nugget of polish on my big toe. Something coral. I had a dim memory of an expensive pedicure, and some faceless woman bending over my foot, cradling it as though it was her own child. Now look at it. More like a Dickensian vagabond.

I dressed quickly in my borrowed clothes, but it was unsettling. If I started noticing things, where would it end? All winter I'd been keeping my gaze on the floor, just doing one thing at a time. If I started looking around me – who knows what might happen?

I went downstairs to prepare the breakfasts. The kitchen cupboards were papered with timetables, lists, instructions. There was no need for me to think for myself, and that's what made it perfect.

I turned the sausages and added bacon to the pan. The tomato went under the grill and I opened a can of baked beans. The full English breakfasts were for the couple in Room 1, the nicest room in Glebelands Guest House; a big bay window on the first floor, overlooking the village and the sea. There was one other guest, in the single – Room 6 – and he'd ordered porridge, which wasn't too taxing, even for me. I went into the dining room to check the tables I'd laid up last night, and I could hear the couple in the room above me, moving around. I made sure both kettles were filled and turned them on. This was my favourite time of the day, before the guests came down and I actually had to talk to people. This was the time of day when I thought I could cope.

Now the couple from Room 1 were on the stairs and I ran to look at the register – what was their name? Janice had been very strict about that, *always call them by their name, little things matter to the customer.*

'Good morning, Mr and Mrs Harper!' I said, standing up straighter as they came in.

They were a pleasant looking couple, tidy and trim with no gloss. She had salt-and-pepper hair, or rather salt-and-cinnamon. She'd been a redhead but obviously didn't mind going grey.

'Good morning to you, Isabel, are we here?'

'That table, yes.'

'Oh, you're so lucky to live in Gorran Porth,' Mrs Harper said, settling herself. 'Have you been here long?'

'I, well, I don't really live here,' I said.

She looked at me in surprise. 'But here you are!'

'I was staying next door,' I said, pointing vaguely, 'and I got to know Janice – this is her guest house – and then she needed to take some time away...I'll get your coffee.'

While the coffee steeped I looked down at my feet again, now decently covered in a pair of Converse I'd found in a stranger's wardrobe. I'd been trying not to think about the future and definitely was not keen to address the past, but suddenly I was counting backwards. It must have been about six months since my last pedicure. Pedicures were the first thing I gave up. Then I stopped getting my hair cut. My chin-length bob was sharp and precise, and it took a lot of maintenance to keep it that way. One day, I just didn't go to an appointment. I have no idea why. A week or so later I cancelled a manicure. A month after that, I stopped going to work. By then, showering was a major effort. Eventually, when there was nothing else to give up, I stopped getting out of bed. Don't judge me. Not yet.

The timer pinged again and I stopped remembering and looked at the list Janice had left me.

The Harpers were clattering away in the dining room – cereal bowls, fruit juice, all the rest of it. I took the coffee to their table.

'I hope you slept well?' I said, 'There was an incredible storm last night.'

'Is that what it was?' Mrs Harper said. 'We heard a lot of banging about, didn't we, Jim?'

Jim nodded round a mouthful of Shredded Wheat.

'And breaking glass, too,' Mrs Harper said, helpfully.

'Oh dear.' I looked out of the window. The large house next door – The Manse – was my real priority, not the guest house, even though I was actually living in Glebelands Guest House and running it until Janice returned. Passing myself off as a competent, responsible person.

'I think that other gentleman might have taken a tumble too – judging by the noise,' Mrs Harper said quietly, raising a conspiratorial gaze to the ceiling.

'The other gentleman? Oh! The man in Room 6?'

'Yes. We met him when we were coming in yesterday. He was going out. He didn't want to chat though, he looked as though he was in a hurry. Then we saw him again, on the harbour wall last night, didn't we, Jim?'

Jim nodded again.

'And we heard him come in, and what a

racket he was making.'

'Drunk, probably,' Jim spoke, at last.

'Oh, Jim, we don't know that. He might just have been clumsy!'

The timer pinged again.

'Ready for your breakfasts? I'll fetch them now.'

While the Harpers were tucking in, I stirred the porridge for Room 6, and looked in the register. I'd written the name in myself, the man had been in a hurry to get to the bathroom. 'Long journey!' he'd said, looking pained, and I'd just taken the cash and written his name in the book.

Derek Moffat. I couldn't recall his face.

I went back to the table to see if the Harpers needed anything else.

They had their maps out and were planning their day. The village of Gorran Porth isn't on the road to anywhere, unless you could walk on water. But the South West Coast Path passes right through it, and even in March there had been a trickle of hearty types with rustling outdoor gear, resting their weary legs at the guest house before heading off for the next little village. That's why Janice didn't just close up, and that's why I stepped in, though how she persuaded me I couldn't quite remember.

'You're booked in for two nights?' I wondered out loud to the Harpers.

'Yes that's right. We like to break it up a bit, don't we, Jim?'

Jim nodded.

'So I'll see you again for breakfast tomorrow. Same thing again?'

'Lovely, thanks,' Mrs Harper said. 'It doesn't look as though the other gentleman is going to eat his breakfast, does it?'

'No. No it doesn't. But he only asked for porridge, so...I'm really sorry he disturbed you.'

'Oh good Lord! That's not your problem, is it, Jim?'

Jim shrugged.

'No, no, you've got to expect this kind of thing.'

'Well, all the same – ' I started.

There was a ring at the doorbell.

'I hope you'll have a lovely day, enjoy your walk.' I hurried to the door.

I could see through the frosted glass that it was the postwoman, her bright jacket like a beacon. I opened the door.

'Morning, my dear,' she said, pushing her fine brown hair back from her red face. 'Phew! Warm for the time of year, mind.'

'Hello,' I said. I'd seen her before, of course, in the distance. She pushed a pair of bulging trollies and she seemed to go up the steep hill without breaking a stride. She was breathless now though.

'Post?' I said.

'No!' she said. 'That's the thing. I just been past The Manse – next door, and there's a window broken in the porch. Yes.'

I craned my neck to see past her to the Georgian house next door. It belonged to my boss, and when I'd stopped going to work, he'd arrived at my flat and given me an ultimatum. He was paying me to work for him, and if I couldn't do that on the 23rd floor of The Shard, I could damn well go and house-sit for his holiday home in Cornwall, until he figured out if he was going to sell it or give it to one of his plentiful ex-wives.

Behind me I could hear the Harpers going back up to their room and I turned and gave them a cheery wave.

'Do you want to come in?' I said to the postwoman.

'Well, I've got a minute,' she said, and she barrelled past me down the passage and into the dining room.

She was taller than me, and she looked full of life and energy, her hair wild and her face glowing. She was maybe about my age but she worked outdoors most of the time and that was written on her skin. Under her long grey shorts her calves were strong and businesslike. She looked capable and energetic and slightly ruthless. She sat down in the dining room and I went back out to the kitchen.

'Coffee? Tea?' I called out, stirring the porridge again as I passed the stove.

'Cup of tea, lovely.'

I filled the pot and brought a mug to the table. She was sitting where the man in Room 6 should be, but I still couldn't hear any sounds of movement from above.

'I'm Pat, by the way,' she said.

'You're kidding me.'

'What?'

'Post*woman* Pat?'

'Oh. I'm used to it.' She gave a big smile, her head on one side, not attempting to hide how thoroughly she was looking me over.

'I'm Isabel. I'm looking after things, until Janice gets back.'

Pat nodded. 'We were dead impressed when we heard Janice was leaving you in charge. She's never done that before.'

'Hasn't she?'

Pat shook her head. 'No way. She usually shuts down for a few weeks to take a holiday. Not that she does that very often. You must be something special.'

'It wasn't a holiday, though. It was unexpected.' I wasn't sure how much of Janice's business she wanted shared around the village. I went to the side window to look out again at The Manse.

'I need to get round there,' I said. 'I'm responsible. I need to check what's missing, call the police.'

'Go now!' Pat said, flapping her hands at me.

'I can't. There's a guest who has to come down for his breakfast. I don't think he's even awake and he knows very well what time he should have been here. Mr Harper thought he was drunk last night. He's probably sleeping it off, but I'm not here to pander to him, I'm here to cook his breakfast.' I stopped. I don't think I'd spoken so much in one go since I'd arrived in Cornwall. I gave a little cough.

'Who is Mr Harper?' Pat said.

'One of the other guests.'

'Ah. Right. Have you thought about going up to see him?'

'Who?'

'The man with the hangover. You could take his breakfast up to him, then your job's done, and you could go round to The Manse.'

'That seems sensible.'

'I'm noted for it,' Pat said, smiling blandly.

'He's only having porridge. I could do that.'

'Well. Problem solved. In the meantime, if you like, I could call my nephew, Horatio.'

I just looked at her.

'He's a Community Support Officer. On account of, we're so far from the nearest police station. You'll want a crime number for the broken window.'

'Oh my God. That would be amazing! Thanks so much. I'm really grateful.' To my absolute horror, my voice was wobbling. She pretended not to notice, and got out an ancient mobile phone and started tapping. I cleared her mug and teapot away while she left a message – by the sound of it – for Horatio.

'There's a patchy signal round here,' she said as she put the phone away. 'So he might not pick up instant.'

'OK, Well, I'll give Mr Moffat a call, then I'll give him his breakfast, then I'll go and examine the damage in The Manse. I hope there's nothing missing. I'll have to call my boss.'

'Oh, he IS your boss then,' Pat said. 'We wondered.'

'Who wondered?'

'We,' she said, trying to look innocent. 'The whole village.'

'What did you think he was?'

'Well,' she shrugged, 'He has got a reputation.'

I laughed. I couldn't be offended at her suggestion, it was just too ridiculous.

'He has got a reputation,' I agreed, 'for only dating women in their early thirties. And I'm fifty.'

'Are you?' Pat looked interested. 'So am I. Twins.' She laughed again. 'You're wearing a bit better though.'

'No,' I said. I wasn't being polite. She wouldn't say that if she could see my feet.

'Yes, I don't mind, I'm an outdoorsy type,

see, with my job. And my horse. You're probably more the indoors type.'

I nodded. I couldn't argue with that. I straightened my apron. 'I'm going to go upstairs and wake Mr Moffat.'

'Shall I wait?' Pat said, 'In case he wakes up grumpy?'

I nodded again. That was really thoughtful. 'D'you mind? Just for a minute?'

She followed me out of the dining room. 'Right you are.' She pointed. 'You go on up, and I'll wait here, at the bottom of the stairs.'

I went up very quietly. The stairs were old and creaky, but I'd been there long enough to know how to do it.

I knocked on the door. 'Mr Moffat,' I said. 'Mr Moffat, I need to serve your breakfast now, there's been an emergency and I need to leave the premises to deal with it.'

I put my face against the door to listen for any movement.

I turned back to Pat and she started up the stairs, less carefully than I had done.

I rattled the door handle. 'Mr Moffat!' I said, not quite shouting. I didn't want the Harpers getting involved.

'Try the door,' Pat said. 'He might have gone out for a walk.'

I did. It opened. I put my head round the side of the door and stopped. Pat was close behind me and I took a step into the room. She slipped in and I shut the door silently.

We looked down at where Mr Moffat lay on the mock Persian rug in front of the wardrobe. The rug was dark red, and the wooden floor was dark too, so it was difficult to tell exactly how much of Mr Moffat's blood was lying there with him.

I looked at Pat.

'Hmm,' she said, standing with her hands on her hips and rocking slightly. 'He won't be needing his porridge.'

CHAPTER TWO

Mr and Mrs Harper were out in the hallway, getting ready to leave for the day. I tiptoed to the door and opened it a crack to watch them.

'They've gone,' I said, finally, turning back into the room.

Pat hadn't moved. Neither had Mr Moffat.

I stepped closer to her, though Mr Moffat wasn't going to be doing anyone any harm now.

We waited there for what felt like ages, and finally I realised nothing more was going to happen, unless I made it happen. I looked around the room. The bed was slightly rumpled, as though he'd rested on it before going out. It hadn't been slept in, though. The sheets were taut and the pillows smooth, qualities which Janice regarded as essential. She wouldn't have left me in charge if I hadn't been able to pass the bed-making test. I inched past Mr Moffat and opened the wardrobe. Nothing. No clothes hanging, no overnight bag or toiletries.

'No belongings,' I said.

Pat looked at me, silent.

'I'll have to ring someone, won't I? I mean, a relative? He'll have to have a wallet, and the information will be in that.'

She nodded. 'Try the bedside table.'

I stepped right over Mr Moffat and the Persian rug. There was nothing in the bedside table, and nothing in the small chest under the window.

'He's definitely dead, I suppose,' I said, more in hope than anything else.

'He's dead alright,' Pat said. 'Look at that head wound.' She pointed, decisively.

I leaned over him, expecting to see a neat round hole somewhere obvious.

What there was, though, was a jagged hole, above his right ear, clotted with hair and blood and something I didn't want to think about.

'He didn't die here, though,' Pat said. 'Or he was already dead when they made that hole.'

I gaped at her.

'Obvious, isn't it.' She gestured at the body like a magician's assistant, and then round at the room. 'No splatter.'

'Splatter?'

'Oh yes. Yes, you'd have blood splatter all over, with a wound like that.'

'Oh my God,' I said. I would have sat down on the floor, suddenly, if it wasn't for the fact that Mr Moffatt was already there. 'How do you know that?'

'Well, you know, all them shows on the telly,' Pat said.

'What shows?'

'You know, all the crime shows. They always tell you about the direction of the knife blow or the height of the shooter and the time of death and all that stuff. Proper science, it is. If he was alive when they made that hole in his head, there would've been a massive –'

'– Splatter,' I said. 'Can we agree, we won't use that word again?'

Pat nodded and patted her lips. 'You won't hear it from me. I'm just saying. Not saying. You know.'

'I have no idea,' I said. 'But I'll take your word for it.'

'I'm no expert,' Pat said. 'But I do know that. Still, let's leave it for Horatio.'

'Yes. He'll know what to do,' I said, as much to myself as to Pat.

'Well. I wouldn't go that far.'

I looked at her and she went on quickly, 'I've got to finish my round, as well. Dimity Price, up in Harbour View? She's thirteen today, loads of cards. Will you be OK if I leave you?'

'I will. If Horatio's on the way.'

'Yes. He'll be on the way, don't you worry. They've had a lot of damage though, from the storm. Trees down, a lorry over on the A30. Sand on the roads, all sorts.'

'It *was* bad, wasn't it.'

'Hmm.'

We took a last look around the room, both of us avoiding looking at Mr Moffat. I felt my legs were a bit shaky as I went downstairs, but Pat looked robust and cheery.

'I'll be off on my round now, but I haven't got much more. I'll be back soon as I can, promise.'

'Oh, I don't want to put you out,' I said.

'Have you got anyone else to call?' Pat said, though we both knew the answer was no.

'I'd love it if you came back,' I said.

'Right you are.'

CHAPTER THREE

After she'd gone, the house was silent and still, but not with the sense of an empty property. Mr Moffat was sending out some kind of faint signal and I was picking it up. I felt restless and twitchy and I went back to look at the register where I'd written his name. No address, and he hadn't wanted a receipt. I struggled to remember him checking in, but he interrupted something when he'd arrived, and I'd wanted to get back to it. I walked around the house distractedl not really doing much until I ended up back in the kitchen.

I turned the porridge off and was about to throw it in the bin when the doorbell rang.

I was suddenly quite nervous, but the person in the glass appeared to be wearing a uniform of some kind. As I walked up the hall, a faint voice called out.

'Hello! Miss...Isabel? This is Horatio.'

I opened the door to see a slight figure with a fluorescent tunic belted over navy trousers. As he came in, I could see a massive blue and white label on his back, proclaiming him to be a 'Police Community Support Officer'.

He was what I think people mean when they say 'fresh-faced.' Pink and flushed and very young. But something about the uniform gave him a certain power and that comforted me. We shook hands, and I introduced myself.

He took out a little notebook and wrote it down.

'Come through to the kitchen, can I get you anything? Cup of tea? Bowl of porridge?' Was I sounding a bit hysterical?

'Bowl of porridge sounds lovely, thanks.' He seated himself at the table.

Well, he was certainly unflappable. Then I realised, as I put the dish in front of him, that we'd called him to deal with a broken window.

'Lush!' he said, circling the bowl with squeezable honey. I waited until he'd had a few mouthfuls. No point spoiling everyone's day.

'When your aunt, Pat, called you,' I said, 'there had been a break-in, next door, The Manse.'

'Broken window, she said, in the Big House, that's what we call it. The Manse.' He looked up from the bowl.

'Broken window, yes, that's it. We don't know if there was also a break-in. Let's not get ahead of ourselves.'

'Oh yes, coulda been the storm, see, very

windy all yesterday, rising to a peak about 2am. I'll go over there now, take a look round, but don't you fret, Miss.'

'The thing is, officer, um, Horatio,' I said. 'There's now something else.'

'Oh yes?' He was looking around him.

'Tea?' I said.

'Oh, lovely, thanks.'

I got up to put the kettle on. And from the kitchen I called back over my shoulder,

'There's now a dead body in Room 6.'

I put two sugars in Horatio's tea myself and stirred it. He was writing in his notebook but I could see his hand trembling and his face was putty-coloured and looked slightly clammy.

'Here you are,' I said. 'Try and have a few sips. I shouldn't have sprung it on you like that.'

'Why didn't Auntie Pat tell me?'

'She didn't know, then. She came in to tell me she'd seen the broken window, and then she called you. But Mr Moffat didn't come down for breakfast, so she offered to stay with me while I tried to wake him up.'

Horatio took a gulp of tea.

'And you couldn't wake him up.'

'No.'

'Are you sure he isn't asleep?'

'Well, pretty sure. Don't you want to take a look?'

Horatio shuddered. 'Not me, no. I'll call it in, and officers will be here to take a statement and look at the crime scene and, you know. All that.'

'All that. Right. OK. But while you're here, could you take a look in The Manse? Only I'm house-sitting for my boss, and if there's been a break-in, well, I don't know how I'll be able to tell him.'

'Don't you live here now?'

'I'm *staying* here. While Janice is away. But I really should be staying in The Manse. Looking after that. That's why I came to Gorran Porth in the first place.' Well, that was a complete lie, wasn't it. I'd only just realised it. The Manse had been standing empty for months, years even, and my boss had only packed me off here on a pretext. Something else I was only noticing now. I rubbed my forehead.

'I'm only over here because I took on the cleaning, for Janice, so I already knew how things worked, a bit.'

'That's right!' Horatio looked triumphant. 'Clarice slipped on a chip and broke her arm, and all her ladies – that she cleans for – were left high and dry.'

'Right. So I took it on, to repay a favour Janice did me...look, is any of this relevant?'

He looked at me seriously. 'You just never know,' he said. 'You never know, until later.' He flipped his notebook closed. 'Let me phone this in. Right now.'

'Great. I'll just go upstairs and check the Harpers' room, straighten up. You finish that tea, won't you?'

The Harpers were pleasant people with nice habits, and I didn't need to do much; make up the bed, flick round the bathroom with a damp cloth, empty the bins and put the tea-tray outside the door to remind me to restock it when I came back upstairs. I lingered over the making of the bed and the various little efforts that Janice liked to put in. I didn't always agree with Janice's way, but Glebelands Guest House was her business, and I understood what a responsibility I'd taken on. Janice had given me a lot of training before she trusted me. People in my old life were paying hundreds of pounds for 'mindfulness' sessions. They could have just spent a day with Janice, making beds again and again, to achieve her hospital corners, arranging the towels to look like swans. The work was warm and meaningless, and full of comfort.

As I came down the stairs, I could see that Horatio was out by the front door, with something crinkly. I went to look. He'd spooled blue and white tape across the front door, attaching it to the sign which said *Glebelands Guest House*, and he was tying it in a criss-cross pattern to the old boot scraper at the side of the porch. The tape said: *Police – do not cross.*

'That's a bit dramatic,' I said.

'It IS dramatic.' Horatio looked at me, wide-eyed, and I could see the resemblance to his Aunty Pat. 'A person is dead. In this house! Possibly, murdered.'

'What? Murdered? No, no. Just dead. He's just dead.'

'Natural causes?' Horatio looked hopeful.

I rubbed at the goose pimples which had sprouted on my arms.

'No. I don't think so,' I said. 'Of course not.'

'I'll go over to The Manse now,' Horatio said. 'You wait here for the police.'

'Yes, of course. Or I could come over with you?'

'No. Safest if I go alone. But, is there a door key?'

I went into the kitchen and took my keys off the rack behind the door. All the room keys were on there, plus the keys for the heating oil tank and the wood store and the front and back doors of the house. I always put The Manse keys on the spare hook at the end. I gave him the whole bunch.

'I'm so glad you are here, Horatio,' I said. 'It is so good to know there's someone keeping us safe, right on the doorstep.'

He went off, looking brighter, bouncing on the balls of his feet, like a small boy looking for adventure.

I closed the front door behind him and went back to the kitchen. From here I could see the back of The Manse. The two houses had come to an arrangement, some years ago, to give up a slice of side garden, cover it with gravel and use it as a shared parking area. The Harpers hadn't arrived by car – they'd walked – so the space was empty at the moment and I could see clearly into the side window of the huge kitchen of The Manse. I saw a dark shadow pass the window, and then Horatio came clearly into view as he left the kitchen through the back door and moved into the garden. He was certainly being thorough.

I caught sight of the register and recalled Horatio's comment about it being dramatic. It was. It was a serious business. A person had met his end in this house, while I slept. *Wait. What*? Someone had been in the house last night, and had murdered one of my guests. I sat down suddenly on the kitchen tiles. My reflection in the oven door stared back. I looked a wreck. My hair was wild and my apron was askew. Janice would be livid if she could see me now. She'd left me in charge of her home, her business, and I was sitting around with a dead man in Room 6 and police hazard tape round the front door like a clear message to prospective guests: *don't stay here. Bad things will happen to you.*

CHAPTER FOUR

I was breathing slowly and deeply, trying to quiet the buzzing in my head, when the front doorbell rang. It was Pat, looking askance at all the police tape.

'Horatio's been busy I see. I'm just finishing up, I got to put my trollies away, then I'll come back up. You OK?'

I nodded. 'Horatio took it badly though.'

'He's soft, that boy.'

'He must have put up with some teasing, being called Horatio?'

'His father wanted him to join the navy. Being a Community Support Office is the closest he'll get to a job in the services. He should by rights be going to art college – he's a good painter.'

'Is he?'

'He does a lovely watercolour. I'll get off now. Here, hang on.' She reached into her pocket and offered me a Penguin bar.

'Thanks.' I looked at it curiously. Almost without thinking, I ripped open the wrapper and took a bite. It seemed to be the most wonderful thing I'd eaten in ages and I stared at the bright blue wrapper, transfixed.

As Pat turned her trolleys to leave, a black car came slowly along the lane. There were four people in the car, all men, all in suits. Their faces turned towards me as the car purred past. One of them gave a friendly wave and a smile and the car pulled in towards the front door. All the men got out and Pat turned back to me, her eyes wide. 'Shall I wait?'

'Go, and come back,' I said. She nodded. 'Hurry!' I mouthed at her and she turned, trolley bumping behind her as she rushed off down the hill.

The first man, the one from the passenger seat came towards me, his hand outstretched.

'Good morning, I'm Detective Inspector Smith.' He flashed his badge with his free hand.

'I'm Isabel,' I said, surrendering to a firm handshake and chewing frantically.

'I'm sorry for the unpleasantness you've had, it must all have been a terrible shock.'

'Yes, I suppose. I think I haven't really taken it in.'

'Hmm. Why don't we go and have a little chat, and let the experts take a look.'

I tried to swallow a chunk of Penguin and led him towards the kitchen.

'Is this your business?' he asked as we got settled at the dining room table.

'No, I'm just house-sitting, well, business-sitting I suppose, for the owner.'

I could see Horatio still in the back garden of The Manse. I suppose he'd come across and introduce himself in a minute. I hoped the policemen would be kind to him. They seemed to be in a different league from his still boyish frame and emotional response. They looked bigger, fitter, more confident. But you'd expect that, wouldn't you? I mean, that's what the people of Gorran Porth were paying their Council Tax for. I could hear the other men from the car making their way upstairs, though I was sure I hadn't told them where Mr Moffat was.

'You got here very quickly,' I said.

'We were in the area when we got the call. Cases like this, we don't like to leave people hanging around. Very distressing.'

He certainly had a lovely bedside manner. I hoped he would take as good care of Mr Moffat as he was taking of me. I started to relax a bit.

'Now, let's get some detail, shall we?'

'Would you like a cup of tea, would they like one upstairs?'

'In a bit, perhaps. Let's let the team get to work.'

I nodded. 'I suppose they've got to do photos and measurements and all that stuff.'

He laughed, showing perfect white teeth which matched the snowy collar of his shirt. He really was exceptionally well-dressed.

'It isn't quite like the TV,' he said, 'but yes,

we will gather as much information as we can. Do you know the name of the deceased?'

'Mr Moffat. Um, Derek Moffat.'

'Right. And, do you have any contact details for him? Phone number, anything like that?'

'No. He just arrived and asked if we had a room, yesterday, and I did have a room and he paid cash so, I know I should have filled in the details, but I just wrote his name in the register.' Was I sounding as panicked and shaken as I felt? I thought from his face I probably was.

But he nodded in an encouraging manner.

'Am I going to get into trouble? I know I should have got his address, but I was right in the middle of something and I wanted to get back to it. I'm sorry.'

'No, no, don't you worry about that. What were you in the middle of?'

I looked out of the window again. Horatio was no longer visible next door.

'Isabel? What was it you were in the middle of?'

'Nothing. I wasn't doing anything. I was just sitting. And I wanted to go on doing it. I actually resented him a bit, for knocking at the door, and bothering me. He wasn't booked in, you see, in advance. He just turned up. Unexpectedly.'

He said nothing, just kept that level gaze on my face. I was beginning to feel a bit flustered. Was it getting hotter in the dining room, or was it just me?

'How did you come to be running this business, Isabel? Someone else's business?'

'Is all this relevant?'

'Probably not, but I can't leave until my boys give me the all-clear upstairs, and I'm finding you very intriguing.'

'Well, I'm not. I'm not at all intriguing.'

'Tell me then.'

I sighed and rolled my eyes. 'I was staying next door, house-sitting for my boss. I had to get out because his brother and his kids were coming for the February half-term, *he said*.' Though they didn't actually arrive. 'So I needed a place to stay, and Janice gave me a room, very cheap. Then her cleaning lady broke her wrist, so I took over the housework for her and she gave me the room for free. And I sort of, moved between the two houses, as I needed. Then two weeks ago Janice's sister who lives in Chelmsford, stepped on a piece of Lego – her granddaughter's Lego, obviously, not hers, and it went septic, so Janice has gone to help out. See? I told you it wasn't intriguing.'

'Don't put yourself down, Isabel.'

He was a strange one alright. He must be one of this new breed of fast-track graduate-entry officers. There was nothing about him which suggested time on the beat, being vomited on by prostitutes, or whatever it was that beat coppers did. I couldn't quite decide if I liked him or not.

There was a ring at the front doorbell and I leaped up.

'I'll get it. Could that be more of your team?'

He shrugged and spread his hands wide, but he followed me a little too closely for comfort.

I could see it was Horatio and I introduced him to Smith when it was obvious they didn't recognise each other.

'Sir!' Horatio shouted, standing up as tall as he could.

'Great work, really well done,' Inspector Smith said, shaking Horatio's hand. 'Did you put the tape up? That was quick, quick and decisive.'

'I did,' Horatio said, flushing with pleasure.

'I wonder, though, if you might take the tape down, now. Just so that Isabel, and Janice's business of course, doesn't attract any unwelcome attention. What do you think?'

'Right, right. I'll do it now. And...is there anything else you need? Anything I could do to help?'

'Hmm.' Smith looked thoughtfully at Horatio. 'Did you take any notes of the crime scene? Did you examine the body?'

Horatio looked crushed. 'No, I...'

'Horatio insisted we kept the crime scene uncontaminated, didn't you, Horatio?' I said.

He nodded, not looking at me.

'So, no-one's been in the room?' Smith was controlling his disapproval very well, I thought.

'Well, I looked into the room, obviously, and saw that he was dead, and immediately sent for Horatio.'

'Yes,' Horatio nodded. 'That's what happened.'

'Well done,' Smith said again, to Horatio. 'Really very well handled, and I shall make sure I say so in my report.'

Horatio seemed to get a little taller. 'Right. I'll go and take the tape down.'

'Oh, and you might do one other thing,' Smith said, 'just take a look around, go round the block a few times, make sure no-one's watching the house, or parked strangely, that kind of thing; well, you know, as well as I do.'

'I'm on it, sir,' Horatio said.

We sat back down at the table. After his dealings with Horatio I liked Smith more. He seemed kind, and it was so good to be able to stop worrying, and let him be in charge. This is what people wanted from an authority figure, wasn't it? I was beginning to feel a bit peckish. I usually ate my breakfast after I'd cleared away behind the guests, but even if there had been time this morning, I wouldn't have felt like it. I had the other half of Pat's Penguin in my apron pocket but it seemed a bit rude to fish it out and finish it.

'Would you like some toast?' I asked Smith. 'Or maybe something more. Bacon sandwiches?'

'That does sound lovely,' he said, smiling widely. 'Let me go and check on my team.'

He went off up the stairs, and I noticed he was wearing expensive shoes under his very classy suit. They'd all looked smart when they left the car, but two of them had overnight bags with them, so I guessed they had those paper suits and plastic shoe things with them. I didn't watch the TV shows that Pat obviously loved, but I'd lived in central London long enough to have seen some crime scenes. They were being very quick and quiet and I was starting to feel a lot calmer. They would contact Mr Moffat's family and break the news, which was what I was most worried about.

Smith came back down, looking slightly concerned.

'Is everything alright?' I asked.

'You mean, apart from the dead body?'

He must have noticed I looked shocked. 'Sorry, just a little police humour. Inappropriate. Bacon sandwiches all round, if it isn't too much trouble.'

He followed me into the kitchen and I was annoyed to find how much it bothered me that I was wearing jeans belonging to a teenage boy, and a faded and tissue-thin Def Leppard t-shirt.

'Can I ask you some questions?' I said.

'Fire away, Isabel.' He was leaning against the kitchen door but it was the heat of the grill that made me feel a bit crowded and hot.

'Well, Mr Moffat was murdered,' I said. 'Here. So, someone was in the house last night, intent on murder.'

'What makes you say he was murdered?'

'Well, the blood. On the carpet. And the fact that he's dead. There's a hole in his head.'

'Ah. You had a little look, did you? Isabel?'

'Well, I had to establish that he was actually dead, and not just sleeping in. I mean, he could have been asleep, hungover, anything.'

'Hm. Well, you did see from the doorway that he had a large head wound? As to how he received the head wound, we'll have to conduct tests when we get Mr Moffat out of your way. He might perhaps have fallen on the way home? Or fallen in the room?'

'It was a stormy night,' I said, wanting desperately to agree with him.

'Exactly. Lots of damage all over the region. I don't think you should worry unduly at this stage, though that's all off the record, of course. Do you need to let that room again quickly?'

'No, it was very unusual to have that booking. I probably won't let it again for weeks. Maybe Janice will be back.'

And what would I do then? Back into The

Manse or was it time to move on?

'Isabel,' Smith said, stopping that train of thought. 'Could I ask you to keep Room 6 empty for a week, and don't clean it or go in there, in case we need to collect more evidence?'

I nodded, and turned the bacon over. I filled the kettle and brought down the biggest cafetière from the top shelf.

'Coffee?' I asked.

'You read my mind, Isabel,' he murmured. I turned the extractor fan on.

CHAPTER FIVE

He went out again to call his team for breakfast, and while he was upstairs Pat arrived.

'Who are they?' she said. 'Are they the murder squad?'

'They don't think he was murdered. He had a head wound, but he might not have been murdered.'

Pat frowned. 'No,' she said firmly. 'That's not right.'

'Please don't use the word splatter, again,' I said. 'Not in front of the experts. I've made them all breakfast, d'you want some?'

'Ooh, bacon, nice.'

Smith came back into the dining room and looked slightly ruffled at Pat being there. I introduced them and told Smith about Pat reporting the broken window and being there to help earlier today. I could see the exact moment he warmed up.

'Isabel is fortunate to have such a supportive friend,' he said, which left her looking delighted.

His phone let out a discreet ping and as he

turned away to answer it, Pat looked at me behind his back.

She jerked her thumb at him. "Andsome!' she whispered. 'And he isn't even in uniform!'

'Come on in the kitchen, help me make up the sandwiches.'

Smith put his phone away and left the room, moving more quickly than I'd seen him before. He rushed up the stairs and came back down with two of his men. They were still in their suits, so I guessed the one left up there was the technician doing the forensics. We worked quickly, keen to know what was going on.

'Breakfast!' Pat said, putting the plates down in the dining room.

'Have you got ketchup?' one of the men asked.

'Ooh, John doesn't drink coffee, do you, John?' Smith asked one of the men. 'Have you got any Earl Grey?'

'I'm sure we have. I'll look,' I said.

'I'll come with you.' Pat followed me.

Back in the kitchen I heard the front door open and close, and another voice joined the police in the dining room. Whoever it was didn't stay long, but headed upstairs.

I found some Earl Grey tea, but when I went out only Smith was there.

'Duty calls,' he said, looking apologetic. 'They've had to check one more thing,'

He had his back to the door now, and

looked slightly less relaxed than before. I guessed the late arrival must have been senior to him, and maybe he was in trouble for bacon butties and a bit of fraternisation with the locals.

'I hope everything's alright,' I said.

'Perfect. Fine. Absolutely.'

'I'll start, shall I?' Pat asked, sitting down in front of the stack of bacon sandwiches.

'I've got some questions for you,' I said to Smith. 'And you've probably got more for me? Do I need to do something official? Like, a statement?'

'Oh, I'll be in touch, I'll probably be back actually. If that's OK.'

I could see Pat, out of the corner of my eye, nodding slowly, her mouth full of bacon.

'Yes,' I said. 'I'd like to know, about Mr Moffat.'

'Of course.'

I heard the front door close again and then a vehicle door slammed. Obviously the senior officer hadn't stayed long. Well, why would he when Smith and his team were doing such a great job?

Then there were more footsteps coming downstairs, heavy and weary.

Smith looked at his watch.

'I need to get moving, I'm sorry to say.'

'So soon? Have you done all the things, you know, the photos and stuff?'

'Absolutely, you've been so helpful, Isabel.'

'Right.'

He turned to go and as I tried to follow him down the hallway, the phone in the kitchen rang. Pat jumped, and he smiled at us. 'You'd better get that, Isabel, life must go on. It seems harsh, I know.'

I tried to signal to Pat to go after him, see him off at the door, but she was engrossed in the bacon. I answered the phone with a quick gabble but there was no-one there, just a strange empty sound, like a deserted room. Once I was sure there was no caller there I slammed the phone down and raced from the kitchen, along the hallway and out of the front door. Too late; the big black car and the very smart policeman had vanished back into the Cornish landscape. I closed the door and stood in the dim hallway, feeling uneasy and trying not to think. I looked up and surprised a glimpse of myself in the mirror over the hall table. I really ought to brush my hair.

CHAPTER SIX

I was still in the hallway, thinking about Inspector Smith – and my hair – when Horatio came rushing up to the house.

'Have they gone?' he asked, leaning over on the hall table to catch his breath.

'Just gone. Did you see anyone? Like he asked you?'

'Only that writer chap. Nick.'

'I don't know him.'

'You don't know anyone, hardly,' Horatio pointed out. He was quite right. In London, I knew hundreds of people, hundreds out of millions. In the village of Gorran Porth, a village of about 200 people – in my reckoning – I knew three. Janice, Horatio and his Aunty Pat. I went shopping, I bought supplies for the breakfasts. I'd had a load of firewood delivered but I'd managed to do all that without really making contact with anyone. I thought about the handful of guests I'd dealt with since Janice left me in charge. It was a struggle to remember any of them. I wouldn't forget Mr Moffat in a hurry.

I turned away, quickly.

'Come on, there's some breakfast left, if

you've got space after the porridge.'

We sat down with Pat.

'Horatio,' I said. 'What about next door, The Manse?'

'No sign of anything missing,' he said, 'but you need to get over there and have a look, I can't really tell. Got some lovely things, hasn't he? Nice paintings and that.'

'He has. I don't know why he doesn't take it all back to London, he hasn't been here for years.'

They both nodded at that. I supposed everyone in the village knew who owned the house. Sir Dougall Spence was one of the most famous businessmen in Britain. My boss (or was he my ex-boss?) had his fingers in some large pies. Some were meaty and some were fruity but they were all expensive, and juicy.

'It was his missus who mostly decorated it, wasn't it?' Pat asked.

'I think so. Not the current wife. The one before that, I think.' I hadn't really taken too much notice of the house in Cornwall. Why would I? I liked holidays in the sun, with city breaks in the winter to soak up the culture. Why would I want to hide away in a little fishing village in Cornwall?

'I'll go over to the house now, I suppose,' I said.

'Have they finished upstairs, or are they coming back?' Horatio asked.

'They seemed to have finished,' I said. 'It

was a bit quick, wasn't it?'

'Did they take a statement?' Horatio wondered. 'Did they give you a crime number or any paperwork?'

I looked at him, dumbly.

'Did they do fingerprints?' Pat said. 'They should have taken our fingerprints, shouldn't they?'

'They don't know we went in the bedroom.'

'But you live here,' she said, 'they need to rule you out as a person of interest.'

Horatio nodded.

'Unless,' Pat said, 'You ARE a person of interest, to Inspector Smith.'

Horatio looked from Pat to me and back again.

'Don't take any notice of your aunt,' I said. 'We just enjoyed meeting each other.'

'He was looking at you, Isabel, like a seagull looks at chips,' Pat said, narrowing her eyes at me.

I shivered. I hated seagulls, with their sharp beaks and cold eyes.

'Still,' Horatio said, 'I think Aunty Pat's right. They should do fingerprints and that.'

'Have they taken him away?' Pat asked, looking up at the ceiling.

'Well, I hope so. I think so.'

'But they came in a car,' Horatio said. 'How did they take the body away?'

As one, we stood up and trooped up the stairs, in silence. We all took our time reaching the door of Room 6, but I'm proud to say it was me who stepped forward and turned the handle.

Mr Moffat was gone, and so was the Persian rug. The room was slightly different, not just the rug but a detail I couldn't quite place.

'What's that smell?' Horatio said, very quietly, as though afraid to disturb something.

'Lemon Pledge, that is,' Pat said.

'We don't use Lemon Pledge at Glebelands Guest House,' I said. 'Janice is quite strict on the lavender and beeswax policy.'

'Still. They've done a nice job,' Pat said. 'Left it lovely for you.'

'But they asked me to give them a week, in case they need to come back and do more tests.'

'That's alright then,' Horatio said, obviously keen to get out of the room.

The doorbell rang and we all jumped.

'Quick,' Pat said, 'Don't let's be caught in here.'

'Don't go downstairs!' I said. 'You'll be seen through the doorway. Wait on the landing, I'll go down.'

As I reached the bottom step, my heart started to pound. I put my hand on my chest, I could feel my pulse though the thin, over-washed t-shirt. Something was wrong, very wrong indeed. I think I even let out a little groan, because Pat shouted down the stairs behind me.

'Buck up!' she said.

There was a blue flashing light coming through the front door, and a dark figure tapping on the glass.

'Police!' came the cry. 'Are you alright in there, Miss? We've had a report of a crime.'

I opened the door. I could hear Pat and Horatio coming down the stairs, and I felt slightly light-headed. I stared at the two men on the front step and it was suddenly so obvious. They looked pale and tired, they had dark Cornish hair and the younger one was a little bit overweight. They both had notebooks at the ready. They were wearing dark suits, baggy at the pockets, slightly shiny at the knees. The older, taller one looked as though he hadn't ironed the once-white shirt beneath the jacket. He was the one who had knocked on the door. He stepped forward and told me his name. Detective Inspector Pirran Trenoweth. I couldn't say anything. He asked me a question which I couldn't understand. He asked me again.

'Are you alright, madam? Is there any danger in the house?'

'No. There's no danger.'

'We had a report of a death. Unexplained.'

I opened the door wider and waved them in. They had the pale and slightly doughy faces of people used to working under extreme stress and eating from corner shops. They showed me their cards on the way into the property.

'Something terrible has happened,' I said.

'Let's have a seat, miss,' the shorter one, Reynolds, said, 'and you can tell us all about it.'

I took them into the dining room. Pat and Horatio were at the bottom of the stairs now and they followed us in. We all sat down round the table and they wrote down all our names in their notebooks.

I started. 'Something terrible has happened.'

Pat looked at me, worried.

'You've mentioned that,' Trenoweth said. 'Why not start at the beginning.'

'I'm looking after this bed and breakfast, and this morning, one of the guests was late down for his breakfast.'

'Porridge,' Pat said.

We all turned to look at her.

'Sorry. Nerves.'

The taller policeman, Trenoweth, smiled at her.

'Not to worry, madam. It takes people in different ways.'

'Pat arrived, with the post,' I said, 'and told me that there had been a break-in next door, – The Manse – which I'm meant to be house-sitting.'

'You are a busy one,' Trenoweth said, writing it all down.

'And then Aunty Pat rang me,' Horatio said. 'To tell me about the break-in.'

'Yes,' I said. 'And in the meantime, I went upstairs, and Pat came with me. We went up to see if everything was alright with Mr Moffat.'

'The guest who was late.'

'Yes. He is late, now. Sorry.' It was my turn to be subjected to stares.

'So, you go upstairs to see Mr Moffat...'

'Yes. And he was dead. In Room 6. Wasn't he?'

Pat nodded. 'Dead, he was. And there was some blood, on the rug but nowhere else in the room.'

I looked at her sternly. I felt the word 'splatter' was hovering in the air.

'And then the police came and took him away,' I said in a hurry.

CHAPTER SEVEN

They put down their notebooks and looked at me.

Trenoweth was the first to speak. 'What police? From another station?'

'No. Actually, I think, now, not really police at all.'

Trenoweth looked as though he was trying to stay motionless, but a slight sneer whispered across his face.

'I'm sorry!' I said. 'Things like this don't happen to me. To us.' I looked at Horatio and Pat who nodded loyally.

'So, let me get this right,' Trenoweth said, tapping his pencil against the notebook, 'there was a dead person in Room...6? Room 6. But some people came and took him away. Pretending to be police.'

'It does sound incredible,' Pat said. 'Now I hear it out loud.'

'And did anyone except the two of you actually see the body?'

Horatio looked a bit miserable. Trenoweth stared at him then started writing again: 'Community Support Office number 5223, did you see the body?'

'Horatio told me we should preserve the crime scene,' I said.

That wasn't going to do it for Trenoweth.

'Really. So you didn't actually see if there was a dead body in Room 6?'

Horatio shook his head.

I was beginning to feel a bit sick. Something very strange had happened, and I just wanted these two police officers – who looked solid and safe and unflappable – to take care of it, and make it go away.

'And who do we think the deceased person is?' Trenoweth said, flipping over to a new page in his notebook.

'Mr Moffat,' I said. I got up and brought the register back from the hall table. 'I wrote his name in here, because he checked in really quickly, all in a hurry.' I spun the book round to face them.

Trenoweth traced the name with his finger. 'Mr Moffat. Address? None. Telephone number? None. Car Registration? None. Hmm. Not left us a lot to go on, have you, Miss?'

'Sorry. I was busy. Not busy exactly. Doing something else.'

'How did he pay?'

'Cash.'

'Did you give him a receipt?'

'No. I would have done that this morning, when he checked out.'

'But he'd already checked out,' Trenoweth said, with a thin, shark-like smile.

We all stared at him.

'Sorry,' he said, sarcastically. 'Nerves. Things like this don't happen to me. I don't generally get called out to a murder scene and find that someone's been there before me and sorted it all out.'

The other officer coughed and spoke up. 'Shall we take a look at the scene, sir?'

I got the feeling he'd said 'sir' for our benefit. They were probably on first-name terms where there were no civilians around. Especially idiot civilians who couldn't hold on to a dead body.

Trenoweth nodded and jerked his head at me. I led the way. Pat and Horatio trailed after us, but stopped at the bottom of the stairs. I climbed, very conscious for the second time that day, of a desire to brush my hair. I thought longingly of the bottle of expensive fragrance on my dressing table at home, in London. Then I felt furious that it mattered to me, when larger, more elemental things were happening right under my nose.

We stopped at the door.

'Room 6.'

'Can you unlock it for us?'

'It isn't locked.' I reached over and opened the door then stepped back to let them in.

They stood in the corner, inside the door. Just as Pat and I had done.

Trenoweth sniffed the air.

'What's that smell?'

'Lemon Pledge.'

'Nice,' he said. 'Very nice. Helpful. Thoughtful. Thorough.'

'Oh,' I said. 'Fingerprints.'

'Yes. Or in this case, no.'

He went further into the room and gestured for me to step into the doorway.

'Where was he? When you found him?'

'On the rug. There was a rug there. It was dark red, but darker red where...where he was.'

'He'd been bleeding.'

'His eyes were open and I was sure he was dead, so I didn't go any further. His face looked, well, he looked a bit...mottled. And his mouth was open. And he had a hole in his head.'

They perked up at that.

'A hole?' Trenoweth said. 'You mean a gunshot wound?'

'No. Sorry. No, not like that. More...jagged. Pat might be able to describe it better.'

I looked down at the floor miserably.

'Where's his luggage?' Trenoweth asked.

'He didn't have any.'

'None at all? He must have had a toothbrush or something like that?'

'I can't remember what he had when he arrived, but this morning, when we found him, there was nothing here.'

The other officer tried the wardrobe and the bedside table and chest of drawers. They were all empty.

'So he checked in with no luggage?'

'I can't remember seeing anything. I mean, I would have noticed if there was a suitcase, because I took him upstairs to the room and he would probably have carried it up, or left it down in the hall and gone back for it. But he might have had something in his hand. Or over his shoulder. I didn't really notice.' I trailed off.

'Seems to me,' Trenoweth said, 'there's a lot you didn't notice: the information you should have been recording in the guest register; the issue of a receipt for payment in cash; a description of the guest's luggage and – now what's that other thing, oh yes, – the identification of the 'police' who came and took the body away.'

I nodded. 'I'm really sorry.'

'Right.' He brushed past me and clumped down the stairs. Pat and Horatio scampered out of sight into the dining room.

Trenoweth sat back down at the table. Reynolds must have been taking notes because I heard him moving around upstairs.

'What can you all tell me about the mysterious police officers, with their lovely housekeeping habits?'

'They arrived in a car,' I said.

'Blue one,' Pat said. 'Dark blue.'

'Was it?' I said. 'I thought it was black.'

'Blue/black,' Trenoweth said, just under his breath.

I looked at Pat. Her face had a look of bewilderment and slight humiliation. I was sure I looked the same.

'Make and model? Registration number?' Trenoweth looked at us. I looked at Pat and she shook her head.

'Officer Marsden?'

'I was next door,' Horatio said. 'There had been a break-in and I went to look, because Isabel couldn't leave here, not with...you know.'

'So you didn't see the car arrive.'

'No.'

'And they didn't see you?'

'No.'

'So how did they know where to come?'

We all squirmed a bit but Horatio sat up straight.

'That was my fault,' he said.

Trenoweth just raised an eyebrow.

'I put incident tape round the door, see, to keep the...'

'...Crime scene nice and lemony clean. Yes, I see that now,' Trenoweth said.

'I think you're being a bit unfair,' I said.

'Horatio did his best. We all did our best. They looked very plausible. They behaved like I imagine proper police would behave.'

'Oh? And how was that, Ms Blunt? How do proper police behave?' Trenoweth was looking calm and friendly, but I could see this didn't extend very far below the surface.

'They were very kind,' I said.

'They were very well dressed,' Pat said.

'They thanked me,' Horatio said, rather sadly.

'So: kind, well-dressed and grateful,' Trenoweth said. I wanted to hit him.

The other officer came back into the room and gave a tiny shrug in Trenoweth's direction.

'Detective Sergeant Reynolds,' Trenoweth said, 'apparently, all it takes to be considered an experienced police officer is to be kind, well-dressed and grateful.'

'Rules us out, then,' the younger officer said.

'Actually,' I pointed out, ' what they had – and what fooled us – was *authority*. The one in the front, anyway, he had natural authority, and a feeling, like an aura of power. That's what did it.'

Trenoweth looked interested at that. 'How many of them?'

'Four. But then,' I turned to Pat, 'Another one came in, didn't they?'

She nodded. 'I heard a door slam. Like a car

door, but not exactly.'

'Yes,' I said. 'And there were more footsteps going upstairs.'

'A second vehicle.' Trenoweth wrote this down. 'Don't suppose,' he turned to Horatio, 'there's any chance...'

'The only vehicle I saw go past was the pasty van, which comes into the village almost every day, but I was on the top floor of next door, and I only saw the corner of it from the attic window, and then it was gone.'

'But the driver of that van would have gone right past here!' I said. 'If we find them, we can ask – '

'There's no WE in this matter, ' Trenoweth said. 'There's only us.' He pointed to Detective Sergeant Reynolds and back to himself. 'And there's you.' He pointed slowly at the three of us. 'You, who had a dead body in your premises, and who lost it.'

I ignored that. 'But, the second vehicle is the one which took the body away!' I said. 'That's obvious, so the driver of the pasty van which Horatio saw, would have seen it, they would have slowed down to get past, they might even have a description! This is so obvious!'

Trenoweth closed his notebook and stood up.

'I'll decide what's obvious, Miss Blunt,' he said. 'I'll need you all to come into the station at your convenience, of course. Truro. We'll take statements there. By early next week, if you please.'

'That's it?' I said. 'Aren't you going to DO something?'

'Oh yes, miss,' Trenoweth said. 'I'm going to find out if anyone's reported Mr Moffat missing, and then I'm going to tell them he's probably dead, but we don't know how, why, or where he is now. That enough activity for you?'

The younger one gave me a card, a police card with his name and number, and Trenoweth's name and number handwritten underneath in green biro.

I thought about handing him a Glebelands Bed and Breakfast brochure, we always had some on the hall table, but decided against it. They would find us if they wanted us.

CHAPTER EIGHT

I stood on the doorstep and almost waved as they drove away. As the brake lights blinked at the corner of Glebelands Lane and they took Lestoon Road up and out of the village, I wanted to wave for them to come back. I turned into the house and saw a flash of red at the other end of the lane, then it was gone. The Manse opposite looked calm and quiet. I wished I'd never left it. I'd have to get the broken window replaced and take a good look through the house myself. I was sure Horatio had been thorough, but he wouldn't know where everything was – how could he? I just hoped Sir Dougal hadn't been using the house to store anything too valuable.

I went back into the dining room where Pat and Horatio had cleared the table and straightened the chairs.

'I suppose you'd better be going now, had you?' I said.

'I don't like to leave you,' Pat said.

'Don't worry, I'll be fine. I'm really glad you were here today. Thanks.'

'Oh don't mention it. It's been possibly the most exciting day I've had in a long time. No disrespect to Mr Moffat.'

'It was all my fault!' Horatio said, sitting down with his head in his hands. 'If I hadn't put tape round the door, they wouldn't have stopped here!'

Pat sat down next to him and put her hand on his shoulder.

I went into the kitchen to put the kettle on.

'Don't get in a state, Horatio,' Pat was saying. 'This is a funny business, and there's better brains than ours to figure it out.'

I made the tea and carried it into the dining room.

Pat poured the first cup for Horatio. 'Here you are, love. Have a nice cup of tea, and put it all out of your mind. That's all we can do.'

'Is it?' I asked her. 'Really?'

'Well, what are you going to do?' she said. 'You've got a business to run, and the house next door to look after, and whatever else it is you do.'

'I don't do anything.' I sipped at my tea. 'Ever since I got here, on Christmas Eve, I've done nothing.'

Horatio lifted his head. 'You go for walks. Everyone's noticed.'

I nodded. Oh yes, I'd borrowed a pair of walking boots that I'd found in The Manse, and I walked to the beach every day – Deadman's

Beach, how apt. Sometimes I walked down to the village and along the harbour wall, and I did a bit of bed making and some loading of the dishwasher. That's all I have to show for my time here.

I slammed my cup down into the saucer. 'I'm going to do a lot more than walk this off.'

Pat and Horatio looked nervous.

'I came down here to hide,' I said.

'Who from?' Horatio whispered.

'I knew it!' Pat said. 'I said to Janice, 'she's on the run, she is,' and Janice said, 'well, she can poach an egg, so she's staying'.'

I put my head down on the dining room table, exhausted with the effort of expressing something I could hardly explain to myself. I could feel Pat and Horatio hovering near me.

'I am not on the run,' I said, into the tablecloth. It smelled of starch, and the lavender bags in the linen cupboard. It was rather pleasant. Maybe I could just sit here for a couple of hours and see what transpired. Something about the clean, comforting scent reminded me of Ivan. Ivan, on the last day in London. Ivan, who had never opened a can, or dunked a tea-bag in a mug, suddenly rolling up the sleeves of his handmade shirt, attempting to clean up my kitchen: pulling stinking dead flowers out of a vase and looking around uncertainly, failing to spot the overflowing bin.

I sat up quickly, scorched with shame,

startling us all.

'I AM on the run,' I said. 'From myself.'

They looked blank. I looked into their lovely guileless faces. 'Never mind,' I said. 'Long story. But I'm telling you this: I turned away from Mr Moffat, when he checked in. I was too busy or too lazy or...something. I didn't even look at him to see his luggage. I looked at him for longer when he was dead than when he was alive!'

Pat nodded. Horatio looked terrified. I wondered if electricity was shooting out of my head – that's how it felt.

'I'm not going to fail him again,' I said.

'Who?' Pat said.

'Mr Moffat!'

'You can't do anything for him now, poor soul,' she said.

'I can. I don't know exactly what. But there must be something, and something is always better than nothing. Isn't it?'

They looked totally unconvinced.

I took a sip of tea and smiled at them, trying to look calm and rational and not at all insane. 'I'm going to need a hand, though.'

They had to go, of course. Horatio wanted to write up his notes on the day, and Pat had a husband – it turned out – called Trevor, and she was heading home to see him. It was mid-afternoon, getting dusk-ish by the time they left.

We'd made a plan, though, and it had given me a sudden jolt of energy. Pat had called her cousin, Petey, and he was banging a piece of hardboard over the broken window in The Manse, until I could get a glazier to come. They were all very busy, they said, after the storm. Petey looked to be in his sixties, with blue eyes blazing out of his tanned face. Well, probably weather-beaten rather than tanned. But he was as brown and muscly as a piece of beef jerky, all sinews and joints, no flesh on the bone. He'd turned up a few minutes after Pat had left, cheery and helpful, and he was whistling tunelessly to himself outside.

Back in the guest house I straightened up after the endless cups of tea, and laid the table for the Harpers' breakfast tomorrow morning. I was glad they would be there, sleeping in the house tonight and having breakfast as though nothing terrible or mysterious had happened. I checked the fridge – enough of everything for the morning. As I closed the door I spotted it, held up with two magnets – one from Windsor Castle and a one lurid Ace of Hearts, from Las Vegas. The Second Envelope. I took it off the door and replaced the magnets. Janice had left me lists of instructions – how to time a perfect English breakfast, who to ring for more eggs, how to use the ancient top-loader washer. And she'd left this envelope and told me I'd probably never need to open it. I knew how to contact her, so it wasn't that. I went into the large room at the front of the house – the one with sea views and downy sofas and old paperbacks the guests had left behind. I didn't get comfy though but sat at the writing bureau and reached for the letter knife and opened the second envelope. I unfolded the single sheet of cream paper and read it, and read it again. Finally, I got up, feeling exhausted and calm. Everything was all clear to me now.

I took Petey a cup of coffee. I could see some lights out at sea – a fishing boat returning to harbour, I guessed, and I hoped they got back before total darkness. When I first moved here, the sea frightened me. Actually, everything frightened me. The lack of street lights, the quietness, punctuated by strange yipping and rustling sounds from the shrubbery behind the house. I soon learned to love the look of the sea, though. I could see it clearly from my attic bedroom.

I could have taken any bedroom – there were six in The Manse – but something about the sloping ceiling and the small low window made me feel secure and comforted. Every morning I could wake to the sea, milky white in the dawn, or grey in the mist, and every night I would look out at the complete blackness, the void, and my thoughts would narrow down again, to the width of my tiny attic bedroom.

'All done!' Petey said, swigging his coffee. 'You didn't ought to have come out here, you'll catch a chill.'

'I'll be fine, thanks,' I said. 'What about you?' I pointed to his jacket, hanging on the front door handle.

'Got me thermals on,' he said. 'Ankle length. Never without them, October to Easter.'

'Good to know,' I said and offered him one of the £20 notes the dead man had paid with.

'Ooh no, not that much.'

'I'll have to go in the house – '

'No, no, no, don't you worry about that. You buy me a pint in the Smuggler's tonight.'

'How do you know I'll be there?'

'You're meeting Pat, aren't you? S'what she said.'

'Yes. I am meeting Pat there, and Horatio. And I'll buy you a pint.'

Petey handed me the empty mug and went off, swinging his jacket over his shoulder.

CHAPTER NINE

I let myself into The Manse and turned on the hall light. The house felt quiet, but safe. It didn't feel as though anything had gone wrong in here. I trusted Horatio to have done a thorough job of checking. Something told me he was better with empty houses than dead bodies.

The Manse had been a Georgian rectory, and it had elegant square rooms and was, naturally, beautifully decorated. The first wife of my boss had brought the children here every summer, I knew, and she'd cared for the house. I don't know why she didn't get it in the divorce, though she did get the St Tropez apartment so maybe she wasn't too bothered. The last redecoration had been in all the magazines: *Coast, Country Living*. You've probably seen it, if you're into that kind of thing. It was just before the divorce, so maybe she was trying to spend Dougall's money. She'd filled the house with paintings, mostly seascapes, and the chairs were all reupholstered in the colours of the sea and sand. I looked round the sitting room. The silver picture-frames were still there; wouldn't they have been prime targets for a housebreaker? I went into the kitchen.

The knives were all still in the block, though maybe the average house burglar wouldn't have known how much they were worth. There was a Wedgewood trinket pot on the windowsill, and a Bose radio on the worktop – plenty of opportunity for a quick-fingered thief with transport issues.

I went on through the house: the morning room, the utility room, the little sitting area on the first floor landing with a Tiffany lamp on a side table and an Eames chair with a blanket thrown over it. All still in place, all just as I'd left it when I last lay there to read. I went into the two back bedrooms – the ones used by the boys who had been teenagers when they last came here. I wondered what they thought about this house where they'd spent their happy childhood holidays. Did they ever want to return? Did they wonder about all their summer clothes, left in the wardrobes? I hoped not. I was wearing most of them.

When I'd arrived from London – on Christmas Eve – I had the clothes I stood up in: a work suit which was suddenly too big for me, and a pair of high-heeled court shoes. In my overnight bag I had a pair of silk pyjamas, a cashmere dressing-gown and eight pairs of La Perla knickers. What had I been thinking?

By Boxing Day – although I'd managed to light the wood-burner – I was getting a bit cold in my suit jacket. I couldn't spend all day in bed with a hot-water bottle, so I swallowed my natural inclinations and went scavenging. In the back bedrooms, the boys had left all their jeans and t-shirts, flip-flops (no good to me then), walking boots, socks, surf shorts, even a wetsuit. The younger boy – Ethan – was thirteen when he'd left, and his jeans were too small for me, but the shirts and t-shirts were fine. The older one had been fifteen, and his jeans fit me adequately for my new life. I'd been wearing those clothes ever since, without questioning my choices, until today. Now I was on the hunt, looking for something new to wear. Tonight was a big night – well, a big night for me. I was going out.

There was one room in the house I'd never examined closely. The master bedroom. If felt wrong, somehow, to find out too much about the private life of my boss. I'd worked for him for twenty-nine years, or to put it another way – two divorces for him, and a stratospheric rise in salary and stress for me. When I'd started, I'd been a secretary. By accident rather than design I became his personal assistant; then I was his executive assistant, and by last Christmas Eve, when I'd walked away, I was the director of the executive office. I had 10 Downing Street in my phone book, and thought I'd had a quiet day if I got home from work in time for *News at Ten*.

I opened the door and stepped into the master bedroom. I went in every week to open the windows for a bit, but this was different.

In the massive oak wardrobe there were only women's clothes. Obviously Sir Dougall hadn't spent much time with his children, but I already knew that about him. There were some pretty little summer dresses – it would be months before it would be warm enough in Cornwall for those. There were some linen trousers, long flowy skirts and a few pairs of jeans. Well, wearing women's jeans would be a step up. I undressed and tried a pair on. A bit long, but fine. I opened the drawers in the built in dresser. Plenty of t-shirts and some folded cardigans. The wooden moth balls clattered as I sorted through the drawer and the noise made me jump. I ended up with a pale blue cashmere over a white t-shirt and my faithful walking boots.

I went into the en-suite bathroom and opened the cabinet over the sink. There was enough Chanel No. 5 in the bottom of a bottle for quick spritz. There was a sample size of moisturiser and I rubbed some on my face. It sank in, as though being poured over the Sahara. Maybe time to buy some of my own, tomorrow. There was an expensive hairbrush and I dragged it painfully through the mass of tangled hair. I tied my hair back with a black ribbon I found on the dressing table, and went downstairs. I looked at myself under the unflattering overhead light. When I was forty-five I'd approached my looming fiftieth with my usual action plan. I'd prepared, planned. I spent more time and money on myself, and took up running. I put photos of film stars in their fifties on my fridge, to inspire me. Now the Hollywood figure I most resembled was Yoda.

I stuffed my pockets with the money Mr Moffat had paid me, and a few pieces of paper torn from an old notebook. I had the house keys for both houses, and I pulled an old Spence Barbour coat over the borrowed clothes and set off down the hill.

Gorran Porth is a small village – very pretty, but hard to find. There's a crescent of beach and a curving stone jetty and when the tide is in the fishing boats bob and buck inside the arm of the harbour. When the tide is out, there's more room for children and dogs, and you have to be careful not to get entangled in the long dripping green ropes which stretch from the anchor points in the earth to the buoys where the boats tie up.

It is a very dark village. No street lights, and although the houses are close together, when they have their blinds and curtains drawn it can feel as though you are being shut out. I hated it the first few times I came down here. I preferred to walk on the higher moorland at the back of the village, where I caught the last fading glimpses of sunlight on the sea, and there were no doors to be closed against me.

I was a bit early, so I walked carefully

out along the harbour wall and turned to look back at the village. The windows of the Smuggler's Arms were orange and welcoming, and I could see the porch lights I'd left on in both the houses, high up on the hill. The sea looked black, fathomless and the temperature was dropping quickly. I wondered about Mr Moffat. Where was he now? He wasn't feeling the cold, wherever he was, but I hoped he was retaining some dignity. Our paths had crossed, impossibly, and he was part of my life, now.

It was too cold to wait any longer, and I walked back along the harbour wall towards the pub.

CHAPTER TEN

Inside the pub was warm and there was a lovely smell of chips, and floor polish. I leaned against the bar until a small blonde woman had finished pulling a pint.

'Can I help you, my love?' she asked, click-clacking over to me on chunky high heels.

'Gin and tonic, please,' I said. 'Wait! No. Sorry. Half of pint of cider.' Everything was different in my life, time for me to be different too.

She passed a honey-coloured glass over to me and I peered along the bar to the gloom at the far end. 'Petey?' He raised his glass. 'And whatever Petey wants,' I said to the woman. 'I'm Isabel, by the way. I live...well, I'm up at Glebe-lands.'

'I know,' she nodded, 'You're helping Jan-ice. She told us all about you.'

'Did she?'

The woman nodded. 'I'm Demelza. I'm running the pub, for now.'

'Nice to meet you.'

We both turned as the door opened and Horatio came in, struggling out of his waterproof coat. He wasn't wearing his police uniform now, just basic jeans and lumberjack shirt. He looked even younger and lighter without the borrowed gravity of his uniform.

'Isabel!' he said. 'Demelza.'

She turned away and reached for a pewter mug. 'Usual?'

'Ta, thanks.'

'Let me get this for you, Horatio,' I said. 'We've got lots to do.'

By the time we got settled at a corner table and Pat had arrived and been served with a pint of stout, the pub was filling up. I could see why it had to be the focal point in a village like this. There was a large room upstairs, Horatio told me, where parties and events could be held, and frequently were. From birth onwards all the villagers had some connection with the Smuggler's Arms.

'Alright, Isabel,' Pat said, 'How are you?'

'I'm fine,' I told her. 'I've opened the second envelope and now everything's clear.'

Pat nodded but I could see the look she darted at Horatio.

'I'm not crazy,' I said. 'Janice left me a second envelope, and she said I might never need to open it, because it was only for emergencies. But this, this is an emergency. Even Janice would think so.'

Pat looked sceptical. 'I think she probably means how to fix the dishwasher,' she said gently, 'or how to order a delivery of firewood?'

I shook my head. 'No. That's the kind of thing which was in the first envelope. All the day-to-day stuff, how to run the business, things like that. This is different.'

I unfolded the paper and put it on the table between us.

'This,' I said, 'is a way of thinking. A philosophy. The Way of the Second Envelope.'

'Isabel,' Pat said. 'You have met Janice. Does she strike you as the kind of person to have a philosophy?'

'And yet here it is,' I said, turning it round so they could read it.

Horatio frowned at Janice's loopy handwriting.

'Number one,' he read out, '*All the small things add up to the big thing.* What does that even mean?'

'Go on,' Pat said.

'Number two, *Put yourself in their shoes.* Whose shoes?' Horatio looked bemused, but I could see the beginning of a glint in Pat's eye.

'OK,' she said. 'I'm getting it, I think. She's telling you how to run a guest house and how to deal with problems, but that's not going to solve a crime, is it?'

'Maybe not,' I said. 'But, maybe. What she's given me is a template. A way of thinking about things. Look at number three: *They aren't always right but it doesn't really hurt to let them think they are.* Well, isn't that the only way to deal with Trenoweth?'

'What's number four?' Pat said, and I let out a sigh of relief.

'Number four – *Prepare for the worst and you'll be ready for anything.*'

'Hmm.' Pat took a sip of her drink. 'Cheery. All these years I've known Janice.'

'Have you, though?' I said. 'Because look at number five: '*You don't really know what's going on, unless they tell you.*'

Pat nodded slowly.

'That's a good one,' Horatio said. 'We're not supposed to jump to conclusions, or make assumptions.'

'Exactly. You see?' I turned to him. 'We can use these rules to – well, I don't know what, really, but I've got to try. Are you in? It will be OK if you aren't, honestly, but it would be better if you were.'

Horatio looked pained. 'I'm in trouble with the police. They say I didn't do things properly. So if we could sort this out, it would be great for me.'

Pat looked at Horatio with narrowed eyes and then at me. 'We didn't even know you before today,' she said, 'so I'm not entirely sure why, but I'm in.'

'Right!' I said raising my glass in a toast. 'Here's to us, sorting it out.'

'I've been making a list,' I said, getting another crumpled sheet out of my pocket. 'Firstly. How did Mr Moffat get here?' They nodded at that. 'Someone must have seen him.'

'Secondly. If he was murdered, in the bedroom, why was his body stolen? He was already dead.'

'Thirdly, the fake police, they were driving past and saw the police tape. But they were already so close. They were in the area. So they knew roughly where Mr Moffat was. How did they know that?'

'I got a theory,' Horatio said. 'But go on with the list.'

'Fourthly – '

' – There's a fourth?' Pat said.

'And a fifth.'

'Alright, you go on.' She took a long swallow of her drink.

'Fourthly,' I said again, 'linked to firstly, why didn't he have any luggage? Was he not expecting to stay overnight? And why trek up the hill to Glebelands, when the pub has rooms and so does the Harbour View Guest House?'

Horatio and Pat nodded.

'And fifthly and finally – there's nothing missing from The Manse – but can it possibly be a coincidence that there's a broken window in the porch, right by the door handle, on the same night someone gets murdered in the house next door? I mean, we're not exactly in a crime hot-spot, are we?'

I sat back, and picked up my cider.

'You look different,' Pat said. 'What have you done?'

'Put some face cream on, and some perfume,' I said.

'Is that what that is?' Horatio said, sniffing the air like a bloodhound.

Pat and I rolled our eyes.

'Let's hear your theory,' Pat said to Horatio.

'I think the fake police already knew where to look because they killed him, or at least one of them did. Either in the room, or close by, and they wanted to take the body away so there could be no forensic evidence.'

He was whispering, and we leaned in closer.

'Good!' I said. 'That's the kind of thinking we need.'

'So why didn't they take the body away last night?' Pat said. 'Once they'd killed him.'

'Too difficult?' I wondered. 'Too noisy? Maybe didn't have anything to put him in? Maybe they were conscious of the noise. Mrs Harper said she'd heard a commotion.'

'Ooh,' Pat said, 'if she'd put the light on, or said something, they might have heard and got scared.'

I nodded. 'Right. We're on the right track.'

'And, difficult to pass themselves off as police in the middle of the night,' Horatio said. 'If anyone spotted them.'

'Right. But to be out looking for him the next day, and have a way to take him away. That's quite organised. Isn't it?' I said.

'Oh my good God!' Pat said. 'Organised. You know what that is. Organised crime. That's the Mafia that is. Oh my good God.'

Pat suddenly looked hot and queasy and started fanning herself with the plastic bar menu.

'I don't think it has to be the Mafia, Aunty Pat,' Horatio told her. 'I think there's other kinds of organised crime. Like the Tongs. And gangs in London.'

'Oh my good God!' Pat said again, fanning faster. People in the bar stared at us. My eye snagged on a tall man in a red waterproof at the bar, who conspicuously was the only person not looking over at us.

'You alright, our Patty?' Petey shouted.

I tapped the table in front of Pat. 'Get a grip,' I said. 'We're not dealing with the Mafia and I think a Chinese gang couldn't go undercover for long in Gorran Porth.'

Pat waved at Petey and gave him a fake thumbs-up.

We all sipped in silence for a minute and tried to calm down. I had a thought.

'Organised crime is always about money,

isn't it? Drugs, prostitution, stuff like that, making money for someone.'

They nodded.

'Well, you'd know best, you two, if that was happening here.'

They thought about it for a bit.

Pat shrugged. 'I can't see anyone making lots of money down here, only the people who own holiday lets, and they mostly aren't local.'

'Oh' I felt slightly deflated then something occurred to me. 'So maybe Mr Moffat was on the run, hiding out. That's why he didn't have any luggage. Maybe it was totally random that he came here.'

'How did they find him, then, the fake police?' Pat asked.

'I don't think it was random,' Horatio said. 'And I don't think it was a coincidence. I think you're right about that.'

I looked around at the bar, filling up now, and with a pleasant buzz of conversation.

'Horatio,' I said quietly. 'Who is that man at the bar, with the red coat on?'

'He's that writer chappie, Nick.'

'Didn't you say you'd seen him, when the fake police sent you out to check the area?'

'He was walking up the hill. He goes walking a lot. Like you.'

'I saw him too,' I said. 'As the real police were leaving, I just saw a bit of his coat at the end of the lane.'

'Must have been a long walk,' Horatio said. 'I must have seen him on the way off, and you saw him on the way back.'

'And now he's in here.'

'Well it might be a small thing, but they all add up,' I said. 'Another drink? I'm going to the bar.'

CHAPTER ELEVEN

I gave Demelza our orders – plus one for Petey – and stood next to Nick at the bar as I waited.

'Hello there,' he said, turning to face me.

'Hi.'

'I've seen you around in the village – never seen you in here though.'

'No, my first visit.'

'Really? How long have you been in the village?' He had nice eyes, I had to give him that.

'I've been here about three months,' I said, 'how about you?'

'Yeah. Couple of months.' He was drinking beer and he licked at the foam on his top lip.

'And what do you do, Nick?' I asked, in my brightest cocktail party tone.

'I'm a, well, I'm trying to write a novel.' He shrugged out of the red coat and folded it up, dropping it at his feet.

'How fascinating.' I was sure Pat and Horatio were watching me, their gazes hot on the back of my neck. 'What's it about, or is it difficult to talk about?'

'No, not difficult. Fancy a drink?'

I couldn't look away from his eyes. He was wearing an Arran jumper over shoulders that were broad and solid looking. *It would be very easy to rest your head on one of those,* I thought. Everyone should have a shoulder like that in their lives. A good smile too.

'I'd love to hear all about it,' I said. 'Another time?'

'Sure.' He looked round to see where I was going to sit, and gave Pat and Horatio a nod.

I got back to the table and put the drinks down.

'He's ever so handsome,' Pat whispered.

Horatio turned to look.

'Don't stare!' Pat said to him. 'Rude!'

'I'm not going to be taken in by a handsome face again,' I said. 'That 'Smith' really knew what he was doing when he charmed us.'

Pat nodded. 'My Trevor isn't handsome, really, but he's never stolen a dead body. Not as far as I know.'

'Pat,' I said. 'Who is that woman with Petey? And have I upset her in some way?'

Pat didn't need to turn round. 'That's Winnie. The love of Petey's life. Whiny Winnie we call her. She's probably giving you the evil eye because you bought Petey a drink and you're the most glamorous person in Gorran Porth. At least tonight.'

'Thanks,' I said, almost certain Winnie's feet were more glamorous than mine.

'Why do you call her Whiny Winnie? Is she just generally miserable?'

'Generally, yes,' Horatio said. 'But she spreads it around. Like a cold.'

'You know the type,' Pat said. 'Always got a pot of lentils on the stove, and does what she calls 'art' with bits of driftwood. Knits her own cardigans, but never quite finishes them. Makes her own yoghurt in an old thermos.'

'Honestly,' I said, 'I can't say I do know the type.'

'To be fair,' Horatio said, 'I do know people who make their own yoghurt who are quite cheerful.'

Pat turned to him. 'Do you? I'm not sure I do. But I do know people who make their own clothes and don't look like a partially thatched roof.'

'This isn't solving the crime,' Horatio said.

'No.' We both nodded. 'But I'm having a lovely time,' I said.

The fug of the Smuggler's Arms was disturbed by a blast of cold air as someone came through the door and we turned to look. Voices were raised in greeting and a plump man waved over at Pat and Horatio.

'Uncle Nat!' they shouted.

The man waved generally around the bar and lurched over to us. He had a full torso, but small, slightly bandy legs, and he resembled a barrel balanced on a wishbone. He walked like a person who has a marked difference in the length of his legs but the trouble, I suspected, lay in the mismatched pair of boots he was wearing.

He pulled out a chair at our table.

Pat introduced us and I shook his hand. It was large, and slightly gritty. He was wearing a black jumper stretched tight over his massive bulk and his eyes – blue like Horatio and Pat's – were set in folds of plump red face. He had a shock of white hair, slightly too long and extravagantly curly, so he resembled a rather glum cherub. I offered to buy him a drink but Demelza was already coming over to the table with a large glass of milk.

He took a big sip while we watched him.

'Had to come in for my supper,' he said finally, banging the pint glass down on the table. 'Pasty van didn't deliver. Terrible it was. I was out by the gate, and he went right past me! I've had no lunch, no tea, had to get the truck out and come down here for my supper!'

'The pasty van?' I tried not to sound too excited.

'That's right. Pasty van.' He looked around him, and Horatio passed him a menu which he flipped open for Uncle Nat to read.

I started at Pat and Horatio. 'The pasty van,' I said slowly. 'Which went past the house this morning. Just as the *police* were there.'

There was a long moment of silence, while Nat looked at the menu, and Horatio and Pat looked at me.

'Oh my God!' Pat said. 'Uncle Nat, we need to speak to the driver of the pasty van. He might have some information we need.'

''tidn't a he, usually.' Nat said. ''Tis normally little Kylie, lives up Roche.'

'But it wasn't today?' I asked.

'Ah. Be a poppet and order me the gammon and egg, would you? With no onion rings, but I'll have a side order of mushy peas.'

I got up and went to the bar, where Demelza was already waiting to take the order.

When I got back to the table, Horatio had taken up the interrogation.

'Who was driving it, Uncle Nat – could you see?'

'No I could not, but it wouldn't have been little Kylie driving like a maniac like that. If our Polly had been asleep in the lane she would have died for sure.'

'Dog,' Pat mouthed at me.

'So if it wasn't little Kylie, who was it?'

'I couldn't say. But whoever it was, they should have stopped at my gate. I've got an arrangement. They should have stopped and dropped off my pasties. Same as always.'

'Uncle Nat does like a pasty,' Pat said to me. 'And he has them specially made – without onions – and the driver always stops at his gate and drops them off on a Thursday. And Uncle Nat always has one with chips for his Thursday tea, and one for his Saturday lunch, and one for his Sunday tea. Don't you, Uncle Nat?'

He nodded his massive head and the curls bobbed like ringlets on a Jane Austen heroine. He looked slightly less glum now, with the promise of gammon and chips on the horizon.

'And then on Monday he has to fend for himself.' Horatio took up the story. 'But on Tuesday, the van comes through the village again, see? So if the van didn't stop, and Kylie wasn't driving it...'

'*They* were driving it,' I said. 'Which means the pasty van didn't drive past the fake police – the pasty van was being driven *by* the fake police. Oh! Oh. That's why the phone rang – remember? The phone rang as they were leaving, but there was no-one there? They didn't want us leaving the kitchen, or we'd have seen.'

Pat nodded, her eyes solemn.

'But why did they want a pasty van?' Horatio asked.

I just looked at him. Demelza arrived with the gammon and eggs and Uncle Nat picked up his cutlery like a man who hadn't eaten in a week.

'Rule 2, Horatio,' I said. 'Janice's rule 2. *Put*

yourself in their shoes. Why did they need a van?' I whispered. 'What did they need to carry that they couldn't fit in the car?'

Horatio's face went ashen and he looked at Uncle Nat's supper uneasily.

'Oh my good God!' Pat said again. 'They put that poor man in the pasty van!'

'What man?' Uncle Nat said, at high volume

'No-one!' we chorused.

Everyone in the bar looked over for a moment. Probably wondering what the mad London woman had said to upset three local worthies. I caught Nick's eye, and although he turned away quickly to make conversation with Demelza, there was something there which made me shiver.

CHAPTER TWELVE

That second half-pint of cider was a mistake. I don't know when I turned into such a lightweight – maybe it was the sea air, or maybe the long time I'd gone without drinking, but this morning I felt muzzy and tired. And my throat was sore. It had been months since I'd spoken to anyone, much. So I hadn't slept well. I had been thinking about Mr Moffat bouncing about in the back of the pasty van. I thought about poor little Kylie. Where was she? How had she been persuaded to let the fake police use her pasty van as a hearse? Or maybe she hadn't had a choice? A wave of sickness washed over me.

Out in the dining room I could hear Mr and Mrs Harper chewing and swallowing, slurping and murmuring over their breakfast. How I got that cooked and served up was a miracle. They were lovely people though, kind and patient, with a gentle curiosity. I didn't notice that yesterday, and I realised I was already paying more attention. Maybe Mr Moffat had done me a favour, though I'd rather he was still alive. I made myself a mug of tea and went to talk to the Harpers, this time really interested, instead of just doing what Janice had ordered. I noticed how the pale yellow colour of the walls made the most of the wintry light, and how the blue china and copper pans hanging on the wall looked harmonious and cheerful. How had that escaped me for months? I turned the radio on quietly, another of Janice's suggestions – people don't feel overheard if there's another noise in the room, she explained. I retuned it. I'd had it on a cool and restrained classical station, but now I wanted to hear the local news. A cheesy song drifted into the room and I knew a comforting local voice would eventually follow.

'Is everything alright?' I asked the Harpers, standing in the doorway and sipping.

'Lovely, Isabel, thanks,' Mrs Harper said. 'No breakfast for the other gentleman?'

I choked on a mouthful of tea. 'Sorry!' I said. 'Just a minute.'

When I got back from the kitchen, mopping at the spilt tea on my chest, and wiping my eyes, they were buttering their toast and chatting quietly.

'He, uh, he checked out,' I said.

'Ooh, you don't mean he did a runner?' Mrs Harper was wide-eyed.

'No. No, he'd paid. He just intended to stay for the one night. But he...he departed.'

'Ah. Well, Cornwall isn't for everyone, is it? I mean, we love the walking, but at this time of year it can be a bit bleak. And he wasn't really dressed for it. Not like his friend.'

'His friend?' I said, trying to sound calm. 'Did he have a friend in the village?'

'Gossip,' Mr Harper said to his wife, with mock sternness.

'Oh shut up, Jim. Take no notice of him,' Mrs Harper laughed. 'I just meant, when we saw him, down in the town, he was chatting very closely. With a man. And it seemed like they knew each other, but they seemed so badly matched, if you know what I mean?'

I smiled and made a 'go on' sort of face at her.

'Well, the man, your guest, he was a little chap, wasn't he. And he looked as though he'd come straight from the office.'

'Yes, that's right,' I said. 'I remember now. He had one of those sleeveless jumpers. And a tie. Bit old-fashioned.'

'That's it,' Mrs Harper said. 'And the other man was tall, very tall. Very good looking too. Quite put me in mind of Poldark. And he had proper waterproofs on, and good boots. I noticed particularly, because we wear the same brand, but he's got the newest version. Our coats are navy blue, you see, and he's got the red coat, very pricey. I'm not boasting, mind, but we take our walking seriously, and we know. He had very nice boots. New. Well, newish. And a Torrent-beater coat, bright red.'

I brought them a new pot of coffee, desperate for them to stay. Mrs Harper seemed happy to chat but her husband was looking out at the sky, and rustling his map.

'You're off today,' I said, a bit stupidly. 'Walking to, where was it?'

'St Agnes, nice long stretch.'

'Lovely.' I looked round the room, looking for inspiration. 'Maybe you'll see the tall man in the red coat, if he's a walker too?'

'I've seen him already!' Mrs Harper said. 'I went down into the village before breakfast – to post some cards – and he was on the harbour wall.'

'Oh?'

'There was such a ruckus in the village shop, something about pasties. It must be so entertaining living in a little village like this.'

'Hmm.'

'He had binoculars with him.'

'Who?' Mr Harper said.

'The man!' his wife said. 'Keep up, love, the man in the red coat.'

'Birdwatcher maybe?' I said, acting casual.

'Not really the morning for it, though,' Mrs Harper said. 'Not with all that sea-mist. No, he won't see much 'til lunchtime.'

I was struggling to keep the conversation going when I heard the flap of the post box and I excused myself and went to see Pat.

'Come in?'

She peered up the hall behind me at Mr and Mrs Harper going upstairs, moving quickly like escapees. I felt a tiny bit guilty.

'I'll come back,' Pat said, 'after my round. Horatio's rung the pasty company, asking to speak to little...to Kylie.'

'That's brilliant!' I said. 'Well done, Horatio.'

'He's a proper nosy parker, that boy. Not too bright, but nosy.'

'I've got more news too, from my guests.' I pointed to the ceiling. 'Let's talk after your round.'

'Right you are.'

I went out onto the step to wave Pat goodbye. Had it really only been one day? My life, which had seemed so ordered, so very tightly controlled in the small area between the two Glebelands Lane houses, was now unravelling.

I've never cleared the dining room quicker than I did then. I raced around the kitchen too, loading the dishwasher, putting things back in the massive catering fridge. The few supplies I had for the guests looked a bit pathetic in there, but the thought of the fridge – and the house –

full, was something I just couldn't contemplate. Mr Harper put his head round the door to say goodbye and thanks and give me the key for their room. I waved them off from the doorstep. They were wearing their high-tech walking kit – though not as high-tech as Nick the writer, I now knew. It was misty, still, and there was a lot of moisture in the air. Not exactly rain nor precisely fog, but something in between. Something uniquely Cornish.

As soon as they were out of sight, I put the door on the latch so Pat could get back in. I rushed upstairs and stripped off the Harpers' bed, kicking the bedding downstairs where it lay in a snowdrift at the bottom of the stairs. I raced round the bathroom scrubbing and wiping. I brought more sheets from the cupboard on the landing and made up the bed and restocked the tea-making tray. Standing back in the doorway I looked critically at the room. Only the bed to make up, and a quick vacuum and that would do it. Finally the room was done and I opened the window a little to keep it fresh, and put the upstairs vacuum cleaner away in the cupboard on the landing. As I closed the door, I heard a sound.

'Pat?' I shouted downstairs. There was no reply. I was sure I'd heard a door; was it the front door, or some kind of movement deep within the house? I was warm from the housework, but it felt as though a strand of cooler air had seeped up the stairs. I debated what I should do. Eventually I moved towards the top of the stairs slowly, trying to avoid the creaky boards. I tried to breathe as shallowly as I could, though really I felt like sobbing. Suddenly, the front door was darkened by someone walking across the front path. I could see a slight form in the frosted glass.

The door handle rattled and Horatio's sweet innocent face came into view.

'Isabel?' he called out.

I ran down the stairs and astonished him with a big hug.

'I thought I heard someone in the house,' I said.

'It was only me, trying the front door. You probably shouldn't leave it on the latch.'

'I'm alright, really. I was just scaring myself. Phew! Come on, I'll make you some breakfast.'

I led him towards the kitchen, reaching down to pick up the pile of sheets I'd kicked down the stairs. And there, right on the corner of a pillowcase which had landed flat on the floor, there was a clear wet boot print.

I dropped the sheets and straightened up. I grabbed Horatio's arm and pointed.

'Footprint,' I whispered. The print was drying rapidly, there was no mud or gravel on the print, just moisture.

Horatio took out his phone and took a photo of the print.

'Good thinking,' I whispered, giving him a thumbs up.

We both stood there, unwilling to go any further into the house.

Horatio looked at his phone. 'I could ring 999,' he mouthed at me.

'How far away are they?'

'Twenty-three miles.'

I rolled my shoulders slightly and took a deep breath. I opened the dining room door as quickly as I could, and jumped into the room, screaming at the top of my voice, 'Aaaaah, get out of my house!'

There was no-one in the room and no sound from the kitchen or the utility room beyond.

I was gasping for breath now, really panicked, but really angry too.

Horatio stepped into the room behind me.

We went forward slowly into the kitchen. I stood stock still and looked behind the door. Still nothing. I tiptoed further down the dark passage which led from the kitchen into the utility room. The back door was open, swinging slightly in the cool morning air. There was another boot print on the pale flooring, just in front of the mat. I looked out of the door. The mist was really close around the house, anyone could be out there, and I thought they might loom up out of the whiteness at any time. There was no sound of running footsteps, no screeching car racing away. If it wasn't for the photo on Horatio's phone, there would be nothing to suggest there was anything other than a middle-aged woman and a very young man, scaring themselves senseless.

CHAPTER THIRTEEN

When Pat arrived a bit later, Horatio and I had made serious inroads into the bottle of cooking sherry I'd found in the kitchen cupboard.

'Alright then?' Pat said, her hands on her hips. 'Making an early start, are we?'

'We've had a shock, Aunty Pat,' Horatio said, 'Terrible, it was.' He shuddered.

'Not as bad as yesterday, though,' I reminded him.

He shrugged. 'The dead body couldn't do us any harm.'

I nodded. 'It was scary, Pat. Someone was in the house.'

'No!' She sat down at the table and looked at the sherry bottle. 'Tell me all about it!'

'I was upstairs, vacuuming, so they could have been in here for ages. They could have come up the stairs – I wouldn't have heard them! Then Horatio arrived, I think that's what frightened them off.'

'So that's more scary than yesterday, when an actual murderer was in the house?' Pat asked.

I reached for the sherry bottle, and Pat lifted it out of reach.

'Have you got something to report, Horatio?' she asked.

'I have. I've got plenty to report.' He got his notebook out and put it on the table.

'I've got lots to report too,' I said, holding my empty sherry glass above my face.

Pat got up and went into the kitchen. I heard her putting the kettle on.

'Nice cup of tea!' she shouted, 'that's what you both need. We've got a lot to do.'

'Where can I get my hair cut?' I asked her.

She came back in with mugs and a milk jug.

'Down in the village, or you could get the bus into St Austell, more choice there.'

'Who's in the village?'

'*Maison la Plage*, by the bus stop. Mavis, she's really called.'

My heart sank a bit and I pulled at my split ends.

We waited until the tea was poured and then Horatio started.

'I rang the pasty company and asked to speak to Kylie. They said she was off sick. I asked if she'd been off sick yesterday and they got a bit suspicious, but they said she had been. They had a relief driver lined up anyway, he was working in the bakery, so they just got him to take over her route. Only, he hasn't been seen since, and neither has the van. Or the pasties.'

'Everyone's talking about it,' Pat said. 'On my round.'

'They aren't talking about us, are they?' I said. 'And poor Mr Moffat?'

'Ooh no, no-one seems to know about that, but they're all up in arms about the pasties.'

'We need to talk to Kylie. We need to find out if she really was poorly, or...or something worse.'

Horatio and Pat nodded. I really regretted the cooking sherry now, I was starting to feel a bit light-headed.

'Horatio, do you know where we can reach Kylie? Didn't Uncle Nat say something about her living in – '

' – Roche.'

'Right. I think we need to go there. We need to make sure she's OK.'

'I could drive us there,' Horatio said. 'But you'll want to get your hair cut?'

'Hang on!' I said. 'Didn't you just say the hairdressers is by the bus stop?'

Pat nodded.

'One of the things on my list is to find out how Mr Moffat got here. He didn't drive, and he didn't walk. Maybe he got off the bus.'

Pat got up and went out into the hall,

coming back with the phone book from the hall dresser. She started flicking through it.

'Have you got things to report?' she asked.

'Oh, yes, that scare has driven it out of my head. You'll never guess what Mrs Harper told me. She saw Mr Moffat last night, on the harbour wall, talking very closely with Nick the writer.'

'No way!' Horatio looked amazed.

I nodded. 'And they saw him – Nick, obviously – again this morning, with a pair of binoculars. Down on the harbour wall again.'

'He wouldn't have seen anything this morning,' Horatio said. 'Very misty.'

'I know.' I could feel my heart pounding. Was that the sherry, or the stress? 'Let me get my haircut booked in, then we can make plans to see Kylie, then we've got to take a long hard look at Nick the writer.'

'I'll take a long hard look at him,' Pat said.

'Aunty Pat!'

'Well, he is...isn't he?'

'Focus!' I said. 'Let's focus.'

'Have you told Janice?' Pat asked.

'Oh God. No. Do you think I should? She'll worry. She'll be livid. She'd never use Lemon Pledge, she thinks spray polish is an abomination.'

'I don't think that's going to be her number one concern,' Pat said. 'Just don't tell her. She won't hear about it all those miles away.'

'She'll hear about it when she gets back,'

Horatio said.

'Not if we don't let it slip.'

'It won't stay secret for long. Once the pasty company gets wind of what happened.'

'Oh God. Again,' I said.

'So don't tell her right now,' Pat said. 'I mean, what is there to tell her, really? It isn't like there's a bloodstain on the floor, or police camping on the front lawn. As long as the guests are happy. When are the next guests arriving?'

'Sunday. Just two of them at the moment. Coming for a wedding on the Monday.'

'You've got a few nights off then. You can come down the pub and meet my Trevor, he's heard all about you and he wants to meet you.'

'What's he heard? About Mr Moffat?'

'Me and Trevor have no secrets,' Pat said, a bit primly. 'But he won't tell anyone else. I've sworn him to secrecy.'

'Can we get on?' Horatio said. 'Only I've got a few things to get done, before Monday.'

'Oh, Horatio.' I put my hand out and patted his arm. 'I feel so bad for you. You're in trouble with the real police.'

He nodded miserably. 'Or, we could just call them the police. That's why I want to sort this out. Find out what's going on. I'm suspended until further notice.'

'That's terrible!' I looked to Pat, who looked as outraged as I felt.

'Well, it all might be sorted by Monday,'

Horatio said, 'and we can't give our statements until then, and they can't meet up and decide what to do about me before then.' He trailed off.

Pat had found the phone number for *Maison la Plage* and she pointed to it, handing me the phone.

I telephoned Mavis the hairdresser and she said to come down now, her newest stylist was free right then.

So we all set off down the hill together, me to *Maison la Plage* and Pat and Horatio to their own homes.

'Rendezvous in one hour,' I said. 'Harbour wall.'

'Righty-ho,' Pat said. 'Shall we have a secret signal?'

'What for?'

She pursed her lips. 'Just for the fun of it? No, no. Alright then.' And off she went, hands in pockets.

CHAPTER FOURTEEN

Maison le Plage was a predominantly purple salon, very small, only two sinks and two chairs, but it looked freshly decorated and I was greeted warmly. The cape, when Mavis flung it round me, smelt of perm lotion and peppermints, and Mavis herself was charming and friendly and I thought she probably looked after Janice's platinum French pleat. Then she told me her newest stylist would look after me, and she called out 'Marc' and he came through the bead curtain at the back.

He had a Mohawk, and lots of piercings in one ear. He wore leather trousers and a t-shirt so tight it looked as though it had been sprayed on him. I relaxed at once; I'd be in safe hands here.

Marc, 'with a C' he told me, soon had me purring with delight as he worked warm water through my hair.

'Been in the village long?' he asked.

'Few months. You?'

'Few weeks. Water alright?'

'Yes, lovely, thanks. What brought you here?'

'Boyfriend. Got assigned down here. Head teacher.' He lowered his voice to a whisper. 'Failing school. Rescue mission.'

'Right.' I nodded with some difficulty. He wrapped my hair in a warm towel and we went over to the oval mirror.

Marc took the towel off and fluffed at my hair disapprovingly.

'When did you last have it cut?'

'Months. About...five months, probably.'

'What was it like?' He lifted my chin with one hand. 'Was it...was that a fringe?'

I nodded. 'It was a bob.' I gestured at my jawline. 'Very neat, very precise.'

He pursed his lips. 'Mmm. Well, what would you like to do? Are you actually *growing* it?'

I sighed, feeling slightly defeated. 'I'm not growing it. Not really. I'm not doing anything, I was just...leaving it there. But I got a sudden urge for a haircut. Whatever you think is best, I'll go along with.'

'Honestly?' He pulled at a long strand.

'Go for it.'

He rolled my hair into a thick coil and reached for the scissors. His eyes met mine in the mirror. I smiled.

Ten minutes later Mavis came back in.

'Marc,' she said with a gasp, grabbing at the door frame. 'Let me just take a look at your lady.' She rushed over, slightly sideways, like a crab in a nice two-piece.

Marc stood back, smirking.

'It's fine, Mavis,' I said. 'I'm really happy with my experience at *Maison La Plage.'*

'Are you?' she said. 'Well, I knew you would be, only I did warn you, Marc, you can't expect everyone to want your styles down here. It looks as though you've struck lucky this time.' She gasped for air at the end of it and off she bustled, looking furious and relieved in equal measure.

'Your styles?' I asked him.

'Yeah. Just like yours, I guess,' he said, fluffing my hair at the back and making some precise snips.

'So, what happened?' he said.

My heart thudded. Did he know about Mr Moffat, could he tell just by looking at me?

'In my experience,' he went on, 'as a hairdresser, women have drastic cuts when something's happened.'

'Oh!' I laughed with relief.

'So which was it? Divorce?'

'Not exactly.'

'Ooh. Mysterious. Disaster of some kind then.'

I sighed. 'There was a disaster, for someone.'

'OK, I won't press it now, but you'd probably rather tell me than Mavis.'

I nodded. 'Can I ask you something? You see the bus stop outside?'

'Hmm.' He reached for a razor and started slicing away at the blunt ends of my hair.

'Did you notice anyone get off the bus the day before yesterday, anyone you didn't recognise from the village?'

'You mean the guy who met the Pirate King?'

'The what, the who?'

'Well, I call him the Pirate King. Don't tell me you haven't noticed him. Hottest guy in the village?'

'Tall. Dark.'

Marc nodded and gave me another smirk in the mirror.

'Wears a red waterproof?' I said.

'Right. I call him the Pirate King 'cos he's got that look. Naughty.'

'He's called Nick. He's a writer.'

'Ha! Right. And I'm an astronaut.'

'You don't think he's a writer?'

'Well, he'd get a bit more writing done if he stayed indoors more. Nick the wanderer more like.'

I nodded. 'I've noticed him a lot, you're right, out and about. Well, only in the last couple of days.' There was a reason for that, though, wasn't there? 'And you say he met a guy off the bus?'

'Not met, exactly. They kind of ran into each other. Sort of...' He straightened up and looked out of the window and I turned my head, as though I could see them too. 'Like the guy off the bus asked for directions or something, and Nick started talking to him. Weird, now I think of it. I mean, you don't just strike up a conversation like that, do you? Very odd couple they made. Not a couple, I mean. The guy on the bus was ordinary, he was a bit pale, flabby. He had a little bag which I noticed because it was red and black and it looked like it matched the Pirate King's outfit.'

I frowned at my reflection in the mirror. There was no doubt then that Nick the writer and Mr Moffat had some connection by that evening when Mrs Harper saw them on the harbour wall. I turned back to the mirror. I gulped. My hair was really short.

'Don't look so worried!' Marc said, flicking his fingers through my hair. 'Bit of undercut, just here? Might as well, for good measure.'

I nodded, distracted. 'What happened then? After the Pirate King ran into the guy off the bus?'

'Oh, didn't see any more after that. My 3 o'clock came in. Shampoo and set.'

I winced.

'I know,' Marc said. 'And all for love.'

I paid for my hair and bought some styling

wax and gave Marc a tip. He gave me a hug, and said, 'Come by any time, just for a chat, maybe?'

'I will. And I'll tell everyone where I got this amazing cut.'

'Oh, they'll know,' he said, opening the door for me.

He blew me a kiss as I left, and I could see Mavis watching through the bead curtains, one hand clutching her pearls.

CHAPTER FIFTEEN

I felt slightly cheerful, with a tiny dose of new-haircut happy as I went down the narrow cobbled street. The houses pressed in on either side, but through the slits and gaps between them I could see blue sea, and sky. The early mist had blown away and the day was blustery now, and fresh. I lifted my face to it and took in great lungfuls of sea air.

I sat on the harbour wall and waited for Pat and Horatio. I tried not to think about Nick the Pirate King, and Mr Moffat and little Kylie. If I just thought about my haircut, and keeping things ticking over at the guest house, I could stay calm. But when I did let myself think about everything that had happened since yesterday morning, I felt a flutter of something else: under the panic and the fear and the sheer humiliation of it all, I felt alive.

Horatio was the first to arrive, looking around and not seeing me. Twice his eyes slid over me, even though I'd only seen him an hour ago. I waved.

'Sorry, Isabel,' he said, walking gingerly on the slippery cobbles of the harbour wall. 'I didn't recognise you. You didn't go for a trim, then.'

'No. All in, that's my way.'

'All off.' He flushed. 'Sorry. It looks very nice. Very, um, modern.'

I could see Pat in the distance, hurrying, and I stood and started walking towards her. She stopped when she saw me.

'Oh,' she said. 'Oh, Isabel. You look amazing. Like a warrior queen. Hang on, has Mavis had a stroke?'

'It wasn't Mavis,' I said. 'It was Marc. Very different.'

I rubbed my hand up the side where the hair was bristly short. 'Very different.'

We all sat down on the harbour wall, Horatio in the middle.

'Is it always so quiet here?' I asked them, waving up at the little bungalows on the hill. 'I never see much coming and going.'

They stared at me.

'It's the winter,' Horatio said. 'It'll pick up, after Easter.'

I still wasn't convinced.

'You do know,' Pat said, 'no-one lives in those houses.'

'What? No! I didn't know that.'

Pat sighed. 'They're holiday lets.' She pointed behind us.

'Look. Coastguard's Hut, Harbourside Cottage, Sail Loft, Flat about the shop. Then up on the hill, starting with the yellow one, see it?'

I nodded

'Yellow one, that's Honeysuckle, that's a couple of teachers from Exeter. Then next to that, number four, that's a family, come every summer, but don't let it out. Then number 6, Harbour View – with an agency, number 8 – ah, Mrs Prosser still lives there but once she's gone, well her kids will sell it, they won't want it.'

Pat looked mournful and I could understand why.

'So those houses are empty now?' I asked her. 'But they'll be busy in the summer?'

'Well, before the summer generally, spring-time. But still...' She trailed off.

'That's...well. It's awful. But I'm really conscious, I'm living in a holiday let.'

'Yes you are,' Pat said. 'And I don't blame anyone who wants to sell their house, they've got to get a good price, but look at it. Dead.'

'And the pub,' Horatio said. 'Not sure how much longer that can keep going.'

'Or the shop,' Pat said. 'And once that goes...well, you'll be able to buy a plastic bucket and spade come August, but good luck getting a pint of milk in November.'

We sat on, huddled against the cold, and I felt sad for the little village, a place I'd previously held in slightly low regard. It was like when you flew somewhere and gradually all the hazy and distant places got clearer and more human the nearer you got. I'd been hovering over Gorran Porth, but now I was at ground level.

'This is a bit wet,' Pat said. 'My bum's getting damp.'

'We could go somewhere else?' I said, conscious that I didn't really know anywhere else, besides the pub and the corner store. Oh, and now the hair salon. My knowledge of Gorran Porth, and my contact with people in it, had tripled in the past day, all thanks to poor Mr Moffatt.

'What's the plan?' Horatio said.

'I think we should go and see Kylie, if we can find her,' I said. 'We need to find out if she didn't drive the van yesterday on purpose, or if she really didn't know what was going to happen.'

Horatio nodded. 'And shouldn't we try to find the other driver, the guy from the bakery who took over?'

Pat reached into her pocket and drew out three Tunnock's tea cakes. We took one each.

'The other driver,' she said, 'He might be one of them, one of the Mafia.'

We both stared at her then went back to unwrapping our tea cakes.

'Are we calling them that?' Horatio asked me.

'Whatever Pat likes,' I said. 'It doesn't matter who they are, it matters what they did.'

'Well I've left Trevor at home,' Pat said, 'watching his box-set of *The Sopranos*. For research.'

'Great. All back to yours for spaghetti, then,' I said, leading them off the harbour wall and round the corner to the little parking area behind the beach shop.

We climbed into Horatio's car which was a disgusting mess of sweet wrappers, old fish and chip trays, socks, baseball caps and drink cans.

'You've had a tidy up, I see,' Pat said, buckling herself into the back seat. I turned to look at her – *not really*, she mouthed back at me.

'Aren't there rules about this?' I said, peeling a sweet wrapper off the bottom of my shoe. 'Police rules?'

'I ride my bike for police work,' Horatio said.

'Can't get that messy,' Pat pointed out.

Horatio gestured to the car's ancient stereo and I found a 1960s compilation CD in the glove compartment and turned it on. We felt quite jaunty as we climbed out of the village and out across the moorland, the sea on our right, grey and slightly cross looking. The sky was mostly clear, with a few wind-torn clouds stuttering along at the horizon. Dusk would descend all too soon and I welcomed the trip out of the village, especially with the company I had. Horatio and Pat made me feel safe; they were easy to talk to, they didn't judge, they weren't pretentious and they were part of something bigger. Not just family, I thought, but place. Place and time.

'I still don't understand,' Pat said, leaning forward, 'why did they want to take his body away? If they are the ones who killed him.'

'I've been thinking about that,' I said. 'I looked at the house, the hallway and the stairs. Smith said he might have died from a head injury, but if he did, he'd have done that in the room. He couldn't have come back from the town with a head injury and got all the way to Room 6 without leaving a trace. He'd have been bleeding.'

'Head wounds always bleed a lot,' Horatio said. 'We know that from Youth Club.'

I didn't ask.

'So he was killed in Room 6,' Pat said. 'Why not just leave him there? And, sorry to go back to splattering, but he must have been killed – in the room – and then someone made that hole in his head. And why? That's just showing off, that is. If he was already dead. Why take a risk?'

We all mused on that.

'Even if he was dead,' I asked her, 'wouldn't the person who, you know, made the hole, wouldn't he have – or she, I suppose –'

'Wouldn't they have got blood on them?' Pat said.

I nodded.

'Hmm. I'll have to have a think about that,' Pat said. 'I think you're right though, because them cows are dead, and there's always a lot of blood.'

I stared at her. 'What cows?'

'Up the slaughterhouse,' she said. 'They're dead. Only blood comes out, doesn't it. Like when you see a badger on the road, or something. But there's no heartbeat, so there's no real...' She looked at me for permission. 'Splatter.'

'Unless,' Horatio said, 'they took the body away because...that's just their way.'

'Tidy? You mean?' I asked.

'Well. Not tidy in itself, but maybe that's their style, you know? Maybe they just like to tie up all the loose ends, take control.'

'But they needed the pasty van at short notice,' I said.

'We've been assuming they set it up in advance,' Pat pointed out. 'But what if Kylie was really ill, and what if the boy from the bakery took over, and what if they...oh my God. They might have kidnapped him and stolen the van. He could be... oh my God. Stop the car.'

'I'm not stopping, Aunty Pat!' Horatio said, stepping on the accelerator. 'But I'm going straight to the bakery.'

CHAPTER SIXTEEN

At the next junction we swivelled in a circle on the gravel at the side of the road, and Horatio wrestled the car around. The thick layer of rubbish on the floor resettled with a slight sigh. Pat and I were holding on with both hands to whatever we could grab on to.

'Don't kill us, Horatio,' I told him. 'That won't help anyone.'

He was brilliant though, braking and accelerating in harmony with the twisting lanes. There are no hedges in this part of Cornwall, only high, unforgiving banks of stone and earth, topped with meagre furze. One brush with that and we'd have been heading straight after Mr Moffat.

We finally reached the major road and it was a massive relief to turn onto the smooth black surface. Horatio picked up speed and Pat and I loosened our grip on the car. I closed my eyes for a bit, trying not to think about the pasty van and the poor volunteer driver.

Horatio was slowing and I opened my eyes and looked around me. He was turning off the fast road and into a small industrial estate. There was the usual mix of car repair places and light industry, but the largest business by far was a blue metal structure at the end, surrounded by high wire fences. There were a number of white vans inside the fencing, all with the title Penwithick Pasties in blue paint. There was a matching blue sign above a closed loading bay, and only the front door – marked 'reception' – was open.

Horatio parked in the visitors' bay and we rushed into the building. We leaned on the counter and Pat banged on the doorbell set into the counter.

'We're closed!' We could hear someone moving in the room beyond.

Pat pressed the bell again, this time keeping her finger on it until a small man in a blue boiler suit came round the corner. The boiler suit had Penwithick Pasties embroidered on the chest pocket, above the name 'Malcolm'. He was wearing a white mesh trilby, with a little hairnet stuck on at the back.

He put both his hands flat on the counter and stared at us, bleakly. His face was slightly jowly, and shadows under the cheeks and beneath his eyes gave him a rather sinister, nightmarish cast.

'We're closed.'

'Sorry,' I said. Pat and Horatio had taken a tiny half-step back. I guessed I was in this now, for better or worse

'We aren't here to bother you. We just need to ask you something. About yesterday.'

'Look,' Malcolm said. 'I've had people in here all day asking something about yesterday. Mostly asking where the blinkin' pasties are. I've had every corner shop from Luxulyan to Portscatho giving me grief about their stock. I've been working all day and all night – making more pasties. I'm very sorry if you didn't get your delivery, but like I've told everyone, one of my drivers has stolen one of my vans.'

'Has he though?' I said. 'I mean, we think the van might have been stolen, yes, but not by one of your drivers. Well, we don't know for sure. But has the driver been seen since?'

'Well, he wouldn't hang around, would he?' Malcolm said. 'He's probably off up country, selling the van. Selling the pasties too!'

'Was he from round here?' Pat said. 'Local family?'

Malcolm shuddered. 'Don't talk to me about that family. I've had them in here blustering about and shouting, saying how their boy never done anything wrong.'

'Malcolm,' I said, using my most reasonable tone. 'We think your van may have been involved in a crime. We think – it is just possible – your driver has also been involved in a crime, as a victim. Can we tell you what we know, and what we think?'

'Well the police don't seem to think that,' Malcolm said. 'They aren't interested at all. It was my newest van, see, and I hadn't had the name painted on it. So they say that's why the boy chose that van to steal.'

I looked at Horatio. 'You saw the van, going past The Manse?'

Horatio nodded. 'It might have been blank,' he said, 'I only saw the top corner, and they all look the same. I just knew it was the pasty van.'

Malcolm looked impatient. 'Well that's neither here nor there, but the police say that's why the van was stolen, it didn't have the logo on it, so he chose that one.'

'He didn't choose it, though, did he?' I said. 'Kylie was off sick, you asked for a volunteer, how could he have known it would be that van?'

Malcolm took off his mesh trilby and rubbed his forehead. 'I can't hardly think straight,' he said. 'I'm that tired.'

'You need a nice cup of tea,' Pat said. 'And we need to tell you our story.'

Malcolm shrugged and lifted the flap of wood which formed the end of the reception counter.

We trooped inside. There was a small office with filing cabinets and a couple of ancient desktop computers, and a large map of Cornwall on the wall. It was covered with a series of squiggles in different colours, all emanating from the dot where we now stood – Penwithick Pasties. The squiggles appeared to be colour coded. Gorran Porth had a green line going through it – past Uncle Nat's farm, down into the village and back out again. There were green lines into the surrounding villages. Areas further north were red lines, and to the west and east, blue and orange.

'All those green lines,' I said. 'All that one van?'

Malcolm came to look at the map with me.

'Ah. All the same van, but not all on the same day. Thursday, see, that's this line,'

He traced with his finger the line which led from the factory, round the top of the nearest town, down into the first seaside village, back out, along the beautiful coast road and up onto the bleak moor. From there, two villages – pasties for the pubs I thought, rather than shops – then curling round into Upper Lestoon, Lower Lestoon and the farm, then past the two Glebelands houses and down into the village.

'So we think, somewhere on this route, your van was stolen.' I said it as calmly as I could.

'Why?' Malcolm looked amazed. 'Why would anyone want it? No-one even knew what was in it, because the name wasn't on it. Only that idiot boy, first time on the road, I'm telling you, he's the one who's got it.'

'Come on!' Pat shouted from the next room. 'Tea!'

She'd nosed out a little kitchen at the back of the office. There was a small Formica-topped table and six mismatched dining chairs. There was a washing-up rota taped to the fridge, and some jars of tea-bags and sugar with names stuck on them. On the wall was a stern reminder about hand-washing and on the door at the end, a directive warning that only authorised personnel could proceed into the food preparation area.

We sat down at the table and Pat pushed a mug of tea towards Malcolm.

'This is what happened,' I started. I had a brief lapse of confidence, but I pressed on.

'Yesterday, I found a dead body. In the bedroom of the guest house I run. In Gorran Porth.'

Malcolm looked up. He looked only mildly interested, but that might have been the tiredness.

'Horatio, here,' Horatio gave a little wave to Malcolm, 'Horatio is a Community Support Officer. And he took control of the, well the crime scene, and he put police tape all round the front door.'

'Quite rightly, in my view,' Pat said.

'Right. So then a group of people who we thought were the police, arrived.'

Malcolm was still sipping his tea, quietly.

'So they arrived,' I said. 'And they investigated, in the room. We thought so.'

Pat nodded.

'And then a van turned up. And it took the body away.'

Malcolm put his mug down. I noticed it had Mr Angry on it. I hoped that wasn't his usual personal mug.

We all sat there for a bit, the fluorescent tube overhead popping and fizzing quietly.

'Lovely smell!' Pat said, suddenly. 'Lovely smell of pasties.' Horatio nodded. I could see him looking around, slightly wistfully. I tried to stay focussed.

'They weren't really the police, though,' Malcolm said, thoughtfully.

'No. We know that now.'

'How did you find out?' he asked me.

'The real police turned up. A bit later.'

'Nasty,' he said. 'Embarrassing.'

'Yes. Quite. So, what we're thinking is, one of the first group to arrive rang someone else, and they found a van, and they stole it, and drove off with Mr Moffat in it.'

'Who is Mr Moffat?' Malcolm asked.

'The, uh, the dead person,' I said.

'In the pasty van,' Malcolm said. 'In with the pasties.'

I gave him a bit of space to think that through. Pat poured more tea. Malcom gathered his thoughts.

'So the lad was kidnapped? Is that what you're saying? Or... or worse?'

I looked over at Pat and Horatio. Had we thought this through? Why hadn't we just dialled 999 as soon as we'd worked it out? Because we hadn't worked it out, had we? There was no more reason to think this than to believe as Malcolm did, that the boy had run off to sell the van. The van which collected Mr Moffat might have been standing by ready, all we had to go on was the coincidence, and the angry pasty customers.

'Do you know where the last delivery was made?' I asked Malcom. 'You said people had been ringing in since their delivery didn't turn up.'

Malcolm got up and went back into the other room, and we could hear him dialling the phone and speaking to someone.

'Smell them pasties?' Pat said quietly.

'I know. Fresh,' Horatio agreed. 'Got anything to eat, Aunty Pat?'

Pat showed him her empty hands.

Malcolm came back in with a scrap of paper. 'I've called my wife. She takes the calls, see, and she sent the drivers out this morning with the replacements, as many as we could. We couldn't make enough, and we couldn't get round to everyone because we still had the normal Friday rounds to do.'

He sat back down and took another gulp

of his tea.

'Right. The last delivery was to Star Stores, at the holiday park in Church Point, that's close to you, isn't it? Gorran Porth?'

'Yes, that's really close to us. Uncle Nat must have been his next call?' I wasn't too clear on the geography of it.

'No,' Pat said. 'Village stores first, surely, then back up the village and out, along past Uncle Nat's.'

'How far is that?' I asked her.

She pursed her lips. 'Mm. Gotta be two miles, at least.'

Malcolm was watching us.

'We know the criminals were driving the van when it went past Uncle Nat's – sorry, Lower Lestoon Farm. Because, firstly, they didn't stop with his special order.'

'No onions,' Malcolm said, 'very peculiar.'

'Right. They didn't stop with the special order and they were driving really quickly. But on those two miles, Pat, some of it would have been past houses. They couldn't have stopped a van and got the driver out and taken over the driving, all without being seen, could they?'

'St Stephen's,' Horatio said.

Pat looked at him and nodded slowly. 'Yes, that's where they did it. St Stephen's.'

Malcolm spread his hands out. 'What? What are we talking about now?'

'You know – St Stephen's, the church,' Pat

said. 'There's a little pull-in, people often stop there to look at the view, and the road turns, you have to slow down. If they were waiting there and they got the call and the van went past, well, we'll have to go there, now. Won't we?' Pat turned to me.

'We should. We should go there now, before it gets any darker.'

'Well. This is all very Juliet Bravo,' Malcolm said, 'but I still think that lad's up country – Exeter. Maybe even Bristol.'

'What's his name?' I asked.

'Tyrone.'

'We might not find him,' I said. 'It might be too late.'

The others nodded and Malcolm stood up when we did.

'I'm not convinced,' he said. 'But I'll follow you, I'll be in my van.'

CHAPTER SEVENTEEN

It was darker and much colder when we returned to the car. This time I got in the back and let Pat sit with Horatio. She could navigate, I'd sit there and worry.

We pulled out onto the smooth fast road, almost deserted now except for Malcolm's lights behind us.

We drove through the outskirts of a town, St Austell I guessed, and then the orange street lights fell away behind us and the dusk pressed in. There was a faint line of paler grey on the horizon, and that's where we headed.

'Isabel, there should be a torch in the back, in the pocket somewhere,' Horatio said.

I found it, and I fumbled around in the litter at the back and found a fleece sweatshirt and put that on. It smelt slightly of dog, but I was starting to shiver and I was glad to have the extra layer. I gripped the torch until my hand hurt.

Horatio was driving fast and we skidded slightly as he almost missed the turnoff. We climbed off the main road and up over the moor. Snatches of landscape were revealed below us as we curved and twisted, Malcolm keeping pace behind. We dropped slightly above Gorran Porth and Malcolm started to slow down. Ahead was a church, small and squat, almost hidden in a clump of scrubby trees, leaning away from the wind. There was a rough mossy wall around the graveyard and a small lay-by in front, as though the church had picked up its robes and taken a half-step back from the road. In full daylight we'd probably see tyre tracks in the leaf-mould and mud at the edges of the space, but the huge empty sky was filing with gloom.

Malcolm pulled in behind us. Horatio and Malcolm left their headlights on and we went through a little gate and spread out into the churchyard and stood as silent as the tomb-stones.

'Horatio,' I said, 'why don't you check the porch and all round the outside of the church first, and we'll check in front and behind every gravestone.'

'Right you are.' Horatio vanished into the twilight.

Beyond the church I could just see the darkness of the sea and in the far distance the comforting blink of a lighthouse. I shivered again. I could hear Pat and Malcolm moving around the graveyard and I found some strength from somewhere and started to move along the rows of gravestones.

'Tyrone!' Pat was calling. 'Tyrone, can you hear us?'

'Come on, lad,' Malcolm joined in. 'You've got us worried.'

Horatio returned from checking the church porch. He'd rattled the door but it was locked.

'Porch is empty, all the doors locked.'

'I wonder if they would have been locked yesterday?' I asked.

'You think he might be inside?'

'No. Just being optimistic, I suppose.' I looked down at a bunch of dried-up flowers on a grave. It suddenly seemed like the saddest thing in the world.

Over in the corner where the two walls of the graveyard met was the humped outline of a compost heap. I picked up the flowers and carried them over. It was made up of grass and leaves and all the cuttings from the flowers the people brought to the graves. And there on the top, was the unmistakable dark shape of a human body.

'Help!' I shouted. 'Help me.'

Pat was the nearest. She thundered over, dodging the gravestones. 'Tyrone?' She reached out a hand and shook him. We both stood motionless, longing with every fibre of our being for a response.

'Shine the torch on him,' Pat said and I did

it with my eyes closed.

She grabbed my hand and directed the beam.

'Oh that poor boy,' It was Malcolm coming up behind us. I could hear Horatio moving in front of me, but I still couldn't look.

'Alive,' Horatio said.

I opened my eyes. Horatio had his hand on the neck of the still figure.

'Are you sure?' Pat breathed.

'Only just, but there's a pulse. Feel.'

I could hear Pat moving. 'Yes! Isabel, feel that.'

Pat grabbed my hand and brought it to Tyrone's neck where I could feel some warmth, and the faint fluttering of his blood. Was that it? That tiny tick of life? Was that the difference between Mr Moffat, and Tyrone?

'What is it?' Malcolm said, 'is it a head injury?'

'Looks like it,' Pat said. 'Look at all that blood.'

And we all looked at where his hair was matted and clotted to the side of his head, his eyes closed and a dreadful pallor in his skin.

'Look at his neck, though,' Malcolm said. 'Look at his poor little neck.' It was blackened with bruises.

'Call an ambulance,' I said to Horatio.

'No, I'll take him in the van,' Malcolm said.

'You can't, you can't put him in the pasty

van.'

'My van's empty, I finished for the day.'

'Isabel,' Horatio said, 'it will be quicker. 'If we call an ambulance it'll have to come out from Truro, and then all the way back. Come on, we got to work out a way to lift him.' Horatio was in charge now.

Malcolm was running back to his van, turning it around and backing up close to the gate with the rear doors open.

'Should we move him?' I asked Pat.

'Got to. Hypothermia'll get him. He's only alive cause he crawled into the compost, nice and warm that is.'

'He is alive, isn't he?'

Pat checked again. 'Still alive. Breathing too, look. That's always handy.'

Horatio ran over with a blanket.

'I reckon we get him in this, carry a corner each. We don't want to bounce him around, I'll go in the back with him.'

'We'll come with you,' I said, 'to the hospital.'

'No,' Pat said. 'They won't want a whole horde of us. We'll get back to the village. Have a think.'

I was too tired to argue.

Malcolm got back from the gateway and we spread the blanket out on the compost heap. We all got together on one side and put our hands in the warm compost and dug out handfuls from under Tyrone, pushing the blanket further and further in until we were halfway. He hadn't made a sound, or a move, but I was pleased to feel the warmth of the compost heap under his body. He must have been outside all night, but it hadn't been freezing cold and the dense yew trees had sheltered him from rain, and sight. If it had been the night before, the night of the storm, he'd surely have died. We lifted his legs and shifted them sideways onto the blanket. Horatio went round to the other side and reached under the boy's shoulders to pull the blanket through. The compost smelt almost obscenely rich, full of life.

We all slid carefully off the heap, and found our footing. Horatio and Pat were on one side, Malcolm and I on the other. On Horatio's command we lifted the blanket and Tyrone was free of the earth. He felt like a dead weight between us – he was thin but tall. We stepped carefully round the nearest gravestone and down the slight slope to the path which rounded the graveyard. Gradually, with tiny footsteps, we reached the gateway. We had to work through one corner at a time, my hand on Tyrone's head to protect it from the gateway. The blanket was wet under his face and so was my hand. At the tail of the van Horatio jumped in and started to pull the blanket in from the rear. Eventually, Tyrone's head was supported by the floor of the van, and we stood back.

Malcolm came round the side and looked at me.

'You saved that boy's life, Miss,' he said. 'I wouldn't have believed it, but you convinced me to come, and here he is. I would have left him out here another night and he would have surely died.'

'I hope we've saved him. I hope so.'

'Come on,' Horatio said. 'Shut me in.'

We closed the doors of the van on him and Malcolm went round to the driver's side. He wound the window down and as he drove away he said it again.

'You've saved that boy's life,' he said again. 'I won't forget that.'

We waved as they pulled away and I huddled a bit closer to Pat.

'You heard him?' Pat said. 'He won't forget it. You know what that means?'

I peered at her in the gloom left after the van's departure. 'No idea.'

'Free pasties. That's what that means. Free pasties, for life.'

CHAPTER EIGHTEEN

We got into Horatio's car and Pat handed me a tissue and I tried to clean the blood from my hand.

'I've got more to tell you,' I said. Pat nodded.

'When I got my hair cut, I asked Marc – the stylist – if he'd noticed Mr Moffat arrive. Because the bus stop is right opposite.'

Pat nodded again and I could her rustling about in the side pocket of the car door. She opened a crackly pack of barley sugar and offered me one.

'And he said he had seen Mr Moffat arrive. Ooh. That's nice. Sweet. I needed that.'

Pat nodded again.

'And you'll never guess who ran into Mr Moffat when he got off the bus?'

Pat turned to me, her cheek swollen with barley sugar. 'Oh my God, Isabel. Who was it?'

'The Pirate King.'

'The Pirate what?'

'Nick the writer. Marc calls him the Pirate King.'

'Mm. I can see where he's coming from, yeah.'

We paused for another few minutes. The sugar was coursing into my blood and the car started to feel warm and cosy.

'So does that mean...' Pat was musing aloud. 'That Nick knew Mr Moffat? And he's been hanging around your house. You saw him, Horatio saw him.'

'And there's more. Marc said Mr Moffat definitely had a bag with him. So whatever was in that bag, that's what got him killed. And whoever killed him took it out of Room 6.'

'You don't think Nick killed Mr Moffat? He's ever so handsome, and proper charming!'

'Look at Smith, we thought he was handsome and charming.'

'We did. And well-dressed, we thought he was well-dressed too. We were wrong about him, weren't we.' Pat sounded wistful. 'Aren't there really any heroes?'

'Horatio's a hero, about now,' I said, looking at my watch. 'And Malcolm. To Tyrone and his family, they'll be heroes.'

'And us, we'll be heroes,' Pat said.

'Yes. Slightly.'

'I bet if we went back to the village now, the Pirate King would be in the pub,' Pat said, starting the car. 'He's in there most nights, according to Demelza.'

'Where is he staying?'

'In Coastguard Cottage. He's renting it.'

'He arrived in the winter, didn't he. Like me?'

'That's right. So whatever is going on, it's been going on for a while. Maybe Mr Moffat was bringing him drugs. Maybe Mr Moffat got killed for the drugs.' She pulled out into the lane and turned down towards the village.

'No. Why would you kill a drug dealer? You'd want him to come back. God, I wish I'd paid more attention. Did Mr Moffat have the bag when he checked in? Why didn't I look at him? I was the last friendly face he saw, and I couldn't even be bothered to look at him properly.'

'Isabel,' Pat said. 'Get a grip, my girl. You've done more than anyone. More than those smug gits in the police. And you found Tyrone. We've got tomorrow and Sunday before we have to go in and give statements, there's no telling what you could achieve yet.'

I leaned my head back and closed my eyes. I thought back to the afternoon when Mr Moffat arrived. He had rung the doorbell and I'd been – where had I been? I'd been sitting in the easy chair in the front room of the guest house, just sitting. So I could see him through the side of the bay window. What did I see? A small man, slightly mousy, official looking. I'd got up reluctantly, I remembered, thinking he'd come to ask something – read a meter, maybe. He was wearing a jacket, and I could see he had a collar and tie and a woolly jumper.

'Oh, yes,' I said. 'Yes. He had an overnight bag with him. It was down by his feet. As soon as I saw it, I realised he was a guest, because I hadn't thought that in the split-second before. And as soon as I realised he was a guest, I stopped paying attention, I just took the money and gave him the key.'

'What about the register?' Pat asked.

I thought again.

'He said he'd fill it in on the way back down, only could he go up to the room now as he needed to get ready to go out. He was meeting someone in the village.'

'And you didn't ask who?' Pat tutted. 'Janice would have asked who. She'd have had his life-story and his inside-leg measurement before he got the key in the door.'

'I'm not Janice,' I said.

'No. Mind you, Janice would probably be dead now too, if she'd been here. She'd have interfered in some way, or made Smith wipe his feet. Generally, she'd have put a spoke in the works, Janice would.' Pat chuckled to herself. 'No offence, mind.'

We pulled up in front of Glebelands Guest House, but I didn't want to get out of the car.

'Nick the Pirate King was watching us yesterday,' I said. 'So he knows Mr Moffat is dead, and he knows the body is gone. But he may not know where the bag is.'

Pat turned to me, her eyes wide. 'Someone was in the house this morning, you said so.'

'Nick? Searching for the bag?'

Pat nodded. 'Isabel. You can't stay there. It isn't safe.'

I looked out of the car window at both houses. They were both dark. I needed to get in there and put some lights on.

'I'm responsible for them. I promised to look after them. I can't leave. We've already had a break-in.'

'And a murder,' Pat reminded me. 'A break-in and a murder. This used to be a nice place. You've brought us down, Isabel, you with your big-city ways.' She punched me gently on the shoulder. 'Come on. Let's go inside and search the houses and put some lights on. Then we can go down the pub, get a hot meal.'

As we worked our way through the guest house, checking each room and opening each cupboard and bathroom door, I tried not to think about how hard this would have been if I'd been alone. Finally we were both back in the kitchen, happy that the house was safe and deserted.

I put some table lights on in the front room, and drew the curtains to close out the night. The house would look inhabited now, at least for a couple of hours.

'Are you going to sleep in here tonight? Or in The Manse?' Pat asked.

'I'm not sure. I'll have a think.'

'You ought to come and stay with me and Trevor.'

'You're really kind, Pat. Let's go to the pub.'

'Let me ring Trevor, he wants to meet us there. Maybe Horatio will have news too.'

'I want to meet Trevor too, but I'm thinking – if Nick is in the pub...'

'Oh no, no,' Pat said. 'He's dangerous he is. Probably. Possibly.'

'We don't know that. And what can he do in the pub?'

'I don't like this. Trevor wouldn't like it.'

'I've got an idea. Why don't I go into the pub and sit on my own. Then if Nick's there I can start chatting to him. And then you and Trevor can come in and sit together, but at another table. And you can watch us, all night.'

'That's a good plan,' Pat said. 'I like that. Shall I drop you down there now?'

'No. I'll go next door, get changed, get a bit dressed up, maybe?'

'Don't go all hussy on us,' Pat said.

'Hardly. Then I'll walk down there, I'll get there by...seven? So you give me a bit of time, then come in with Trevor. If Nick isn't there, or I haven't been able to talk to him, we'll just have a nice night in the pub. Just a normal night in the pub.'

Pat wanted to go through The Manse with me, checking and securing it, but I managed to persuade her I wasn't afraid.

Acting convinced for her sake actually helped. I waved her goodbye in the porch where Petey's repair of the broken window was holding firm, and let myself into the house.

I went straight upstairs to the master bedroom and helped myself – with no hesitation this time – to some black jeans and another cashmere, bright pink, and a pale pink t-shirt to go under it. I showered in the master bathroom and put on my stolen clothes. Another good dollop of Chanel and I thought I was probably smart enough for the Smuggler's Arms.

I took my old clothes down to the utility room and put the expensive and under-used appliances through their paces. I'd come back from the pub to a fresh load of heavy metal t-shirts and boy's jeans, but I wasn't sure I'd ever wear them again. My vanity was coming back to life, with all the other parts of the old me.

I found a nice pair of leather trainers in the hall and put those on. One last thing to do.

The study was locked; it was the only room in the house where I had valuables of my own. Now I went to the hanging rack of keys on the dresser in the kitchen and looked for the key. Inside the square room was a bureau, a leather chair, some bookcases and the paintings and ornaments which scattered the whole house. I opened the top drawer in the bureau and took out my handbag. I hadn't used it since Christmas Eve. I rummaged deep into the bag. There at the bottom was the cool shape of my mobile phone. I turned it on. Nothing, no charge at all. Where was the charger? Upstairs in my attic bedroom, probably, where my overnight bag and the rest of the belongings lay strewn about the floor. Did I have time to go up there now? I decided against it, and slipping the phone into the pocket of my jeans I locked the door again. I put the key back and took my purse out of the deep kitchen drawer in the dresser. I had drawn out £500 when I left London and I still had plenty left. I took some tenners out and put them in my pocket, locked the house and left.

It was so easy to live like this: no handbag, no phone, no...*baggage*. Could I go back? Could I give this up? I was already about to make a big change. When I got back tonight I planned to put my phone on charge and then I'd start calling people. I didn't imagine it would be easy. I'd walked away from so much and now I was moving back into the daylight, like a swimmer kicking up from the bottom of the pool. I'd thought I was Mr Moffat, but I'd really been Tyrone all along.

CHAPTER NINETEEN

The walk down the hill was bracing and it felt comforting to step into the warmth of the Smuggler's Arms. Demelza smiled at me and Petey was there – (still there?) – at the end of the bar and I ordered a half pint of cider and whatever Petey was drinking. No sign of Nick. I got up onto a bar stool, I didn't want to go to a table and get settled in if he wasn't going to materialise.

'Busy night?' I asked Demelza.

'Might pick up.' She shrugged. 'Winter, see. Be alright in a couple of months.'

'Oh yes, tourists. I'd forgotten, it must completely change the village.'

'It does. There's still some don't like it, but most people take the chance to make some money while they can. We should be grateful people still want to have an old-fashioned beach holiday. You'll be busy too, I bet, up at the guest house. When's Janice coming back?' Demelza was polishing the bar while she talked, moving up and down, so I timed my reply.

'I think Janice will be back in a week or two. Maybe. I'll ring her on Sunday.'

'What will you do then?'

I took a long sip of my cider. I was about to reply when there was a sudden blast of cold air behind me and I knew, I just knew, that Nick the Pirate King had come in.

I watched Demelza's face as she smiled at him. There was genuine and not just professional pleasure on her face. And why not? A man like that certainly brightened things up.

I swivelled round on the bar stool.

'Nick!' I said. I hadn't worked for one of the most powerful men in the world and not learnt to take charge of a social situation. 'Please let me get you a drink – I so want to hear about your book.'

'Pint of Doombar,' Nick said to Demelza and sat on the stool next to mine. 'Thanks.'

He took off his red waterproof, rolling it up, and pushed at the sleeves of his flannel shirt.

He looked at me while he took the first sip and I had to look away. Demelza was watching us, a slight sly smile on her face. She wandered off up the bar.

Nick put down his glass. 'Nice haircut. I thought you never went out of the village. You didn't get that round here.'

I was infuriated at his insinuation that I never went anywhere – who did he think he was to comment on that – but I stayed on track.

'I did get it here, actually. There's a new stylist in town, so I went to the salon on Water Street. You know, the one right opposite the bus stop.'

'Ah. Right.'

'Yes, the stylist, Marc, he's new. He's getting to know the place, though, he told me. Of course, he's in a great spot there, to see all the comings and goings.'

'Oh yes?' He looked bland and unruffled.

'So tell me all about your book. What gave you the idea? Have you already written one? Would I have read anything of yours?'

'No, no, first-time author. I came to a crossroads in my life, and I decided to do this, not forever, but I had a bit of cash, enough to keep me going for a few months, so I found a little place to rent down here, very cheap in the winter. What about you, Isabel?'

Being a writer was a very good excuse, I thought. Very handy. Convenient. Because you never had to be seen doing anything, and you could wander round the place thinking, getting inspired.

'Me? Oh I'm not doing anything interesting. I go for long walks, run the bed and breakfast for Janice, while she's away.'

'But that does sounds interesting. All those new people, coming and going. You must see some strange sights, I bet.'

He raised his pint glass and I saw a hard

granite glitter in his eyes as he sipped.

'It really isn't very busy at this time of year,' I said. 'I mean, take yesterday, just three people, one single guy and a couple.'

'Mm?'

'And they've all checked out now.'

He nodded. 'Well. Nice work if you can get it.'

'I've got more people arriving on Sunday though. It was such a challenge at first, getting all the fried eggs ready at the same time. And my back ached the first week after all the bed-making.'

He nodded. 'Writing can be exhausting too, I find myself getting quite hunched up over the laptop. I like the walks around here, I like to take a break and see the sea.'

'I know. I like the high road up over the top and down to the secret beach.'

'Is that what you call it?'

'I know the locals call it Deadman's Beach, in Coffin Cove.'

'D'you know why? I've wondered, I keep meaning to look it up.'

I shrugged. 'Demelza?' She sauntered over.

'Why do you call it Deadman's Beach, and Coffin Cove?'

'Ah, well,' she leaned on the bar conspiratorially, 'they do say, anything which goes in the bay north of Deadman's Point will end up on the beach. 'Cos of the currents, see. I don't believe that myself, I think it was a wreckers' beach, or maybe once there was a big shipwreck and all the bodies washed up there, and the name just stuck.'

'Cheery,' I said to Nick as Demelza went back down the bar.

'They like a bit of drama, I've noticed,' he said.

You don't know the half of it, I thought. 'Tell me about your book then, has it been burning inside you for years?

'I've been thinking about it for a while, but then the opportunity came up to devote some time to it.'

'Have you got an agent?'

'No. No, I'm a long way from that point.'

'Only, I know an agent, so...' This wasn't exactly a lie. Among Sir Dougall's business interests was a massive talent agency.

'Oh, I'm not really ready to show it to anyone yet.'

'But maybe in a few months? Will you be here over the summer? I suppose the rents go up then?'

'I haven't thought that far ahead, I'm just going with it, seeing where it takes me.'

Liar, I thought. Very good-looking liar.

We chatted and sipped for a bit longer, and I dithered over how far to push it.

'Do you want something to eat?' I said, gathering my nerve. 'I could murder a plate of fish and chips. Absolutely murder.'

'Great. Let's find a table.' He gathered up his coat and carried both glasses over to the nearest empty table, right by the log fire. Nice. In other circumstances I couldn't have imagined a better Friday evening, but this man might be a murderer. Or at least know someone who was murdered by organised criminals. Was possibly an organised criminal himself?

He put the glasses on the table and did a slightly clumsy swerve so that he was sitting with his back to the wall. Clever. Not too subtle though, because I'd noticed. He could see the door and the rest of the bar, while all I could see was him. He had a more useful view, but I had an eyeful.

'What would you like?' I asked him, 'my treat.'

'No, the gentleman pays,' he said. 'Them's the rules.'

'Well let's break the rules. You can pay next time.'

He looked a bit rattled, but I didn't care.

'I'm having the fish and chips, with mushy peas, what about you?' I asked.

'I'll have the steak and ale pie, with jacket potato.'

'Right.' I placed the order with Demelza and sat back down at the table.

'So. Where were we?'

'You were telling me,' he said, 'about what

brought you to Gorran Porth.'

No, I wasn't but...damn...he was good.

Two could play at that game. I ignored his question.

'Oh, just excuse me for a minute?' I said. 'I want to buy Petey a drink, he's been so kind to me.'

I went back up to the bar and asked Petey what he'd like. He was sitting with the glowering woman from last night. I hadn't seen her close up before. She might have been about my age, or might have been a hundred years old. Her face was unlined and smooth, but she was slumped over with a look of misery and hopelessness. She had a mass of greying hair, wiry and too long, almost obscuring her face, giving her the look of a wild animal glaring from a thicket.

'This is my girlfriend, Winnie,' Petey said. I debated reaching out my hand but something told me Winnie didn't care to observe the social niceties.

'Hi, Winnie,' I said, being very bright. 'Nice to meet you, can I get you a drink too?' She stared at me and pointed to her glass of cider which was almost full.

'Right. Just one for you then, Petey. Well. Lovely to see you, I won't intrude, I think my supper's coming.'

And I went back to the table, relieved to be back in the company of a possible murderer.

Demelza put our plates in front of us,

handed us some cutlery wrapped in napkins, instructed us to 'enjoy!' and walked away.

He still didn't say anything, but signalled with his glass to Demelza. She brought us both a new drink and we started to eat, in silence.

'Sorry,' I said eventually. 'Didn't mean to abandon you, but Petey did an emergency repair for me, at The Manse.'

'Not to worry.'

'Yes. We had a break-in, or, maybe just an accident. The night of the storm.'

He nodded.

'You were saying,' he said, 'what brought you here?'

'Oh.' *Was I*? 'Well, I think I just needed a break. I'd had a busy year. Well, a busy few decades. I just needed to get away.'

'Everyone thinks something mysterious happened to you.'

'Do they?'

'You're quite the topic of conversation around the place. Staying in The Manse, arrived on Christmas Eve, not seen in public until January 11th or so I was told.'

'Wow. Village life.' I was halfway through my second glass of cider, and told myself to slow down.

'I'm glad there's no big mystery,' he said. 'Although, I'd like you to think that you could, you know, you could tell me anything that was worrying you. Anything at all.'

'Oh? That's a bit forward, Mr...what *is* your other name?'

'Price. Nick Price.'

'Why would I suddenly want to tell you all my troubles?'

'Not all of them, maybe. But we're both outsiders, aren't we? Some people here would call us foreigners, so, if there was anything worrying you, or anything you wanted to talk over...'

'Finished?' Demelza said, leaning on the table.

'Lovely. Thanks,' I said as she cleared the plates.

Behind us I felt the door open and I heard Pat come in, with – presumably – Trevor.

'Friend of yours,' Nick said, gesturing.

'Oh I think she's on a date, with her husband,' I said, giving her a quick wave and turning back to him. 'She's the postwoman, you know.'

'I did know. Not that I get any post, but she's out and about all round the village. She doesn't miss much, does she.'

'No. She found the broken window in The Manse, on the day after the storm.'

'No other damage?'

'No, nothing at all, nothing to worry about. Shall we have pudding?'

Demelza went off to get us some lemon meringue pie and a portion of spotted dick. Both with clotted cream. Well, we wanted to fit in, didn't we?

'Tell me about the crossroads,' I said.

'Crossroads?'

'Yes, you said you were at a crossroads in your life, and you decided to make a change. What were you doing before?'

'Oh, right. I was a civil servant.'

'Really, how interesting. What department did you work in?'

'It wasn't interesting, that's why I decided to take some time away and try something new.'

'Can you go back to your job, are they keeping it open for you?'

'Maybe. What about you, is it true, I've heard you work for Sir Dougall Spence.'

'I do. I did. So tell me more about the Civil Service. Haven't there been some major shake-ups there?'

'It's always being shaken up, that's the problem. New governments have different priorities, and new managers want to do things in a different way.'

'So, that was what drove you to the crossroads – a new manager?'

Demelza came back with the pudding bowls and I could have screamed at her, though once I took a look at the lemon meringue pie I calmed right down, and started eating.

'Good food here,' Nick said, after demolishing half his spotted dick in one go.

'Hmm.' I slowed down. I had to keep this

evening going, I wasn't finding out anything. Should I be more direct? 'Why did you pick this village to move to, do you already have friends here?'

'No, not really. Just...random I suppose. Peaceful. And the cottage I'm renting has great views.'

'So you don't know anyone here?'

He raised his gaze and looked straight at me. 'Well, we both know that's not quite true, Isabel.'

I took a massive gulp of cider.

'I'd like to think I know you,' he said. 'I mean, we've got so much in common, haven't we?'

I picked up my spoon again.

'Both of us,' he went on, 'escaping from London, and both of us seeking a quiet, peaceful life, with no interruptions to the way we've chosen to spend our days.'

I nodded.

He carried on eating calmly.

I heard the door behind me open, and another blast of cold air blew Horatio into the pub. Pat waved him over to her table. I so desperately wanted to hear what he was going to say – was Tyrone alright? Had the police been called to the hospital? When might Tyrone wake up and tell the police something useful?

'Excuse me,' I said, 'I must powder my nose,'

I caught Pat's eye as I passed her table and she joined me in the tiny cold Ladies' at the back of the pub.

'Horatio's just come back from the hospital,' she said.

'I saw him.'

'How's it going with the Pirate King?' She rubbed her hands with glee.

'Going fine, he's telling me lots of slightly plausible lies, but he's not giving anything away.'

'And neither are you, I should bet.'

I nodded. 'Any news, about Tyrone?'

'Too early to say but they sounded optimistic, Horatio thought. But it was a very unusual head injury, he was hit with a sharp implement in the side of his head, above the ear. But he had a very dense skull, apparently. Anyway, his family's there now, all hugging and kissing Malcolm. You know he's going to get all the credit.'

'That's fine,' I said, 'if it keeps attention away from us. I'd better get back.'

'Isabel – ' Pat grabbed my arm. 'You aren't going to do anything dangerous, are you? You aren't going back to his for a nightcap?'

'No. I don't think so. Probably not. No.'

Pat looked fierce. 'Because let's not forget, your new boyfriend might be a hitman.'

We looked at each other soberly for a minute.

'I'll be careful' I said. 'I'll go from here right up to the house.'

'He might follow you.'

'Not with you watching, I don't think he will. How's Trevor, I hope he's not finding this all a bit tedious.'

'Lovin' it. Absolutely lovin' it. Thinks he's James Bond.'

James Bond.

'Wasn't James Bond actually a civil servant?' I wondered.

'A what? What's brought that on?'

'I'm just thinking about the Pirate King – he claims he was a civil servant and I was thinking of a white-collar pen-pusher, which he most obviously wasn't, but now I'm thinking a bit wider.'

A woman I hadn't seen before came into the Ladies' and glared at us.

'You waiting?'

'No. No, you go ahead.' Pat moved out of her way.

'Talk tomorrow?' I said. 'With Horatio?'

'Yes. Enjoy...you know.'

We left the Ladies' together and went back to our respective tables.

Nick watched me approach the table and by the time I sat down I was definitely feeling alive again.

'Why do women always go to the Ladies' together?' he asked. 'What do you talk about in there?'

'Lip gloss,' I said. 'We talk about lip gloss, and celebrities. Do you want a coffee?'

'Fine.' He signalled to Demelza.

'Actually,' I said. 'Pat had some good news. A boy had gone missing, a van driver, a local lad. And we found him, and we sent him off to hospital and he's probably going to live.'

Nick couldn't possibly hide his reaction to that, I noticed, so instead he went the other way and overreacted.

'That's fantastic! That's amazing news. Well. You must be so proud. That's...oh that's great news.'

'Did you know him? The boy? You seem really pleased.'

'No, I didn't know him, didn't even know he was missing, but any life saved, that's a great thing, right?'

I nodded. Now I was going in for the killer blow. 'He had a very unusual head injury. A sharp object, just above the ear. But he had a very tough skull, so he didn't die. Shouldn't be hard to catch whoever did it, might even be able to tie it to other crimes.'

'If the police around here can do their jobs properly,' he said, looking darkly round the bar.

I thought he might have been looking at Horatio but the darkness was gone in a moment and the charming pirate was back.

'This is nasty talk for such lovely company,' he said as Demelza put the coffee cups on the table in front of us, a lovely blue china pot with white writing on it, and matching cups and saucers.

He poured us both a cup and started drinking his.

I lingered as long as I could, taking tiny sips.

'There's another storm coming,' I said. 'I heard it on the radio today.'

'Great. I love that. Tucked up in my cottage, with the wind and rain lashing in. What about you, you must have good views up there at the top of the hill?'

'Yes, nice views from the attics of both the houses. I worry about the fishermen though, don't you? Out there in the storm?'

'They're used to it. They'd call us townies if we worried about them.'

'Yes. Probably.' I noticed he'd finished his coffee quickly and his attention had wandered slightly.

'Do you need to go?' I asked him. 'Has inspiration struck?'

He looked blank and then recovered. 'Yeah. Right. I've had a couple of good ideas. Talking to you has been just what I needed, Isabel. Can we do it again soon? You have to give me a chance to treat you.'

'Sure. Say whenever you'd like.'

'Have you got a number I can call you on?'

I hesitated. 'You can get me at the guest

house, there's a machine there too, if I don't pick up.'

'You've got a mobile,' he said, 'in your back pocket.'

I felt hot.

'But the signal is patchy,' I explained. 'It isn't reliable round here. You must find that in your little cottage?'

'Right.' He stood up and put his raincoat on. 'Look, I'm really sorry to just rush off like this.'

'That's fine, I understand. You've got work to do. Writing.'

'Yeah! You've really been lucky for me.'

Liar, liar, I thought, though it was *my* pants on fire.

I stood up and pecked him on the cheek, mostly for Pat's delight.

'See you soon.'

CHAPTER TWENTY

I wandered over to Pat's table and Trevor stood up and pulled out a chair for me.

'I'm Trevor, pleased to meet you.'

'Isabel.'

He had a lovely warm handshake, and a sun-baked face with twinkly brown eyes and sandy hair. He looked comfortable and confident, sure of his place in the world. I could see what made him such a good match for Pat. They looked alike, in that way that some couple had.

'Sorry,' I said. 'I've messed up your evening rather.'

'Not at all!' Trevor assured me. 'I'm enjoying it. Well, apart from the poor soul in Room 6, of course. I'm not making light, not at all.'

'No, that's fine. We've had our moments, haven't we?'

Pat nodded.

'How was it at the hospital?' I asked Horatio, who wasn't eating, but cradling a pint.

'I kept out of the way, mostly,' he said. 'But

Malcolm's promised to ring me if there's news.'

'Good.'

Pat put down her fork. 'Why has he gone, Nick? I thought you were in there.'

I rolled my eyes at Trevor. 'Stop trying to fix me up with a criminal.'

'Handsome, though.'

I looked around the bar and drew my chair closer to the table. 'He got very excited when I told him about Tyrone. And that's when he decided to leave. I could see it clearly in his face, he couldn't wait to get out of here.'

Pat's mouth fell open. 'Oh my God. You don't think he's going to the hospital, he's not going to finish him off.'

'Aunty Pat,' Horatio said. 'Get real.'

'I don't know,' I said. 'I hadn't thought of that. There wouldn't be any point though, would there? I mean, if they've examined the wound and they know what caused it.'

'They don't know,' Horatio said. 'Very unusual, they said. But sharp.'

I felt sick. 'Why did I tell him? I was just trying to goad him, and now I might have put Tyrone at risk!'

'I don't think so,' Horatio said. 'I really don't. But just in case, let's go and see if he's gone home.'

'Follow him?'

'Not quite.'

Horatio got up and gestured to me.

'Demelza,' he called, 'I'm just showing Isabel the function room, she's thinking about booking it!'

Demelza waved us away.

We passed through the door I'd used earlier to get to the Ladies' and then up a narrow flight of stairs which was concealed by another door.

At the top was a landing, and through the doorway I could see a large empty room. There were tables and chairs but they were pushed to the sides leaving the floor free. There was a small bar in the corner, and a piano on the opposite wall. Horatio didn't turn the lights on, but went over to the bay window and raised the central blind. There was enough moonlight and reflected lights from downstairs to enable me to get across the room safely. I stood in the window next to Horatio. The pub occupied a corner which pointed down towards the sea. I could see through the space between the shuttered café and the closed beach-shop to the roiling water of the harbour. The wind rattled the windows and the street on either side was deserted.

'Wild night,' I said.

'Another storm tonight,' Horatio agreed.

'Where are we looking?'

'There, you might have to lean. That building with the rounded top and all the windows.'

Through the gap which ran behind the beach-shop and the long low boat repair shed, I could see a small building, only the door on the bottom level visible. Above it though, the windows went right round the structure, leaning outwards slightly, like the bridge of a ship. The windows were lit up and I could clearly see a tall shape moving about inside. Back and forth the shape went, in a small trail, a few feet one way, then back.

'He's on the phone,' I said. 'That's how people move when they're on the phone.'

Horatio nodded. 'Landline, though, he's not wandering around. No mobile signal down here.'

'Does he have a car?'

'He parks it halfway up the hill, behind the old chapel.'

'He could still go out,' I said.

'Not without me knowing – I've blocked him in.'

'Horatio! You are good at this.'

'Not really. It was all my fault in the first place.'

'Rubbish. Don't take any notice of Inspector Pirran Trenoweth. He hasn't done anything to help, has he?'

'Not that we know of, but they might be doing a lot, behind the scenes.'

'Let's not forget who saved Tyrone.'

'You did, Isabel.'

'We did, Horatio. We did.'

When we went back to the table, Pat and Trevor had finished their meals.

'He's in there,' I told them. 'And he's not going anywhere near Tyrone.'

'He doesn't look like a murderer,' Trevor said.

'No. Although, do we know what they look like?' I said.

'We don't know he's a murderer. In fact, if he knew the victim, he might be in as much danger as Mr Moffat,' Horatio said.

'Yes,' I said. Something had been nagging at me. 'I'm wondering – '

'Go on,' Pat said.

'Well, Marc said Mr Moffat and Nick ran into each other at the bus stop and started talking.'

They all nodded.

'But Mr Moffatt also met Nick later on the harbour wall. So it wasn't that he was scared of Nick.'

'Did he have the bag with him that time?' Pat said, 'the second time?'

I shrugged. 'But if he was scared of Nick, why wouldn't he just have waited in full view of everyone and got back on the bus? Got out of town?'

'We got to find the bag,' Trevor said. 'We got to know what's in it, that will tell us – well, it will tell us something.'

Demelza came to clear away the plates. 'Anything more for anyone?' she asked.

'That was an amazing meal,' I said.

'We wondered when we'd see you,' Demelza said.

I squirmed a bit. 'We'll, there's always food in a guest house...'

'Hang on,' Pat said. 'You were in the village on Christmas Day!'

I knew I was turning pink. I nodded.

'Oh, lovey,' Pat said. 'What did you have for your Christmas dinner? All up there in the big house on your own.'

'Pat!' Trevor said. 'She's a grown woman. Probably been cooking her own Christmas dinner for years. Right, Isabel?'

Demelza was looking at me expectantly. 'We had a full Christmas spread in here,' she said.

'Oh God. Look, I didn't even really know it was Christmas Day.' I told them. 'I put the television on when I got up and the Queen was talking to me. I thought I was having a hallucination. I really wasn't thinking about food, even when I worked out what day it was.'

Now they were all looking a bit mournful. I guessed Christmas dinner was a big deal round here.

'Anyway,' I went on. 'There was some food in the house. Not perishables. Obviously.'

No-one said anything. Alright, I thought, I'd get it over with. 'I had a Pot Noodle for my

Christmas dinner. OK? A Pot Noodle.'

Pat actually gasped. Trevor's sweet face screwed up in concern.

'What flavour?' Horatio said.

'Does it make a difference?' Demelza said. 'I don't reckon they do a turkey and all the trimmings flavour.'

'No,' I said. 'They don't. But it was hot, and it was fine. And look! I survived.'

'What about pudding?' Pat said. 'No Christmas pudding?'

'Pat...' Trevor said. 'If she had a Pot Noodle for her dinner, she's not going to turn out to have a Christmas pudding with brandy butter, is she?'

'I did have a pudding, actually, and thank you for your concern.'

There was silence. I waited a few moments, then put them out of their misery. 'I had a raspberry Pop-Tart.'

There were groans and shrieks at that, and Petey and Winnie looked over at us. *I'm the centre of this*, I thought. *These people care that I had a Pot Noodle for my Christmas dinner*.

'Promise me,' Demelza said, putting her hand on my shoulder, 'promise me you'll never eat a Pot Noodle again.'

I nodded. 'It was the first, and last.'

'Now,' Demelza said. 'Whether you want it or not, I'm bringing a bowl of sherry trifle over for everyone. Dig in.'

We all seemed to manage to find room for a bowl of creamy trifle, with the kick of sherry in the bottom.

It had the advantage of keeping us all quiet, too, and there was only the sound of spoons and pleasure and chatter in the darker corners of the pub. Finally we returned to the topic of the day.

'What's the plan, Isabel?' Trevor said, pushing his bowl away.

'I'm not sure,' I said. 'We're going to the police some time next week to give our statements, and they might have more information, though they might not share it with us.'

'And Horatio's going in for a bit of a telling off, probably,' Pat said. Horatio looked a bit sick at that.

'Let's hope we've got the upper hand by then, and you'll be off the hook,' I told him.

'I don't see how we can sort it out, really,' Horatio said.

'No. Maybe not. But we just have to keep going, one step at a time,' I said. 'I've still got my list to get through.'

'What's on the list?' Trevor asked, crossing his hands over his chest, and leaning back in his chair.

'How did Mr Moffat get here?' I said. 'Well, we know he came on the bus. But where did he come from?' That might help. And what was he supposed to do with the bag, and did he do it?'

All three of them nodded, looking at me expectantly.

'Right,' Trevor said, rubbing his hands together. 'What's the next step?'

I didn't know, then, but I was about to find out.

CHAPTER TWENTY-ONE

We all left the Smuggler's Arms together, and despite Pat and Trevor's protests I walked home alone. I felt safe – well, safer than I had in the last few days. Tyrone was alive and in good hands, and Nick was in the Pirate King's lair, talking on the phone, but nothing more sinister than that. Glebelands was deserted, no guests until Sunday, and no car in the shared parking. The trees and bushes behind the houses were whipping back and forth in the strong sea wind, and there was the sound of rattling from the buildings, but nothing which would trouble even the most nervous of homeowners. Or house-sitters.

I decided not to sleep in the guest house. I wanted to go up to my attic bedroom in The Manse, the first place I'd gone when I'd arrived here. I'd steal some more clothes from the master bedroom, and just move over to the guest house on Sunday afternoon when the new guests were due to check in.

I let myself in through the front door and turned on the hall lights. Nothing to worry me here. I moved through the house, checking the doors and windows for damage, but feeling relaxed and secure.

Upstairs all was quiet. In my bedroom the carpet and dresser were strewn with the few things I'd brought with me. My overnight bag was open on the floor and I found my phone charger and plugged my phone in. I might not be able to turn it on until morning. It would take hours to deal with the messages which must have stacked up since Christmas Eve, the last time I'd been in touch with anyone from my other life.

I gathered my shoes and clothes up from the floor and packed them neatly in the case, and put the case on the dresser. I'd purposely left this room a mess – an antidote to the deserted rooms elsewhere in the house but now I felt I wanted some order in things. My life was getting more complicated by the day. The hours I'd spent curled up in a chair, staring at the sky, doing nothing, seemed far behind me now.

I looked at my phone. No, I'd leave it until morning.

Snuggling down in my little bed, I was about to turn out the light when I noticed the seascape on the wall. It was my favourite painting in the house and I'd moved it up here, some time in February. I'd put the abstract which had hung in here down in the study, and put this gorgeous thing on the wall where I would see it every morning. It was a line of beach, not particularly sunny, but it had a peaceful look. The vast expanse of it was like something from a new world, fresh and untouched. The painting spoke to me, which was why it was hanging in my bedroom. And now it was hanging upside down.

I got out of bed and went over to the painting. Definitely upside down. I put my face against the wall and peered behind it. There was nothing there. Taking the painting off the hook, I looked at the label. Yes, it was upside down. I turned it back the right way and put it back on the wall and rushed across the room and back under the covers. Who had done that, and why? Someone had been in this room, where my clothes were, my underwear on the floor, my high-heels, unworn for months but still mine.

I pulled the covers up over my head and cowered. My shoulders began to ache from being hunched up. The sight of my mobile phone charging gave me a bit of comfort. At least I could call someone, though I didn't want to. Even if Pat or Horatio came, I'd have to go down through the empty house to the front door to let them in.

Finally I forced myself out of bed and got dressed quickly. I felt stronger then, straight away. I opened the wardrobe and looked inside, locked the door once I'd finished checking it. Getting back up on the bed I bounced up so I could see that the top of the wardrobe had nothing on it. Then I grabbed hold of the armchair in the corner of the room, and heaved it over in front of the door. That felt better. It wouldn't keep anyone out, but it would slow them down. Peering out of the high window I could see the lighthouse in the distance and below me, the roofs of Gorran Porth, sleeping through the coming storm.

I lay on the bed, still fully dressed, my mind whirling. What had we been saying about coincidence? There's no way it was a coincidence that this house had been broken into on the day Mr Moffat was murdered. Not a chance. But who had troubled themselves to come up to the top floor, into the smallest room, the room which contained absolutely nothing of value, and turn round a seascape? There were more obvious paintings to interfere with. Paintings with ships, or houses – they would have been noticed straight away. Why pick this room?

I woke with a start and a stiff neck. I looked at my watch. 4.20am. I must have fallen asleep. So what had woken me?

I looked over at my phone. It was dark. I looked out of the window – everything was dark, but what would I expect to see at this time? I tried the bedside light. Nothing. I looked over to the guest house where Pat and I had left lights burning before we went to the pub. Nothing on in there either. Good. A power cut was not scary, was it? A power cut didn't suggest a malevolent force, out to get me. No. Of course not. Still, no way I was going downstairs until it was dawn.

I got under the covers, fully dressed and lay motionless, listening to the wind. I thought about Nick, who had told me I could talk to him if anything was worrying me. I wonder how he'd react to a phone call about now, telling him I was scared of the dark, and even more scared that he was involved in murder.

The next time I woke up the phone was charging again and the room was warm and filled with pink dawn light. I stood up and stretched and remembered very clearly what I'd thought about as I fell asleep.

I'd turned the painting back the right way, and would have been so easy to convince myself that I'd been dreaming. I stared over at it, trying to decode the message it held. It was obvious that it was a sign. A sign that someone had been in this room. A sign only decipherable to someone who lived in this room, who knew this painting. And why this room? Because it was the only room in the house which was obviously inhabited? A mess of clothes and towels, my make-up and my overnight case, scattered around the room. Whoever had come through the house had sought the one room where someone would see the painting.

I moved the chair away from the door

and gathered up my phone and charger, the few things I'd need for a night next door in the guest house, and went down to the next landing. The master bedroom again, for more cashmere and a rather nice scarf. A short wool coat would make a nice change too, and some cashmere socks for my walking boots. Really, I was turning into a complete criminal and I had no guilt whatsoever. I knew Sir Dougall didn't need anything from me, but I'd think of something to leave in the house when I eventually moved out.

Downstairs I drew the curtains to let the blustery blue daylight in. Suddenly, I stopped, dropping everything in the hallway, the clothes, the phone, everything thudding onto the carpet. The painting that was upside down. The person could have stolen it, or hidden it, or just taken it off the wall. But they'd turned it around, made it the opposite of what it should be. And they'd broken into the house but not stolen anything. So maybe they'd done the opposite there, too. Maybe instead of taking something, they'd left something? Mr Moffat's bag? Is this where it had ended up?

I picked up all the things I'd dropped, with the strong feeling I was being watched. Panic flooded me; I needed to search the house now, but I was scared of what I'd find, and what it might mean. I couldn't shake the feeling that someone was waiting for me to start looking and they'd come in and take from me whatever

I found. If they had to use force, they would. I thought about Mr Moffat and Tyrone, both with head injuries. Someone could strike quickly and with deadly force, and I'd be next.

There was no way I could leave this house now. I went back upstairs and showered and changed in the master bathroom. I chose that one because it had the ensuite bathroom, so I was behind a locked bedroom door and a locked bathroom door. Fully clothed in fresh luxury, I felt a bit stronger. I turned my phone on, and ran downstairs and put my walking boots on. I went round the house drawing the curtains again. If I was going to turn the place upside down, I didn't want anyone looking in. In the sitting room at the front I saw a flash of colour out of the corner of my eye. I went over to the side window. Yes, there in the distance was the red coat, Nick striding out, walking away from the house, map flapping in one hand, rucksack over his shoulder. I wondered what was in that bag – a small sharp instrument, maybe?

Had he been watching the house? If he saw me drawing the curtains again, surely he'd be suspicious. He might turn round and come back, and I wouldn't be able to see him coming. I'd have to work fast.

I ran back upstairs to my bedroom in the attic. I'd already searched the wardrobe. I looked under the bed, and pulled the bedside table out from the wall. Nothing. The dresser was fixed, but I tried all the drawers and looked on the underside of the top surface. Nothing there. OK, this bedroom was clear.

I stepped out onto the landing. There was another attic room, which had been a playroom for the boys. I never went in there, but I had to check it now. I stepped gingerly over the model railway which circled the room. The trains were in the station and all was quiet on the track. There was a large chest of drawers in one corner and I opened each drawer in turn. The top one was full of plastic toys, Lego and odd mascots and figurines. The second drawer was packed with jigsaws and boxed games, Monopoly from New York and Trivial Pursuit in French. The bottom drawer was full of costumes; a pirate's cutlass gleamed up at me and I took it out and swung it round my head. 'Take that, Pirate King,' I said, but the sound of my own voice scared me and I closed the drawer. There was a squashy sofa in the corner of the room, with a reading light over it. My memory of Sir Dougall's sons didn't fill me with confidence that they'd spent a lot of time sitting quietly and reading books, but I pulled the sofa out from the wall and as simply as that, there it was. Mr Moffat's luggage, pushed behind the sofa and left there for me to find.

I pulled the bag out and brought it nearer to the window. It was an ordinary red and black nylon travel bag, two side compartments, one long central space, all zipped closed. My heart was pounding. I felt hungry and sick at the same time. My arms felt useless but I wanted to open the bag.

A loud noise ripped through the house and I almost shrieked with terror.

Someone was rapping the door knocker, confident that they'd be answered, well aware that someone was in the house.

I pushed the bag back behind the sofa and stood up. I couldn't see the front door from this room. There was nothing for it, I'd have to go downstairs.

CHAPTER TWENTY-TWO

Sweating with fear, I opened the front door, fast, and gasped. It was Nick.

'Oh, I've interrupted you,' he said.

'No, just doing chores.' My voice was a bit wobbly, but he didn't look as though he noticed.

'I was passing, going on a walk, and it looked as though you were up, so, I wanted to apologise for rushing off last night. And, just to make sure you were OK after the storm, is your power back on?'

'Oh, don't worry about last night, I'm just glad you were inspired.'

'Right. Right. OK then.' He looked at me intently and I wondered if I was looking as shocked and flustered as I felt.

'Actually,' I said, 'I was just going to go next door, I could cook you breakfast if you like.'

'Full English?' He was smiling now and I could see why Marc called him the Pirate King.

'On the house. I'll just get a few things and lock up here.' I hesitated, wondering if I should invite him in. No. Safest thing was to get him right away from the house. I rushed back into the kitchen, got the keys and came back down the hall. He was still outside, looking as though he didn't have a care in the world.

'You've drawn all the curtains.'

'Yes. It keeps it warmer.' *And it makes people think I'm still in bed* – I thought, *but that didn't stop you, did it, Nick?*

We walked over to the front door of the guest house and I unlocked it and invited him in. I tried to look at the soles of his boots but couldn't manage it. He was looking around, and he stopped at the register on the hall table. He must be able to clearly see the entry in my handwriting, Mr Moffat, but he didn't let on. He flicked back a couple of pages and pretended to read some names.

'Anyone famous?'

I laughed. 'Infamous, maybe?'

I led him through to the dining room and pointed to the main table.

'You can lay that table, please, cutlery and crockery through here.'

He followed me into the kitchen and opened drawers and cupboards and began assembling what he needed. I looked at the key rack on the back of the kitchen door. It was no surprise to see, Room 6 was missing. I was furious, but strangely not scared now. Watching him carefully I got the sharpest knife out of the drawer and slipped it down between the bread-board and the side of the freezer, near at hand. I put the sausages in the pan and then turned to bacon, eggs, baked beans and tomatoes. I put the kettle on and asked if he'd like tea or coffee.

'Whatever you like.'

'I can do one of both, that's what I do for guests, so why not just say what you'd really like.'

'Coffee for me, then, please.'

'Fine.' And tea for me.

In went the bacon, the plates were warming under the grill and bread was ready in the toaster. Nick had finished the table and lounged in the doorway.

'I have to make a quick phone call, if you don't mind,' I said, and he moved into the dining room. It was only giving me the illusion of privacy though, I knew he'd be able to hear every word.

Pat's phone number was on the pad by the phone. I dialled it, wincing slightly. It was early on a Saturday morning to be ringing someone, even after all we'd been through together.

Trevor answered the phone straight away.

'Good morning Isabel,' he said.

'Oh, how did you know...'

'We've got caller ID. We know Janice's number.'

'Right, sorry to ring so early, but I wanted to say, I was going to meet up with Pat at some point today?'

'Right. I see. Pat! Pat, come here quick. Isabel's on the phone.'

I heard the phone being handed over.

'Alright, Isabel love?'

'Hello, Pat, I was just ringing to confirm when we're meeting today.'

'Um, well, I always go to Uncle Nat's in the morning, do a few chores and that, you know.'

'Yes, that's fine for me,' I said firmly.

'Oh my God. Who is it? Is it Smith?'

'No, not at all. Nothing to worry about. Nick called in to make sure I was OK, so I'm just cooking him some breakfast. Then I'll be along to see Uncle Nat at the usual time.'

'I see. Right. So Nick can hear what you're saying, ooh, you are clever, Isabel. I said to Trevor, she's a clever one alright.'

'Great. So I'll see you later. Bye for now.'

I didn't feel particularly clever, but I'd achieved what I wanted. I'd make it clear to Nick that someone knew he was in the house. The trouble is, I'd also made it clear at what point I'd be out of the house. One step forward, two steps back. I plated up the breakfasts, slid the eggs on at the last minute and carried them in triumph to the dining room.

'Here you are, one full English, courtesy of Glebelands Guest House.'

'Nice breakfast,' he said. 'Hope the bed part

is as good.'

I gaped at him.

'Hope the beds are comfy, I mean.' He looked innocent.

'Hmm. We did have a complaint this week, about noise in the night.'

He raised an eyebrow at that.

'Not that kind of noise. A fight, or someone being very clumsy in their room.'

He carried on eating, without a care in the world, it seemed.

I looked at him over the top of my tea-cup.

'You really are very good looking,' I said. 'Didn't you ever think of being a model?'

He pointed at me with his fork, and shook his head, chewing.

'Just a thought,' I said. 'If you didn't want to go back to the Civil Service, I mean. Of course, a good photo on a book jacket will sell copies.'

He shrugged. 'Maybe.'

'What's it about, you didn't ever say?'

'Didn't I?'

'I'd have remembered.'

'Well, I suppose you could call it a thriller, kind of an espionage thing.'

'Ooh. Spies?'

'Spies, yes. Is there any more coffee? I could make it.'

'Go on then.'

I sat back while he went into the kitchen. My phone pressed into me, snug in my back pocket, and I turned it on. The familiar chime made me tense up, but it was too late. The phone was on, and streaming into it was three months of rage, betrayal, disappointment and hurt. I looked at the phone, but listened carefully for the sound of a key being returned to the back of the kitchen door.

'Signal OK up here?' Nick asked, coming back in with the cafetière.

'Fine up here,' I said, 'on the top of a hill. Hopeless in the village.'

'Oh well. I found you anyway, using the old fashioned method, knocking on your door.'

I smiled. 'It was nice of you to think of it. Very thoughtful. I expect you give a lot of thought to everything you do.'

'Mostly, yeah. So, I hear you're busy later. Shame, I was going to suggest we drive up the coast, get out of town for a bit.'

'Sorry, yes, I promised Pat. I've got a lot to do today, and I've got guests arriving tomorrow.'

'Have you?' He looked very interested in that.

'Yes. They booked ages ago, they've got a family wedding in the area.'

'Right. Do people book direct with you? Or, with the owner, Janet? Is it?'

'Janice. If they book through the website, they go through to Janice, and if they phone or call at the door, they do it through me.'

'Isn't that a bit dicey? Couldn't you both

end up taking a booking for the same night?'

'Janice has thought of that. She says it will be OK until Easter weekend, that's when the tourist season really begins.'

'How will you manage then?'

'Janice is coming back. I probably won't be living here then.'

He nodded at that. 'Back to London?'

'No. Maybe. Possibly.'

'Right, nothing like a firm decision.' He laughed, but it was kind.

'I've got a few weeks before Janice comes back. I spent a lot of time here not doing anything, just going for long walks and sitting around in front of the wood burner next door.' I gestured to The Manse. 'I've only really come to know people in the last few days.'

'Oh? What's brought that on?'

'This and that. Various things.' *Which you know about very well.*

'OK. Well, I'd better get going,' he said, 'if you're sure you've got a lot to do.'

'Absolutely. But you can buy me supper some time, in the Smuggler's.'

'Deal.'

I followed him down the hallway and stood on the front doorstep, waving as he wandered off down the hill.

Oh, Nick. I thought. *So handsome, and such a liar.*

I went back into the dining room and sat

down with my phone. There was a red exclamation mark on the screen and the words 'memory full' flashed at me.

I clicked onto the text messages, selected ALL and deleted them. Then I went into voice mail and did the same.

I scrolled through to 'Tanya' and pressed 'call.'

I heard the moment she answered, but she didn't say anything.

'Tanya?' I said. 'Can you hear me?'

'Isabel. Is that really you?'

'It's me. I'm so sorry, I'm really sorry.'

She didn't say a word.

'Shall I ring off?'

'What, and go another three months without speaking?'

'Sorry.'

'Don't say that again. Where are you?

'In Cornwall.'

'Cornwall? England? I thought you'd be in the Maldives at least.'

'No. I didn't go far.'

'I've been so worried.'

'I'm...well, I am sorry, but I'm not going to say it again.'

'I spoke to Dougall and he said you were fine, and not to worry, but I did worry. We all did!'

'I wasn't exactly fine, but I wasn't in any danger. I just needed some time away. To think.'

'Are you coming back to London, Isabel?'

'No. Not to live. Maybe for a visit, if I'm still welcome?'

'Always. But there must be more, don't go now.'

'I'll ring back. I've got loads to tell you. I'm just a bit preoccupied now.'

'Alright. But ring back, yeah? Don't just not say anything.'

'I won't. And, Tanya...'

'Yeah?'

'I'm sorry.'

I'd been dreading that for months, I shouldn't have doubted Tanya, my best friend. She had been, briefly, the girlfriend of my boss. I knew it wouldn't last, she was too old for him, only ten years his junior, but he was between wives and she was very beautiful. We'd kept in touch after Dougall had dumped her and we'd become good friends. She'd been a model and was now the model wife of a famous philanthropist. I'd introduced them, and I'd managed her wedding, (Babington House, honeymoon on the Isle of Skye) and they'd both remained grateful. They had two lovely boys, one of them my godson. I often wondered if Dougall regretted losing her, but he seemed happy enough with wife number 3, and he'd sent a thoughtful wedding gift. I made sure of that.

I looked at my watch. 9.30am. Still early, but still lots to do. I checked behind the kitchen door and rang Pat again.

'He's gone. And he had the key, he took it when he was in here yesterday, when we found the footprint. He had the key to Room 6 and he put it back when I was in the dining room.'

'Oh my God. That proves it. He's a murderer. And you were in the house with him.'

'No, that's the point. It doesn't prove that. Why would he need to look in the room if he'd already been in there? And we know there was no luggage in there when Smith came, because we looked for it ourselves, so he didn't go in there to move it. And...Pat, I know where the luggage is.'

'Oh my good God again! Where? No. Don't tell me. They won't get it out of me, Isabel I swear on that.'

'No-one's going try to 'get it out of you', Pat,' I said, though I wasn't confident. 'Look, I want to come to Uncle Nat's and meet you, but I'm scared to leave the house. If Nick's searched the guest house, he'll try The Manse next, won't he. And I told him when I'd be away, so now I can't leave it.'

'When do you think he searched the guest house?'

'When we were driving to Penwithick Pasties. Must have been.'

'What a rotten lying...being so nice to you,

in the pub.'

'I know. I seem to bring that out in criminals, don't I?'

'I know what we could do, we could get Petey to come up to the house, do a bit of maintenance or something.'

'Would he?'

'Oh, he would, all those drinks you've been buying him? He'd do anything for you, Petey would.'

'Can he get up here now?'

'Trevor!' Pat shouted. 'Go and get Petey, take him up Isabel's, she'll brief him. Did you hear that?'

'I did.'

'Good, he's on his way. Rendezvous at Uncle Nat's 10.30. Well, more like elevenses really, by the time we all get there.'

'Over and out.'

Petey and Trevor arrived just as I'd finished loading the dishwasher. I made Petey a cup of coffee.

'The main thing is,' I said, 'I don't want anyone going in The Manse.'

'Righty ho.'

'So maybe you could do some...pruning? I don't know. Some sort of handyman work? So people know you're around.'

'Right. But I don't have to do the work if there's no-one watching. I just have to leap up, if they appear.'

'Yes. Although, you might not know if they are watching.'

'They might be covert, like,' Trevor said.

'I'm not sure I can deal with that,' Petey said. 'I'm a plain dealer, I am. Always have been. What you see is what you get. I don't want to get mixed up in any funny business.'

'There's no funny business. None at all. But you know the window was broken next door, someone tried to break in.'

Petey nodded, scratching his sunken cheek and frowning.

'So I just want to be sure, while I'm away for an hour or two, that no-one's trying to get into the house. And they might not be trying to break in, they might be really plausible. Believable. It might be someone you know.'

'Ah, right. Alright, I can manage that. Only I don't want any funny business.'

'Petey,' I said. 'I can assure, you, this is not a funny business.'

Trevor gave Petey a firm look and I gave him a spare key to the guest house as well as The Manse. I was a bit worried that he might just sit down and nod off, but he came out of the house to wave us off. I didn't have to make the walk over the windy moors, Trevor was driving Pat's car and we got to Uncle Nat's in comfort.

Pat met me at the doorway of Uncle Nat's

and gave me a hug.

'Are you alright, love?'

'I am. I've got a lot to tell you. But I'm here to work as well.'

'Don't you worry about that. The great thing about Uncle Nat is, he's got very low standards. He wouldn't notice if we didn't lift a finger. Come on in.'

Uncle Nat was sitting at a large farmhouse table finishing what appeared to be a big breakfast. The morning sun was caught in his cloud of white hair so that he appeared to be surrounded by celestial light.

'Come on in, my lamb,' he said, waving at me. 'Come and sit with old Uncle Nat.'

I sat opposite him. The table was covered with farming catalogues, old newspapers, calendars, receipts, bills and letters. The plate – from which he was mopping fried egg with a hunk of bread – rested on a dog-eared *Yellow Pages*. Pat was in the background scrubbing the worktops, and Trevor was bringing firewood through the kitchen in great armloads, taking it to a room beyond. Nat was cheerful, relishing his breakfast. He put his glasses on and stared at me.

'What happened to your hair?' he asked, not unkindly. 'Why is it...like that?'

'Uncle Nat!' Pat shouted at him. 'Rude!'

'No, that's alright,' I said. 'This bit on the side, that's called an undercut, see, it sits under this bit which, if I just flick it over...'

Nat looked sceptical. 'Not being rude,' he said, 'but at your age?'

I laughed. 'I know,' I said. 'And I'm up to a lot more besides a new haircut.'

He stirred his tea with a knife and lifted the mug. 'And what's this I hear,' he asked, 'about a Pot Noodle?'

'Oh. Pat?' But Pat was off upstairs, her arms full of linen.

'We were all here,' Nat said. 'Christmas Day, about ten of us, all round this table, you could have slipped in that corner there, you don't take up much space.'

'But you didn't know me on Christmas Day. I'd just arrived.'

He shrugged, finishing up his fried egg and chasing a few baked beans round the plate.

'What shall I do?' I asked him. 'Give me a chore.'

'You sit there and relax, let them two do all the work.' He cackled at that.

'No, I'd really prefer to be useful.'

He raised his eyebrows at that. 'Useful? Well, you could get the eggs in.'

'Right. Get the eggs in,' I said. 'Get them in from where?'

'From the chickens. Where they come from.' Uncle Nat caught a look at my face and started such a bout of laughing I thought he'd explode. His face wobbled and his eyes closed with delight.

'Right!' I said. 'I'm going.'

He heaved himself to his feet and lurched over to the doorway. I followed him out into the port and he thrust an egg box in my hand and waved me off across the yard.

Opposite the farmhouse was a collection of ramshackle barns and sheds, each containing part of a massive piece of farm machinery. Most of them appeared to have a chunk missing, and they were pitted and scarred, rust running down them like dried blood. It looked like an abattoir for tractors. In the corner of the yard was a large wire enclosure, and there were some brown hens, wandering about listlessly inside. I let myself into the pen and looked at the low dark henhouse. Surely I didn't have to get in there? I heard angry clucking and shrieking inside. No, there was no way I was going in there. I looked over at the farmhouse door. Trevor was coming out to get more firewood. I raised a hand in an enquiring wave and showed him the empty egg box.

'On the side!' he shouted over. I picked my way across slimy ground, avoiding the hens, and there on the side of their little house was a rectangular box running the length of the structure. The roof was felted and had a handle on top. I lifted it and a chicken looked up, enraged.

'Sorry.' She huffed off, and there in the straw was a large brown egg.

I put that one in the box, and there were three more in the other divisions.

I went back to the kitchen, victorious. Pat was there and she showed me how to put the new eggs at the end of a bigger tray, and move the older eggs up to the top.

'How many?' Uncle Nat bellowed.

'Four.'

'Ah. Picking up a bit, after the winter. Good girls.'

'Come on, Isabel, come and help me,' Pat said.

We went upstairs to what was obviously Uncle Nat's bedroom.

We stripped off the bed and flapped new sheets over the mattress.

'Come on, Isabel,' Pat said. 'Spill the beans.'

'Well, I saw him lurking again. Nick. When I got up this morning. He was at the end of Glebelands Lane, moving away. But then he obviously thought of an excuse, because he knocked on the door, even though all the curtains were drawn, and wanted to know if I was alright, you know, after the storm. Oh, and he apologised for going off last night.'

'Tell me about what you found.' Pat passed me some pillowcases.

'I found the bag. In the attic.'

Pat straightened, clutching a pillow to her chest. 'How did it get in there?'

'I'm guessing, when the person broke in. They put it in there to hide it.'

'Mr Moffat?'

'I think so. Because no-one else has had any luck retrieving it, which they would have been able to do if they roughly knew where it was.'

We finished the bed and moved on to Uncle Nat's bathroom. It would have been all the rage in London with the claw foot tub and the big rectangular sink, but this was the real thing. There was a vast black and white photographic portrait on the wall in a heavy dark frame. It was by far the grandest thing I'd seen in the house. The subject of the portrait was a cow. There was something about her calm demeanour and fathomless eyes which resembled Nat.

Pat pulled her rubber gloves on and started to scrub the bath.

I took a spare cloth from her bucket and gave the sink a good clean.

'So Mr Moffat hides the bag,' Pat said, 'and Smith wants it, and Nick the Pirate King wants it. And you've just found it. What was in it?'

'I haven't looked.'

Pat gasped. 'Isabel!'

'I know. But I didn't have time. He rang on the doorbell just as I found it, so I had to hide it again and run down and see him. And I don't want to go back in the house until I know where he is.'

'Good thinking.'

'So I just need to keep it safe until we can get to the police station to give our statements. Monday or Tuesday at the latest, do you think?

I'm going to call a taxi, get straight in with the bag and get out at the police station and hand it over. I just need to keep everyone away from it until then.'

'We'll help you, you know we will,' Pat said.

'Thanks. But people have died for that bag. And been left for dead. You've got Trevor to think of, and Uncle Nat, and Horatio.'

'Yes I have,' Pat said. 'And we're all in this together, and that includes you.'

We finished the bathroom and Pat put fresh towels out. We carried the old linens downstairs to where Trevor was clearing the kitchen table. Uncle Nat was putting on his boots and coat, moving very slowly and lurching from side to side like a trawlerman in a storm.

'Going out to walk the land,' he said. 'You wanna come with me, maidy?'

'Me?' I said. 'Yes, lovely. Unless I'm needed here.'

Pat and Trevor waved me away.

It was hard to walk at Uncle Nat's pace. He was already slow, but he wanted to tell me a story for every square yard of land, and he couldn't seem to talk and walk at the same time. We went out into the lane where he vividly re-enacted the story of the pasty van, rushing past him. Then we turned down a paved track behind the farmhouse and he told me about the cost per meter of the tarmac, and the time it had taken him to earn it back.

'Where does this lead, though?' I said. All I could see in front of us was a large, gently sloping field and beyond it, the curve of Deadman's Beach.

'Down there.' He pointed.

'The beach?'

'The field, where you park for two pounds a day. Bargain, mind you, complete bargain. I must be mad. Then you walk down the track to the beach. 'Tis the only way you can get there, see, unless you'm a rock climber.'

'That's amazing. What's that, there?' I pointed to a whitewashed building in the corner nearest the track.

'Lavvies. Got to have them.'

'That's wonderful. What a perfect business. So simple.'

'Ah.' We leaned on a five-bar gate and looked at the field. 'Come June,' Uncle Nat said, with an expansive wave, 'that'll be all cars, far as you can see, all day until September. Then I lock it up, till the next year.'

'What about that field, over there? What do you do in there?'

'I just leave that.'

'You could do camping. People would go for that, wouldn't they?'

He nodded. 'I'd have to deal with them, though. Can't do that. Thing with the parking is,

I just pay a boy, put up a little shed for them to sit in. And I come out a couple times a day, count the cars, tally the money.'

I nodded. What a nice way to live.

'Do the locals like it?'

Uncle Nat sighed. 'There's no pleasing some people.'

'Oh, dear.'

'Some do, don't get me wrong. There's a burger van goes down there, parks at the end of the track. And an ice-cream van. And Widow Twankey, my neighbour across the way, she loves it.'

'Widow Twankey? Surely not.'

'No, not really, Widow Tansey it is, really and truly, but, what would you do?'

'So why does she love it?'

'Come on. We'll go a bit further.'

We ambled down the track a bit further and I felt the troubles of the past few days fall away. I felt light, and free. I'd made contact with my dearest friend again, and I had new friends. I didn't know what the future held for me, but I'd made some decisions about what it didn't hold. We stopped and looked at the beach.

'There.' Uncle Nat pointed across the beach to a white house high on the green cliff. 'See her house? She does cream teas up there, see, and she's had to build an extension and take on another girl. Lovely girls she had last summer. Swedish. Awful pretty. I drank a lot of tea, and no better than I could have had at home.'

I squinted to get a better look at the house, the other side of Coffin Cove. Only here would the person in a house that far away be described as a neighbour. The beach was deserted except for a slight figure with a dog.

Nat frowned. 'That could be her, the Widow Twankey. That dog's found something. Nice bit of yellow tarpaulin. I'll have that, if the widow doesn't want it.'

And sure enough, the dog was barking at something in the shallow water. Whatever it was, it was moving slowly in and out with each receding wave and the woman was getting closer to it, trying to pull the dog away.

Uncle Nat and I took a few steps closer, though we were still too far away to see clearly what it was.

We could hear though, we could hear the scream the woman let out when the dog got hold of whatever it was and tried to pull it from the water. She shouted at the dog and she waved up at us. I stopped in my tracks.

'Go back to the house, Uncle Nat, get Pat and Trevor to come back in the car. I think that's a body.'

CHAPTER TWENTY-THREE

I set off at a run, gravel flying below my boots, my coat flapping around me. It was hard to keep my footing on the downward path but I slowed down when I reached the beach. I struggled across to the woman, speeding up when I got to firm damp sand. The dog was going mad, but the woman looked ashen and still.

I approached the dog cautiously.

'Bruce!' the woman shouted. 'Bruce. Come here.'

The dog was reluctant to leave its new playmate, but it went reluctantly and sat at her feet.

She stared at me.

'You're that one looking after Janice's.'

'Yes. I'm Isabel.'

'What happened to your hair?'

'What? Really?'

She seemed to pull herself together. 'Look

what Bruce found,' she said, as though pointing out an interesting pebble.

'Yes.' I looked down. There was no doubt. There was a cold, pale face, washed by the sea and lightly dusted with drying sand. The hair was slicked back by water and over the right ear there was a dark cave, a hole in the skull. It wasn't bloody or gruesome, the sea had washed it clean. The man was wearing a t-shirt, which might once have been white, with a logo on it, and below that yellow waders, held up with chest straps. He looked empty and clean.

'Coffin Cove,' I mumbled. 'Deadman's Beach.'

'They do say that, yes.' The woman was standing oddly, her shoulders facing away but her head twisted back to look, the dog still straining to return to the dead man.

'He's dead, is he?' she said.

'Definitely dead.'

'Oh I can't look. I can't look.' She took a few steps backwards.

'Alright. Don't worry.'

'Had I better stay? Give a statement?'

'Probably. I could ring the police now, actually, I've got my phone with me.'

I took out my phone and searched in my coat pocket. Yes, there it was, the card with Pirran Trenoweth's phone number. I started to dial.

By the time I'd left a message and rung off,

Trevor's car was at the end of the track and Pat was helping Uncle Nat out of the car.

I caught hold of Mrs Tansey's arm and took her towards the car.

'They'll give you a lift home,' I said, 'and I'll tell the police how to contact you.'

'You're very forceful,' she said. 'But that's why Janice picked you.'

'Is it?'

'Oh yes. Not everyone can do B&B. I tried, but my girls couldn't cope. We do cream teas, you know.'

'I do, yes. Uncle Nat. Nat. He told me.'

'Don't believe too much he tells you, that's my advice.'

'Right. So here we are.'

I handed Widow Tansey over to Trevor who knew just what to do.

'Hop up there, my love, in the back.' The dog jumped in after her and Trevor reversed carefully up the track to a point where he could turn round.

Pat and Uncle Nat were walking slowly, almost crab-like, to the dark shape in the shallows.

I ran a few paces to catch up with them.

'Mr Moffat?' Pat said.

'No, look. Younger. Fitter.'

'Who is Mr Moffat?' Uncle Nat asked.

'That's the man we found. Murdered, in the guest house,' I told him.

'I can't keep up with you youngsters,' he said. 'Have you told me any of this?'

'No. Don't worry, Uncle Nat. It was a secret. But now it probably won't be.'

Pat grabbed my arm. 'Look. Up there. Red coat.'

Sure enough the tall form and flapping red coat was coming towards us over the sand. Like the rest of us he struggled over the dry top of the beach, but once on the harder wet sand he broke into a run, only slowing as he neared our dismal group.

'What's that?' he said, leaning over as if gasping for breath. I didn't think he was, though. I thought he probably spent quite a bit of time running, and some of that time running towards dead bodies.

'Ooh, don't look,' Pat said. It'll upset you, not a nice thing at all.'

'Good thing it isn't high summer,' Uncle Nat said. 'You'd have had a crowd here.'

'Well, as long as none of us makes a sandcastle,' I said. I didn't move my eyes from Nick's face. I watched him for dear life. My life. He looked at the body as I had done and Pat too, a glancing look, trying not to settle too hard on any one place. Enough to take in the hair, and the jagged black hole in the side of his head. Just above the ear.

My eyes were tearing up, but I still didn't take my gaze from Nick's face.

'Have you called anyone?' he said.

'I've dialled 999 and I've also left a message for...someone. An officer I've had a bit of contact with.'

'Dialled,' he said. 'On your mobile phone.'

'Very good signal on the beach.'

'This poor guy.' He pointed down without looking. 'He obviously got in over his head with something.'

'How do you know that? Do you know him?'

Pat was watching both of us, turning her head like a spectator at a tennis match.

'Do you even know how he died? He might have fallen in the sea?'

'Isabel!' he shouted. 'Take care. Watch out. Give me your phone. Give it to me now.'

I handed it over and moved a little bit closer to Pat.

'Hang on, mate,' Uncle Nat said. 'You can't go shouting at ladies like that.'

Nick ignored him.

'Here, I've put my number in there, under 'help'.' He handed the phone back to me and marched back off the beach, without a backward glance at any of us, and without a last look at the body.

I staggered back up the beach to where the dry sand lay in fluffy lines, and I lay down flat on it. It was cold, but I didn't care, my legs wouldn't have held me up much longer. I heard Pat and

Uncle Nat lumbering after me and I covered my eyes with my sleeve.

'Alright, love?' Pat said. 'Fancy him shouting like that.'

'Here they come, that was quick,' Uncle Nat said. 'They must have been sitting in a lay-by having a cuppa.' Two police cars, with all the markings and flashings, were coming down the track. Two officers got out of the first car and ran towards the body at the edge of the sea. The second car stopped and one uniformed police officer and one man in a suit got out – great, that looked like Pirran Trenoweth.

No-one could walk across a beach in a suit and look dignified, so I felt a bit more confident by the time the second pair reached us. Just as they drew near enough to speak, Trevor drove down the track and stopped at the bottom.

'I'll get Uncle Nat back to the farm,' Pat said. 'But then I'll come back, don't you worry.'

I felt bereft as they left and Inspector Trenoweth sat down next to me.

'Nasty business, Miss Blunt,' he said.

'I know. Horrible.'

'And how do you come to be involved in this?'

I glared at him. 'I was walking on the beach and Mrs Tansey and her dog were there' – I pointed, 'and there was something in the water. And there it is.'

'Well,' he stood up, brushing sand off his

suit – sand which landed on my coat with a sharp hiss – 'I'll go and take a look myself, while you stay right here.'

'Wait! Wait. There's something else. You probably already know about Tyrone?'

'Who is Tyrone?'

'Tyrone, the boy driving the pasty van. He had a nasty head injury, but he survived. I don't know in what state, but he's still alive, he's in Truro Hospital.'

'I'll look into it,' he said. 'Excuse me while I look at the body.'

He went off down the sand, making a phone call while he went. He was still talking as he crouched over the body. His already bad suit would be ruined by salt water if he wasn't careful. He pointed to the hole in the man's head and carried on his phone conversation.

I felt weary and suddenly very heavy. I longed for him to come back up the beach so I could tell him about Mr Moffat's luggage, and Nick – maybe – and let him take care of it all.

He put his phone away as he came to sit down beside me again. This exposed the wet bottoms of his trousers to the beach, and he ended up with a pale strip of sand which he brushed at as he started to speak.

'I've spoken to my colleagues in Truro,' he said. 'No connection, none whatsoever.'

I said nothing.

'Alright, Miss? You look a bit pale. Shock

can be dangerous, you know. I'd better get you home, get a hot drink inside you.'

'No. No thanks.'

'You really don't look good, I wouldn't want to be accused of cruelty to bystanders.' He laughed a bit at that.

'I'm fine,' I said, though I thought I was a bit more than a bystander. 'Everything's fine, thanks. So, that man in the sea, how did he die?'

'Well. I'm not a medical man. We have experts to decide that. I should say he did die of a head wound, but we'll have to see.'

I said nothing, again.

'I'm thinking,' Trenoweth said, 'he possibly had a head injury, maybe from a fall, and he took a tumble. Very crumbly paths around here. Very hazardous and he isn't wearing walking boots.'

'Really. Cliff walking in waders? That seems a bit odd.'

'When you've been in this business as long as me, Miss Blunt, you don't question the oddness of the public. Do you recognise him, by any chance?'

'No. I've never seen him before. But then, I'd never seen Mr Moffat before the day he arrived at the guest house, which was coincidentally the day he died of a head wound.'

'Probably best not to overthink these things,' Trenoweth said, looking out to sea.

He didn't believe me. Or he did, but he

didn't want to admit he believed me. I pushed my hands into my pockets and felt something in there. The second envelope. I turned and looked out to the horizon while I buttoned my coat and wrapped my scarf tighter.

'I know you're right,' I lied, right into his face. 'I know you are. I'm just a bit rattled, that's all. It's been a difficult few days.'

Trenoweth gave me a professional smile and was about to say something more when I turned away.

I wasn't going to break into a run, but it took every ounce of strength I had to walk as evenly as I could over the sand. Once I got to the track, I started to hurry, then realised how that would look from behind, so I stopped and turned to face the beach. I needed to be sure. There he was, Trenoweth, still sitting on the sand, but on his phone again now. The three uniformed officers had pulled the man slightly up the beach, just enough so that the waves weren't lifting his hair and washing the sand from his face with gentle laps. They were standing in a close triangle above him, their hands in their pockets, chatting. I wondered why they remained there, then I saw the gulls overhead, circling.

I shivered again and climbed the track, back to my friends.

CHAPTER TWENTY-FOUR

They were all sitting around the farmhouse kitchen table when I joined them. Trevor passed me a mug of tea.

'Come and sit down, maidy,' Uncle Nat said. 'Is it all sorted then?'

'No. Not really. Thanks though. For asking.'

'Cheer up, love,' Pat said. 'Things are moving, aren't they?' She must have seen something of the desperation I felt. 'Come on, help me get the washing in.'

'In?' Trevor said, 'You've only just put it out.'

Pat pursed her lips at him and picked up her mug. We went outside and Pat led me round the end of the farmhouse to where a low bench rested against the whitewashed wall. Out of the wind, and with the house behind us, it was warm in the weak sunshine.

'What happened?' Pat said.

'Trenoweth is in on it.'

Pat looked at me in panic. 'What are you talking about?'

'He said he thinks the man fell off a cliff path.'

'But...but that hole, in his head.'

'I know. He says he rang the hospital to ask about Tyrone, and he's sure there's no connection.'

'He's one of them? I can't take it in.'

'I don't think he believes what he was saying. He spoke on the phone before he talked to me, I think he was being told what to say, what approach to take.'

'What did you do?' Pat asked me, looking aghast.

'I was about to argue.' I pulled the crumpled envelope out of my pocket. 'And then I remembered this.'

'No, no. Isabel.' Pat put her head in her hands.

'Yes! *They aren't always right but does it really hurt to let them think they are?'*

'So you let him think you thought he was right.' Pat looked doubtful and I did share those doubts.

'I know,' I said. 'I know what you're thinking. But it did seem to calm him down.'

'I can't believe it,' Pat said again. 'What are you going to do with Mr Moffatt's bag, you can't take it to them now.'

'I don't know what to do. I've been wracking my brains over it. There's Smith and his men, Inspector Trenoweth and his entire police force, and then there's Pirate Nick, who was behaving very oddly this morning.'

Pat nodded. 'Very strangely, in my view. Uncle Nat thought so too.'

'And out of those three groups, one of them must be good, surely. One of them must be honest? I just can't tell which.'

'Whatever's in that bag,' Pat said, keeping her voice down, 'must be worth a lot.'

'I have to get back there,' I said. 'I can't leave poor Petey to keep them out.'

'What are you going to do?'

'I'll hide it again. I'll have another think.'

We sipped our tea in silence. On any other day I'd have thought this was a treat. A new friend, a new place to sit in the sun. I thought about Tanya, who I had ignored for three months. She was still my friend, still in my life. I looked at Pat's comfy jeans and supermarket trainers. What would Tanya think if she ever met Pat?

'You're a good friend, Pat,' I said.

'Oh, what's brought that on?'

'Just thought I'd say it.'

'Here, you're not going all fatalistic on me, are you?'

'No! No, of course not. Just been a funny morning.'

'That's true. Why don't you stay for lunch?

Uncle Nat's best heifer is about to calve, we might have a new arrival by tea-time. They're so cute when they're brand new. You've got to see it.'

'I've got to get back, got to relieve Petey.'

'If you think that's best.'

Out in the lane, a black van kicked up dust as it lurched past the yard and off down the track to the beach.

We looked at each other.

'That's what a body should go in,' Pat said. 'Not a pasty van.'

'Hmm. I want to give you my mobile phone number,' I said.

'Right. Let's go and write that down, and I'll get Trevor to drop you back to Glebelands.'

'No. I'll walk. I'm safe enough, and I need to think.'

'If you say so, Isabel. But not too much thinking. That never ends well.'

I set off back over the moor, stopping at the highest point on the lane to lean on a gate and look back. There were still figures on the beach, and I supposed their vehicles would be at the end of the track. The farmhouse looked quiet, though I could see puffs of wood smoke making their way from the chimney to be lost in the pale winter sky. Seagulls were still whirling above the beach as I turned away and hurried off.

The walk did me good, I felt out of breath

and a lot more cheerful by the time I got to Glebelands.

Petey was at the front of The Manse, sitting on the front doorstep, eating an apple.

'Alright,' he said, gesturing with the apple. 'All quiet. No-one came by.'

With that, Winnie came out of the house, surprising me.

'Winnie,' I said.

'Well, yes, Winnie, came to keep me company, didn't you, girly.' Petey gave her a resounding slap on her ample behind, and she lifted her top lip to bare her teeth.

'Just went in to use the bathroom,' Winnie said to me. She looked a bit more droopy in the daylight than she had in the pub. She pushed her hands deep into the pockets of a maroon cardigan and waited with bovine patience for Petey.

'Winnie's having a new bathroom, when Trevor's free,' Petey said proudly.

'Great. Pleased for you. Thanks so much, Petey.'

'I'll be off now then, will I?'

'Thanks. There's a drink in it for you.'

'Ah. See you then, Miss Isabel.'

CHAPTER TWENTY-FIVE

Once inside The Manse I locked the door behind me. I went through the house slowly, checking every window, and making sure the curtains and blinds were all still drawn. I got the key for the study out of the cupboard. I went upstairs really quietly, as though I could be heard from outside the house. In the attic, the bag was where'd I'd stuffed it. Everything looked unchanged, but everything had changed, totally. I no longer had any faith in Trenoweth, Nick had scared me on the beach, and the thought of what had happened to Mr Moffat frightened and upset me. Now, in death, he felt closer to me than when he was alive, and that made me ashamed. All the way back I'd thought about the black van. It was fitting, it was dignified. It should have been the way in which Mr Moffat left Glebelands Guest House. If I'd paid more attention then, none of this would have happened now and I wouldn't be trembling with fear over a black overnight bag.

I dragged it out from its hiding place and tiptoed out of the attic. I paused on the top of the stairs, listening to the silent house. The bag was heavy. I got down to the study, unlocked the door, and then locked myself inside.

Sitting on the carpet, I opened the bag as carefully as though it was a bomb. Inside was a collection of dense, dark blocks, each sealed in heavy-duty plastic. I didn't want to look too closely, but as I picked one up, there was movement in the block, it wasn't a solid entity. I pressed at the plastic with one hand and peered at the top of the block. It was instantly recognisable, dark with a beacon of gold in the centre; mundane and glamorous at the same time. The bag was full of passports.

I put the block I'd been holding back in the bag and looked around. There was the bureau, which locked, but I wasn't sure the whole bag would go in there. I reluctantly removed the blocks, one by one. Once I'd loosened them from the bag I counted out fifteen blocks, formed from tightly packed passports. There were about fifty in each pack. Worth killing for? Worth dying for? Each one was worth killing for, if you needed one and someone else had one, I guessed. It was impossible to know if they were blank or not, and I wasn't about to start unpacking them. My fingerprints were already all over the wrapping, and given what I thought about Trenoweth, I didn't want to get any more involved than I was. Opening all the drawers and the front panel of the bureau, I put the blocks in different places, behind other items. Hidden, if you weren't really looking.

Then I locked all the drawers and the top of the bureau. I locked the study door, and brought the bag into the kitchen. I took a half-used cardboard carton of soup – mulligatawny – from the fridge, and dropped the bureau keys in it, folded the top back together and put it into the freezer.

I opened the fridge. There was a big opened jar of Nutella in there, some relic from a long-ago summer holiday. I pushed the key to the study door deep inside the jar so that it was covered. Then I went into the utility room and fetched an unopened box of dishwasher tablets and an economy-sized bottle of detergent. I wrapped them in towels and stuffed them in the bag and hefted it up and down a few times, testing the weight. I put the bag inside the tumble dryer and closed the door. If someone searched the house and found the bag, they might not open it until they were on their way to freedom. I know – that sounded like a long shot – but I was under pressure.

I looked at my hands. They were trembling, but they were empty. No keys, no passports, nothing to encumber me.

I went out through the front door, locked it and checked it and let myself in to Glebelands

Bed and Breakfast.

In the kitchen I turned on the radio and I let the sound fill the house like sunlight. I started to feel lighter, free. At some point I'd stopped listening to Dido's 'Lament', and started listening to Dido. I made myself some toast and stood at the kitchen counter, nibbling. There was a knock at the front door, and I went to let Horatio in.

'Are you alright?' he asked.

I nodded. 'Fine. Did Pat tell you, about the beach?'

'That's why I'm here.'

We went into the front room and sat down.

'What do you think?' I asked him.

Horatio shook his head. 'How did he get on the beach? But he can't have been in the sea very long, or he'd have been...'

I put up a hand to stop him. I really didn't need any more detail.

Horatio changed tack. 'Did you get a look at him?' What did he look like?'

'Younger than Mr Moffat. Fitter, probably. Looked more like he worked with his body than his brain, like Mr Moffat. And he was wearing – ' I closed my eyes to think better – 'He was wearing, they were like dungarees, but made of a rubber material. Yellow.'

'Waterproof? Like the fishermen wear.'

Horatio nodded slowly. 'And he'd have had to come off a boat, to be on Deadman's Beach.'

'Has anyone reported a boat missing?'

'No. Quite the opposite.' He reached into his pocket for his notebook and flicked it open, turning back through the pages.

'Last week. In Mevagissey. Yes. We had a bit of trouble, see. Here we are.'

'Mevagissey,' I said. 'That's near here.'

'Couple of miles. Local beauty spot, you can't move for tourists in the summer. But still a proper harbour, with fishing boats. Not that there's much this time of year, but this boat,' he tapped his notebook, 'this boat came and went, apparently, every couple of weeks. Then it was gone, and the fishermen don't know where, and they'd like to know, because whatever this chap was fishing for, he didn't put it through the co-op – that's where they sell their fish and they all pay a bit to the running of it. And he had a very shiny boat and all mod cons, satellite and that.'

'Smuggling,' I said. 'He was smuggling out what Mr Moffat was bringing in.'

Horatio looked worried. 'Drugs?'

'No. What's the most precious thing in the world?'

Horatio thought for a bit. 'Diamonds.'

I shook my head and he thought again.

'Gold?'

'No! No. Passports.'

'Passports? Why would anyone smuggle

those?'

'You need a passport, everyone needs a passport.'

'Not if you aren't going on holiday,' Horatio said. 'There's probably quite a few Cornish people don't need a passport. Though I suppose, if you weren't lucky enough to live in Cornwall, you'd have to go abroad for your holidays.'

'But you need a passport for more than that, nowadays. Opening a bank account, buying a house, all sorts of things.'

Horatio looked amazed. 'I hadn't thought of that. And all the immigrants, too.'

'Exactly. You need a passport to prove you exist. And someone's got a supply of them. We're talking big money. Powerful criminals.'

'Why did they kill him, though, the smuggler on the beach? And Mr Moffat. That's going to dry up the trade.'

I thought for a bit.

'I don't know. Maybe they were winding things up? Something must have been different this time. Maybe the person killing them was double-crossing the others?' I rubbed my hands over my face. 'This is complicated. How far out do the fishing boats go?'

'Out, far,' Horatio said with an expansive wave. 'They can be gone for days.'

I stood up and looked out of the window at the slice of ocean I could see, above the roofs of the village. It looked bleak and cold and I didn't want to think of even a smuggler dropping into that. I hoped he was already dead when his waders filled with water and pulled him under.

'Beyond there, though,' I said, pointing out, 'what is there?'

Horatio came to join me at the window. He scratched his face thoughtfully.

'English Channel,' he said, finally. 'And then, the world.'

CHAPTER TWENTY-SIX

Horatio had to leave, which was probably a good thing. He would have worried about what I was planning to do next. I checked both houses, locked them, and double-checked that I'd locked them.

I didn't know how regular the buses were, but I was determined to get to Mevagissey this afternoon. I'd heard about Mevagissey, even before I came to Cornwall. It was a chocolate-box, calendar photo kind of a place, or at least that was the impression I had.

There was a twenty-minute wait for the bus. Marc waved at me from the hairdressers' window and beckoned me over. There was no-one in the salon, so he made me a cup of tea and we chatted about London while I watched for the arrival of the bus. No-one else joined the queue, and no-one was on the bus when I got on. It was a tiny single-decker, so I couldn't get a better view of the landscape as we trundled up the hill and out of the village, but I was surprised to see that the coastal path led there, the wooden finger of the sign pointing the way. I looked up at the hills, probably not an easy walk but I might give it a try when this was all over. We arrived at the stop next to a car park and a shop optimistically selling buckets and spades. Not much call for those today. Mevagissey was made from the same dark granite as Gorran Porth, and the closed and shuttered shops spoke of a winter of carefully guarded privacy. I went down a dark alley between shops and the story was suddenly different. There was the harbour, far, far larger than ours, at Gorran Porth. I stopped on the cobbled front. Had I just thought of Gorran Porth as mine? My home? I turned up my collar and pushed my hands deeper into my pockets.

Mevagissey had two harbours, I saw as I wandered around. One harbour which nestled in the embrace of the town, surrounded by houses and shops – some open – and cottages which climbed in steps of powder blue, lemon and pink, up the hills. I bought a paper cup of hot chocolate from a shop selling newspapers and postcards and tried to engage the person serving in conversation, but they wanted to get back to the tiny TV on a bracket above the counter. So I wandered round the harbour wall to see what lay beyond the gap which led from the inner harbour to the outer. This was a much larger expanse of water, and less crowded with fishing boats. The arms of this harbour were spread wider, not so comforting and close. Beyond the outer harbour the real sea churned, slapping against the stone walls, sending the seagulls complaining into the air. The air was less stormy now and there were snatches of blue sky. Shadows from the clouds scudded over the water, and where the sun broke through the sea glittered and the houses looked cheery and summery. I could imagine the pull of this place on a sunny day. Easy to see why it appeared on postcards and jigsaw puzzles.

I wasn't at all sure why I'd come, or what I was looking for, but I needed to walk back along the jetty and out to the other side of the harbour. Slowly I worked my way round, paying close attention to the boats. They were bigger than the ones in Gorran Porth, I guessed they went further out to sea. They were squat, sea-stained things, with brightly painted hulls and with piles of nets lying like veils on the cramped decks. Some of them had winches and winding equipment at the stern, and they were all decorated with bright pink plastic balls – to stop them bashing into each other, I'd guess. They had sweet names: Sally-Anne, Katy, Queen of the Sea. The sweetness didn't fit with the ugly boats, but I guessed they were named for mothers, wives and girlfriends. I stopped at a bench and sat down to take it all in, and to inch closer to an old man who was reading a paper. He looked up as I joined him.

'Good afternoon,' I said. 'What a lovely day. I can't believe I've never been here before.'

It worked. He put his paper away.

'Never been to Mevagissey before? Where you been all your life?'

I smiled at him. 'I'm new to Cornwall. All these boats, it looks like a proper industry.'

'Ah. Used to be. They still do alright, these boys, but there aren't many of them. The sea can't support any more.'

'I see. So, is everyone here a fisherman, all these boats? Or...'

'No, anyone can berth up, visitors and that, but they have to pay their dues.'

'Of course. And those numbers on the boats, what do they show?'

And so he explained it to me, the code for the home port of the fishing boats. And the visiting yachts and the other little craft sheltering for the winter.

I nodded.

'Well, I'll go for another walk,' I said. 'But now I'll be more knowledgeable, thank you.'

'Ah,' he said. 'I hope you find what you're looking for.' He flapped his newspaper and the wind caught it, the pages struggling to be airborne and a nearby bird startled upwards.

I turned to stare at him but his face was back in his paper and I had no choice but to leave the bench.

The part of the harbour I saw now was

very different from the timeless beauty of the other side. There was nothing charming about the stacks of blue plastic bins towering over the boats. There were piles of lobster pots standing on the harbour walls, plastic netting and nylon ropes snaking over the dark granite. I walked on. There was a large building on a sloping jetty. A sign, which looked hand-painted, pointed me to The Aquarium. There was a boat with a dark green hull and the letters HH57. I'd go back and ask the reading man what that meant. The boat was bigger than most of the others and none of them had HH on their hulls. This boat had a closed structure on the deck, with blinds drawn down inside the windows, and a padlock on the door. Some of the other boats only had a shelter on three sides, with a roof. This boat, HH57, looked more expensive, somehow, even to my unknowledgeable gaze. Out of the corner of my eye I could see two other people approaching the boat, from the opposite direction. A couple of men, both older than me by about ten years. They were oddly dressed – at least for Mevagissey. If I'd run into them in Sir Dougall's office in London I'd have thought they fitted right in. They were wearing shiny city shoes and dark blue coats, one with velvet flashes on the collar. They had the smooth moisturised look of rich people who took care of themselves. I was sure their hands, if I could see them, would be soft, with manicured nails. They were from my old world, a world of money, and appearances. They were out of place. I looked more at home here than they did, with my waterproof coat and walking boots.

Suddenly, they were both looking at me, their faces bright with expectation.

'Hello there!' one said.

'Hello. Lovely day.' I smiled and tried to look casual.

'No,' one man muttered to the other and they both turned away sharply, as though keen to get out of my way. I gave them another smile and wandered off, still looking at them slyly. I wished I had sunglasses to hide behind though they might have looked a bit odd today. When I was far enough away, the two men casually moved away from the green boat, walking slowly around the harbour, though I noticed they didn't get too far from HH57. The next time I looked, they were at the end of the jetty staring out at the water. I wandered back round the harbour slowly, keeping them in my peripheral vision. I wasn't sure what our odd exchange had meant, but it did mean something, I was certain of that.

I got back to the old man on the bench and sat down again.

'Well?' he asked. 'What did you think of it?'

'Very pretty. Where's HH? On the hull of that one?'

'Mm. Not sure. Could be Harwich? Yes.

Probably Harwich.'

'Isn't that a long way away?'

'It is a long way away.'

'Don't the locals mind? I mean, someone coming in from another place and fishing in their waters?'

'They would, if that boat was doing any fishing.'

I paused. 'Why is it here then?' I asked.

'That's for you to find out,' the man said.

I was dumbstruck. 'Oh. Right.' My mind was whirling. Was he exceptionally rude, or did he think I was someone else, like the two men on the jetty? Did they all think I was the same person, or were they all expecting someone different?'

'Who do you think I am?' I said.

He looked at me. 'I don't know you.'

'But you think I'm...someone specific.'

'You are, aren't you? Aren't we all? Specific, I mean.'

I sighed. Very cryptic.

'All I'm saying,' he said, 'is, when you've got a problem, you ring your mates, don't you?'

I nodded, without looking at him. That is indeed what you did. Unless you forgot you had any mates and instead ended up in a seaside village where you didn't know anyone. I sat up straighter. I had mates now, didn't I?

'Can I ask you something else?' I said. He nodded and folded the paper on his knees.

'This morning I was over at Gorran Porth – well, on the beach actually, just round the headland.'

'Coffin Cove,' he said. 'Deadman's Beach.'

'Yes. And, this is unbelievable, but there *was* a dead man. On the beach. He looked like a sailor of some kind, but not a fisherman, you know?'

'And he was dead?' the old man asked. I had a feeling I was making his day.

'Very dead. And I wondered if he came from here.'

I knew he didn't come from round here, Horatio would have known that, but I thought it was worth just casting my line. Oh, listen to me.

The old man shook his head. 'Not heard of anyone going missing. Could have come off a bigger boat, further out. We've had some storms. Might have been swept overboard. They do say that anyone who goes in the water north of Deadman's Point – '

' – Ends up in Coffin Cove,' I finished. It wasn't that though, was it? The man on the beach had been dead when he went into the water, or dying, at least, from a massive head wound.

'Well, thanks for your time,' I said, getting up. 'I'd better be off.'

'You take care now, Miss,' the old man said, opening his paper again.

I looked up at the sky expecting to see it

crowded with dark clouds, as a sudden breeze rippled across the water towards me. I walked off without saying goodbye

There wouldn't be another bus yet so I had some time to kill in Mevagissey. A pub facing the harbour seemed busy and so I stepped inside. It was dark, but warm. I stepped up to the bar and looked around while I waited for the barman to get to me. There were a few people dotted around, some locals, I guessed, and some early tourists in clean new waterproofs. The tone was quiet, and there was a pleasant low gleam coming from the shiny glass floats and nautical pictures on the walls. I ordered a coffee, and went to sit in the window seat, the granite padded against the cold, with a good view of the harbour. The barman put the coffee on the table in front of me.

'Passing through?' he said.

'No. No, I live near here.' How strange that sounded.

'Ah,' He nodded and moved away, his hosting duties done. I sipped at my coffee and watched the harbour. I thought in the distance I could make out the two dark blobs of the men in their coats. The bench with the mysterious newspaper reader was out of sight.

The two strange men who thought they'd recognised me, what was their deal? They were obviously waiting for someone, but it was someone they didn't know, had never seen before. Or at least one of them had never seen before? I quite literally scratched my head. I'd have to get Pat and Horatio thinking about this. I was meeting them tonight, so we'd talk it through in the pub. I learned from working for Sir Dougall for all those years, that sometimes you just needed to share things. In those days, I'd have formed a committee – I'd have gone through the company looking for the best people, then I'd have added a few mavericks, unexpected names on a list I'd present to Sir Dougall. He'd look at it, pass it back to me with a grunt, and I'd get them all together and we'd start talking about the next project – a takeover, a move into a new territory. Who would be on this committee? I had the dreadful feeling that Smith, Nick and Inspector Trenoweth were the obvious experts, but I suspected they were all working for our major competitor. If we were broadly honest and law-abiding people, they were the opposition.

I noticed the two men in coats were walking back along the harbour wall, back towards HH57. Were they interested in that boat in particular? Or was it just coincidence we'd all been standing there? My vision was blocked for an instant as someone walked past the pub window, stopping right outside to light a cigarette. He was wearing jeans and a white t-shirt. I couldn't see his feet, or his head, just the middle section as he leaned in away from the wind, cupping his hand round a bright red plastic lighter. Also bright red, a circular logo in the centre of his white t-shirt. The same logo, on the same white t-shirt, as the dead man on Deadman's Beach.

I left most of the coffee, shouted thanks to the barman and raced outside. Right outside the door of the pub I could see the white t-shirt moving off up the harbour. I reached for my phone and trying to be really casual about it, took a photo of the man from behind. I had a clear shot of the logo, but I wasn't sure I could get in front of him and take his photo without anyone noticing. I stopped to look in a shop window, watching his reflection while he got a bit further in front. He wasn't hurrying but he was moving in a purposeful manner, getting to where he needed to be, but trying to finish his cigarette before he got there. He passed the bench where I'd chatted with the newspaper reader, though the bench was empty now. I sat down and tried to look as though I was fiddling with my phone, keeping my head low, looking ahead at the smoking man. Yes, he was advancing towards HH57, and so were the two men in coats. They looked towards me and I held my phone up to my face and pouted and flicked at my hair and tried to look as though I was taking a selfie. The man in jeans jumped down onto the deck of HH57 and held out his hand to help the two men down. He pointed at something and the second man unhooked a fat blue rope before climbing down onto the deck. The two older men didn't linger on deck but got straight inside and vanished out of view. I put my phone down and got up, moving towards the boat. The blinds on the windows of the wheelhouse went up and it was too late to duck out of view. There was a popping, coughing sound as the engine started, the boat pushed away from the high harbour wall and began to turn. I had to hurry now, running to the sea-wall and climbing up to look over, out to the open sea, waiting to see which way the boat would go. It nosed through the narrow opening, and turned right – down the Channel. South, towards Gorran Porth.

CHAPTER TWENTY-SEVEN

Back on the bus I phoned Horatio and left a message.

'Team meeting – urgent. Meet me at The Manse.'

I rang Pat, and got through to Trevor and told him the same thing. He asked if he could join us and of course I said yes.

I got off the bus in the main street at Gorran Porth and looked through the buildings to the harbour. The tide was halfway out, so I didn't think HH57 would be coming in here to-night, but what did I know about boats? Abso-lutely nothing. As I got close to the top of the hill I could see that Pat and Trevor were already at The Manse, sitting in their car. I waved to them and they joined me at the front door.

'Horatio's on his way,' Pat said. 'He got your message.'

'Good, come on in, there's loads to tell

you.'

We gathered in the kitchen and I opened the lids of the AGA to warm up the room.

Trevor looked around him in interest, while Pat helped me put out some wine glasses and cheese and crackers. I opened a bottle of Sir Dougall's no doubt expensive wine, not that he'd miss it, and as we were settling round the long kitchen table Horatio came in, ruddy with the cold evening, and rubbing his hands.

'Alright, all?'

'Horatio,' I said, 'did you lock the door behind you?'

He looked at me in alarm and went off to check.

Once we were all seated, with wine and crackers, I began.

I told them about my trip to Mevagissey, the man on the bench, the two men who thought they were waiting for me, and the sailor with the logo on his t-shirt – the logo which had been on the chest of the dead man on the beach.

I sat back with my wine.

No-one said anything. Finally Pat spoke up.

'This is getting worse and worse. Normally, after a crime, you expect things to get better, don't you?' She turned to Trevor, who shrugged. 'You do! You expect to find answers, not more questions.'

Horatio nodded. 'Aunty Pat, maybe the

dead men aren't the actual crime. Maybe they're just, um, what do they call it?'

'Collateral damage,' Trevor said.

Pat looked impressed at that.

'You could be right, Horatio,' I said. 'If the crime is the passports, Mr Moffat was killed because he didn't hand them over at the bus stop, or after. So the people who want them, have been looking for them.'

'Are they the people who killed Mr Moffat?' Pat asked. 'And what did the man in Mevagissey mean, about ringing your mates?'

'I've been thinking about that,' I said. 'When you've got a problem, you either call the authorities, don't you, or you call the press.'

'The press?' Horatio didn't look convinced but Trevor and Pat were nodding, thinking.

'So someone in Mevagissey thinks something's wrong,' Pat said, 'and they've called someone to look into it? But what do they think is wrong, they aren't the ones with a dead body in their bedroom, or on their beach?'

'Horatio? What have you heard?' I asked him.

'Well, the usual things. Boats maybe not declaring all their catch, nothing dramatic, not that I've heard.'

'What about a mysterious trawler from Harwich, not going fishing but coming in and out of the harbour?'

'I'll ask. I've not heard anything, but I'll ask.

I'll go and do that now, shall I?'

'Take care, love,' Pat said, and I walked him to the front door. We looked up and down the lane but there was no-one watching. Horatio pulled up the hood of his sweatshirt and vanished into the dusk.

'What about this logo,' Trevor said when I got back. 'Can you draw it?'

I rummaged in the drawer of the kitchen table and found some blank paper and crayons left there from some long-ago summer lunch with children.

'It was red. It was a bit like this – ' I did a rough outline with crayon. 'Was it round, or oval?' I asked Pat. 'You saw the body this morning.'

She shuddered. 'I tried not to look. Uncle Nat, he probably got a better look.'

I carried on drawing for a bit, but it was no good. Logos were simple, but precise. And I hadn't recognised it, so maybe getting a more exact version of it wasn't going to help, if no-one knew what it was.

'Should we ask Uncle Nat?' I said. 'It seems wrong to involve him in this. It could be dangerous.'

Pat and Trevor looked at each other. 'We can't tell him anything,' Pat said. 'He can't keep a secret.'

'We could just ask him about the logo – if he saw it,' Trevor said. 'How about that.'

'Which of Janice's rules are we following now?' Pat asked me, spreading Jarlsberg on a cracker.

'We've got a choice,' I said. 'Could be number 2, *Put yourself in their shoes.*'

Trevor nodded. 'The criminal's shoes? I don't know as I could manage that.'

Pat shrugged. 'What other rule?'

'Well, rule number one is a good one, *All the small things add up to the big thing.*'

Trevor looked impressed. 'I never had Janice down as the cryptic type,' he said. 'I thought she was quite straightforward.'

'She is,' Pat said. 'What she means by the small things is, making the butter into those little curls, stuff like that.'

'Yes,' I said. 'And putting the little jam pots with the labels all facing the same ways, and making a point on the first sheet of loo roll.'

'And what does that all add up to?' Trevor asked.

'The big thing,' Pat said. 'Obvious.'

'Well, not obvious to me,' Trevor protested.

'I think, what she means is, that the general...um...experience of the customer, the impression we make on them, is all made up of those little things,' I explained. 'At least, I hope that's what she meant. Otherwise I've been doing it wrong.'

'You haven't been doing it wrong,' Pat said.

'Hasn't it all been going smoothly?'

Trevor and I looked at her, while she spread another cracker.

'Apart from...' I prompted her.

She looked up, the cracker halfway to her mouth. 'Well. One dead body, against quite a few happy customers. Gotta keep a sense of proportion.'

After a bit more chat and eating, we cleared away the food and wine and locked up the house, and Trevor drove us to Uncle Nat's farmhouse.

Inside his kitchen it was dim and cosy and smelled of food. Uncle Nat was sitting at the table, watching the TV and sipping from a mug of tea, one hand on his massive stomach and his wild white hair showing signs of having been under a hat all day.

'Ah, come and sit down,' he shouted, and turned the TV down. He kept one eye on the manic leaping about of some pair of teenagers, but he listened to his niece carefully.

'Uncle Nat, this morning, on the beach – did you see that bloke?'

'The dead one?'

'Well of course the dead one!'

'Now, Pat,' Trevor said, 'Let's not get our hair off.'

'I saw him alright,' Uncle Nat said. 'What's all this about?'

'Nothing,' I said. 'We were just wondering. He had a logo on his t-shirt.'

'Oh yes?' Uncle Nat said, looking back to the TV. 'That.'

'Yes. So we were wondering...because I can't remember it very clearly, we were wondering – '

He raised a massive red hand. 'Hang on there,' he said, turning his bulk awkwardly to put the mug of tea down behind him.

'Now.' He turned back to the table. 'Where did I put it?' He lifted a broken-spined address book and some pages dropped out. 'Not that.' He moved a pile of tractor magazines, dislodging a piece of toast – 'ah, that's where that went.'

I looked on in horror, and Pat had her head in her hands.

'Here we are!' Uncle Nat roared and we all sat up straighter. '*The Truro Times*.'

He licked his fingers and began turning the pages. Towards the back he found what he was looking for. He stabbed one finger at the page, and turned it round so we could see. Even in black and white there was no doubt. There was the logo, on the funnel of a ship. And the text below the photo read – *'newest arrival in port, Sunbeam Marchesa BV, a car carrier from Spain, due to tie up at Carrick Roads, indefinitely.'*

I looked at the date on the paper. Early February. It was almost a month old. I looked again at the photo. 'What does that mean? Due to tie up at Carrick Roads, indefinitely?'

'We'd better show you,' Trevor said.

Pat nodded. 'Tomorrow, not tonight. Too late tonight.'

I had no option but to agree. Trevor was tearing neatly round the photo while Uncle Nat returned his attention to the silent television.

Pat turned to Trevor – 'aren't you going to see Winnie tomorrow morning?'

Trevor waved his hand. 'She won't mind if I'm a bit later. I'll say Isabel needs something.'

'No!' I said. 'No, don't say that to Winnie. I get the feeling I'm not her favourite person. Let's go in the afternoon

'But then I definitely can't come,' Trevor said. 'I'm pricing up another job at 2 o'clock.'

'Well you go on,' Pat told him. 'We'll be fine, the two of us.'

I nodded. 'It'll be fine, Trevor,' I said. 'What's the worst that can happen?'

CHAPTER TWENTY-EIGHT

On Sunday morning I had my weekly phone chat with Janice. We had an agreement, we wouldn't bother each other all week, unless it was an emergency. Little did I know when I'd made that agreement that I'd be dealing with an emergency so big I couldn't actually mention it. On the three Sundays before this one, all I'd had to do was listen to Janice reeling off the bookings for the week to come. I felt a bit guilty: I was more than capable of managing Janice's website, far more capable than the slightly teenage web designer in St Austell she'd paid to create it, but I hadn't wanted to be connected to the internet, and I'd refused her offer to show me 'how it works'. So I was reduced to taking a weekly phone call and noting down the bookings on a spiral notebook, like an old-fashioned newspaper reporter. Of course if anyone booked unexpectedly, she would ring me, and I was free to take bookings on the door if I'd wanted – which is how I'd ended up with Mr Moffat.

I took the notepad down from the hook behind the door and checked that all the room keys were there, even Room 6 hanging innocently. I hadn't been up to the room since Friday, but I was sure Nick wouldn't have left any trace. The room was lettable though I couldn't see myself showing a potential guest around the facilities – 'here's the en-suite; look at the sea view, oh, and that's where Mr Moffat died.'

I sat down at the dining table, where the conversations over the past three days had ranged much further than extra sausages and the Cornish weather. I flicked the pages of the notebook and listened to the clock on the cooker. I got up to pace up and down the dining room.

When the phone finally rang I nearly leaped out of my skin.

'Janice!'

'Of course it is. Are you alright? Who were you expecting?'

'No-one. Yes, I'm fine. Everything's fine.'

'Fine? I don't think so, Isabel,' Janet said.

I was so shocked, I had to sit down. Who had told her?

'It is a lot better than fine, my dear,' she said. 'A lot better.'

'Oh. Well. Good.'

'We're full. Well, almost.'

'Are we? When?'

'Tomorrow, Monday night.'

'Oh dear,' I said.

'What's that?'

'That's great news. Great. So, I've got the notebook ready, fire away.'

'Right, now you know about the first couple, Mr and Mrs Chapman. Their niece is getting married. And they already asked for a sea view, so they have to have Room 1.'

'Room 1,' I said, as I scribbled in the notebook.

'Now, another couple booked via the website, only today. Isn't that amazing?'

'Yes,' I said. 'Unbelievable.' Janice always pronounced website as two distinct words. Web. Site. She was going on with the instructions.

'A young couple by the sound of it. Mr – where is it? Mr Marks, and his young lady. I don't have her name, but that's alright.'

'Mr Marks and companion,' I noted down. 'And they'll have room 2?'

'Well, as they're a young couple, you could put them in Room 4. The bed isn't bigger but the room is, and there's that little window-seat. By far the most romantic room, I think.'

'That's thoughtful,' I said.

'Those are the little touches, my dear, which make a successful business. You'll get the hang of it.'

'I hope so, Janice.'

'Yes, you'll get the hang of it. Now there's

another couple, but separate people, so they want twin beds, so you could either give them Room 2 and Room 6, or you could separate the zip-together in Room 2 and let them both have that one.'

'I'll do that,' I promised. 'I'll separate the beds. They're only paying for one room, so...'

'Yes, dear. But Room 6 doesn't get used much, might be nice to give it an airing. But up to you. You're the one there.'

'I'll make sure Room 6 is aired before you get back. Promise.'

I made a little note on the notebook – *get rid of the smell of Lemon Pledge.*

Janice had more instructions. 'So the names for the twin beds are, let me see. Duncan Loomes, and Alan Lewis. Loomes and Lewis, they sound like a double-act, don't they.'

'They do.' *And what's more – I think they are.* But I didn't say anything, just took the rest of the details, one more booking, a single man this time, an ornithologist called Mr Lark, (I didn't even bother to comment.) He'd have Room 5, a double bed, but a small room, perfect for one.

'So you'd better flee round, dear,' Janice was saying. 'I told them they couldn't check in before 4 pm, any of them, just to give you some time.'

'Thanks, Janice. Don't worry. I won't let you down. I've been following the rules. They've been really helpful'

'I don't worry about you, ever,' Janice said. 'I know it must all seem terribly quiet after your London life, but I know you are a good reliable worker.'

'Yes. Well, goodbye, Janice, speak in the week if we need to. And, and I'm doing my best.'

'I know you are, Isabel. You'll always do your best. Don't get bored!' And with a merry laugh, she was gone.

After the phone call I was suddenly ravenous and made myself a proper lunch. I always had plenty of eggs, for the breakfasts, so I made a cheese omelette and sat down to eat it at the window table in the front room, looking out over Glebelands Lane. The Manse next door looked solid and stately. I'd be sorry to leave it, but I tried not to worry too much about where I'd go. Down in the harbour the tide was in, and I wondered where HH57 was moored up. It would be out of place in Gorran Porth, though it might be back in Mevagissey. Perhaps it was out on the high seas. I didn't think the two older men were particularly dressed for a long sea voyage, so that didn't seem likely. They seemed more dressed for a business meeting.

I wondered how Horatio was getting on. Was anyone talking to him about what the man on the bench had told me in Mevagissey? Or were they clamming up tight at the sight of a

Community Support Officer, even one about to lose his badge?

I was in the kitchen clearing up when Pat arrived and it felt almost like an adventure as we got into her car and pulled out of Gorran Porth. Pat talked about her job and I realised how much she knew of her community: she could see what was in every porch, inside every front door. She knew who'd had a bit of luck on the Premium Bonds, who had a hospital appointment, who was being chased for unpaid bills. She was the invisible guest at birthdays and she silently observed the shrinking numbers of Christmas cards arriving for the oldest in the village. I couldn't have picked a better companion for this self-induced assignment.

We were driving down winding lanes with few houses on either side. There were the occasional farms and churches, chapels which were now holiday cottages, and fields with a few caravans in, but not much that would be called even a village. The low mist had returned, and the air was white with moisture. It seemed darker than it should be for the early afternoon.

'Where exactly are we headed?' I asked her.

'We're going to look at the Fal. Where that ship is, with the logo on the funnel. Though I'm not really sure why. We thought it was a good idea last night.'

'We did. Well, we'll have a look at it, and then maybe do something more cheerful?

Pat was focussing on the road now but looked slightly distracted. I felt guiltily aware that I was involving people in something unpleasant, possibly dangerous, just to assuage my guilt.

'Pat, you know you don't have to do this,' I said.

'Do what? Open the glove compartment.'

I found a Tupperware container full of slices of Battenberg cake and I passed her one.

'Do this, getting into this...whatever this is.'

Pat nodded. 'I know, but this week we've got to give our statements, and Horatio's probably going to lose his job. So, I think we should keep going.'

I ate my slice of Battenberg.

'After all,' Pat said. 'What would we have been doing, if we weren't doing this'?

'Hmm. I'm not sure that's a good enough reason, but...I'm really glad you are here, Pat.'

'Who did you leave behind?' she asked me. 'In London?'

I reached for another slice of Battenberg and put the container back in the glove compartment.

'Friends, colleagues. My boss. Everyone in the office – people I'd known for decades. Oh, and Ivan.'

Pat nodded, triumphantly. 'I knew it,' she said. 'I told Trevor, 'mark my words,' I said, 'there's some romantic shenanigans there'.'

Oh dear. Well, I'd have to come clean.

'It wasn't romantic, really,' I said. 'I'd been with Ivan for about seven years, and we had a great time. He was clever, and funny and successful. We always had fun. Expensive fun, I mean. Going all over the world, doing exciting things. It was exhausting, and glamorous, and maybe a bit...dark.'

'Ooh,' Pat said, looking a bit troubled.

I pressed on. 'And then, suddenly, I was depressed. I just couldn't do anything. Some people dropped by the wayside, of course. But not my best friend, or my boss. And I thought Ivan would give up, because it isn't as though he needed me for anything practical. But he didn't give up. He kept on turning up, trying to...I don't know. Trying to rescue me. He even – I mean, you'd have to know him to know how amazing this was – he even tried to wash up, in my kitchen. He didn't have the faintest idea, love him.' I could smile at the memory now.

'And did you love him?' Pat asked.

'I did, yes. But when he blocked the sink and flooded the kitchen and told me he wanted to change his whole life, and be with me forever, that's when I realised.'

Pat didn't say anything. I had to just take the final step.

'When I was faced with the prospect of having him all to myself, that's when I realised.

The thing I loved most about him, the thing that made him perfect for me, was that he was married to someone else.'

Pat said nothing. I looked over at her. She was frowning slightly.

I had to know. 'Well?' I said. 'Are we still friends?'

'Why wouldn't we be friends?' she asked, craning her neck to see round a blind bend.

The road became narrower, the scrubby banks on either side getting steeper. The lane turned and became single-track, so that the naked branches met over the top, darkening the road and closing us off from the day.

'I don't know,' I said.

'Because I'm happily married?' she asked. 'So I have to disapprove of someone who isn't?'

'No, not that exactly.'

'I just want the best for you, Isabel. That's all.'

'OK. Well, Ivan was the best thing for me, until he wasn't.'

She nodded. 'There aren't many men like Trevor around, I'll tell you that. I know how lucky I am. And he can do all the jobs around the house.'

'And does he?'

She grinned. 'Once a year. Between Christmas and New Year, when no-one wants a tradesman in their house. That's when I get all the little jobs done.'

She made a slow turn off the road and into a tunnel of trees. At the end of the tunnel, there in front of us was a stretch of dark green water. I blinked and squinted. I couldn't see the opposite bank, because in the middle of the river, inexplicably, was a massive ship.

'How is that possible!' I shouted. 'That's huge, and we're in the middle of the countryside.'

I looked over at Pat. She was looking very pleased with herself. 'I know! It always takes people like that.'

'What is it doing here? How did it get here?'

She pulled into the side of the road. There was a lay-by with about four cars in it, and she parked. 'Ships come up the River Fal, it's a lot deeper there in the middle than it looks.'

'But why?'

'Well, parking. Parking for ships. If people have got a ship and they don't need it, they need somewhere to keep it where it won't come to any harm, and keeping it in the middle of a river doesn't cost anything like as much as keeping in a dock somewhere.'

We got out and pulled our waterproof hoods up. The mist was coming off the river in white clouds now. The bare trees were dripping and the whole scene looked otherworldly. I couldn't take my eyes off the massive metal structure in front of us. We walked down a slight slope to where the road widened into an open yard. There was a corrugated iron boat shed with a high roof and a sloping jetty that led into the river, and some wooden pallets stacked up. There was a set of stone steps leading from the jetty down into the water, and what looked like a pump from an old-fashioned petrol station.

'That's not our ship,' I said.

'No, but there's more.' Pat pointed, and sure enough, as we got to the side of the river, I could see four more ships, moored in pairs. They all had rust-red hulls below the painted upper levels. The ship at the back was clearly the one we were looking for. On her funnel I could see the round red logo. More importantly, tied up to her side, below a door-shaped opening much higher in her hull, was the squat green body of HH57.

I grabbed Pat's arm.

'Hide!' I said.

She looked at me in horror.

'What? Why?'

'That's the boat, the one I told you about, in Mevagissey.'

Pat looked back at the ship and as we stood there, HH57 let out a spurt of smoke and across the water the unmistakable sound of her engine reached us.

We started to step backwards as quickly as we could. We ducked behind the corner of the boat shed.

'We'll have to get back to the car,' Pat whispered.

'I know. Wait until they're getting in the boat, then they won't be paying attention, they'll be distracted.'

CHAPTER TWENTY-NINE

We didn't have a chance to do that. Almost silently, a rich black car arrived in the yard, stopping smoothly by the steps which led down to the water. We were stuck now, we couldn't get out from behind the shed without the driver seeing us.

We moved further along the side of the boat shed. There was a door with a hasp and a padlock, but the padlock was hanging in the loop and I flicked the clasp back and gently opened the door. It was well-oiled and didn't make a sound. We stepped into the darkness. I don't know if Pat was struck by it, but it made me think about the morning we'd found Mr Moffat, both of us standing right inside the doorway afraid to go any further. Now we moved into the boat shed and looked out of the grimy windows. HH57 was moving away from the larger ship, crabbing sideways towards the steps where the driver of the car was standing on the river bank. He raised a hand in greeting.

'Smith,' Pat whispered. 'That's Smith. Oh my good God.'

'That's not all,' I said, turning back from the windows. 'Look.'

There in the gloom of the shed was the humped shape of a vehicle. It was covered with a dark green tarpaulin, but the covering didn't reach to the ground. I could clearly see, above the bumper at the back, that it was a small white van.

'Oh my God!' Pat mouthed at me. 'He could be in there. Mr Moffat.'

'Keep an eye on the window,' I pointed, and she turned back.

I lifted the tarpaulin up at the front as quietly as I could and slipped underneath it so I was hidden from view.

'They're getting closer,' Pat said.

I got my phone out and turned the torch setting on. There was nothing in the front of the van, but we'd known it was new – too new to have the logo painted on. It was definitely the right van, though, there was a Penwithick Pasties order book resting on the front shelf, pressed against the windscreen. I took a photo of that, but there was no signal to send it to anyone.

I slipped out from under the tarpaulin.

'Could you see him?' Pat said.

I shook my head. She gestured towards the back doors of the van.

I shook my head again. 'In a minute,' I whispered. She nodded and we turned back to the river.

Smith – there was no doubt it was him – caught a rope thrown by the sailor I'd seen in Mevagissey. He put his weight to the rope and in the moment when the boat met the steps, the two men I'd seen yesterday came out of the structure on the deck. Smith threw the rope to the sailor and he reversed out into the river, turning HH57 out towards the big ship.

Smith opened the rear door of the car and both men got into the back. Good. That reduced Smith to the level of a chauffeur and that gave me a brief spasm of pleasure.

He got into the car and started the motor, and Pat and I sighed. I hadn't even realised I'd been holding my breath. The car turned round and headed for the lane and we stood up, suddenly released from our tension. The car stopped in the mouth of the lane and Smith got out and walked towards us. I gestured to Pat and we ducked under the front of the tarpaulin where it was longer, bending over the bonnet of the van and keeping as still as we could. We needn't have worried. Smith didn't open the door, he simply closed the padlock, got back in the car, and drove away.

As the sound of the car receded, we straightened up and stared at each other. It was gloomy inside the shed, and now it seemed much colder too.

'I'm so sorry, Pat. I'm so sorry I got you into this.'

'Hey, enough of that talk.' Pat rubbed her arms. 'I don't suppose there's any way out?' She rattled the door half-heartedly. 'No.'

'What about the windows?' I crossed to a long workbench which ran the length of the building.

'Maybe, but we'd have to be sure there was no-one watching from out there.' Pat gestured to where HH57 was tying up once again to the bigger ship.

'What about the jetty?'

Pat looked down at the slimy green jetty, closed off from the river by metal gates which were chained together. She stepped down onto the concrete ramp, arms out for balance.

The padlock was new, and shining, and hadn't been helpfully left open. Water lapped under the gates, bringing the smell of the river up to us: mud, and something more physical.

'Let's get it over with,' I said. 'Let's see if he's in the back of the van.' And I marched over and flung the doors wide.

Inside there was a jumble of upended trays, wide and shallow, with wooden sides and metal corners. Stencilled neatly on each one were the words Penwithick Pasties. Mr Moffat was not in the van.

'Phew!' Pat said. 'That's a relief. I was a bit shaky then. What about you?'

I nodded. 'They probably put him in the river straight away.'

We both looked out. The river seemed to be moving faster now, though the light was fading and it was hard to pick out details beyond the massive pale bulk of the ships. I still couldn't quite take in the strangeness of the sight.

Pat shivered again. 'I could do with a hot flush about now,' she said.

I opened the side door of the van. 'We might as well get in, it'll be warmer.

I looked around to make sure there was no blood anywhere, either from Mr Moffat or Tyrone, but it seemed clean.

'Look at this,' Pat said, rooting around in the footwell and coming up with a blue and white plastic bag. This is Uncle Nat's order. From, you know, The Day.' And sure enough, on the outside of the bag was scrawled 'Lestoon Farm – no onions.'

She put it back down. 'No phone signal?' she asked.

I checked again. 'No.'

'Still, they know where we are. Trevor and Horatio.'

'How long d'you think they'll leave it?' I wondered.

'What time is it now?'

'Twenty past four.'

Pat groaned.

'Could be worse,' I said. 'You were right, it

is warmer in here. And we have got pasties.'

'Not at their best.' Pat pointed out. 'Let's hope it doesn't come to that.'

We sat in silence for a bit. Finally I spoke.

'I think I'll ring my boss today. Maybe tomorrow.'

'Sir Dougall?

'Yes. I thought I ought to tell him, I'm not coming back.'

Pat was silent for a minute. 'Trevor had a mid-life crisis when he was turning fifty. He bought a motorbike. Frightened me half to death. Fortunately, really, the first time he went out on it, it poured with rain and his boots filled up with water, and then the bike broke down and he had to push it all the way from Fairy Cross to Lostwithiel. He sold the bike the very next day and I never had a moment's trouble with him since.'

I smiled in the gloom.

'I was really busy and tired,' I said, 'and one day, everything seemed to become a bit...pointless. And then, Ivan, you know.'

Pat nodded. 'So what did you do then?'

'I stopped going to work, and that was still exhausting, so I stopped getting out of bed. Then Sir Dougall rang me up. Told me to get to Cornwall, have a rest, sort myself out. Keep an eye on the place. He sent a bike messenger over to my flat with a bunch of keys and an address.'

'And you did!' Pat said. 'You sorted yourself

out, and you sorted Mr Moffat out.'

'I'm not sure about that,' I said, 'He's still dead. And we don't really know who did it.'

'Hm. I'm wondering about the other dead man,' Pat said. 'What if he's the one that had to get rid of Mr Moffat, and then he was killed so he couldn't speak?'

I looked at Pat. 'You could be right. But whoever threw him overboard didn't realise he'd be washed up on Deadman's Beach.'

'Couldn't be from round here, then.'

'No. Could be from Harwich.' I gestured out to where HH57 was bobbing gently on the black river.

We sat for a bit thinking about that, letting the time pass and trying not to fret about the wait for rescue. Finally, I gave in.

'I could really do with a pasty. Do you think they're still edible?'

'Might be.' Pat started to undo the bag. 'It isn't hot weather. And they didn't actually go in the van with Mr Moffat, they were here in the front all the time.'

She handed me one. It was cold, and the pastry was tough, but we bit into it with relish.

'Bit dull,' Pat said, 'without the onions.'

'Nice though.'

'Yep. Plenty of them.'

I wriggled around in my seat, to get my phone out of my back pocket. As I moved my leg, I kicked something heavy and metallic.

'Hang on.' I handed Pat my half-eaten pasty to hold, and reached down into the darkness.

My fingers closed around something cold. I brought it up into the slightly lighter area by the windscreen.

'Oh dear,' I said. 'I think this is the murder weapon.'

Pat leaped out of the van and the internal light came on. It hadn't been noticeable before, but it was getting dimmer outside and in. She slammed the door quickly, but anyone watching from the ship couldn't have failed to see it.

'Sorry!' she shouted from outside. 'I can't get back in again.'

I reached up and turned the light out and Pat opened the door carefully. I was still holding the chisel in my other hand. It was about six inches long, it looked fairly new and it was marked with what I was pretty sure was blood.

Pat took the rest of the pasties out of the blue bag and put them on her lap and handed me the bag. I put the chisel inside and tied the handles together.

'D'you think they saw the light?' Pat said. 'Getting pretty dark now.'

'We'll soon find out,' I said, 'they'll come over to investigate.'

'Another pasty?' Pat asked.

'Maybe in a bit,' I said. 'First I need to find something to wipe my hands.'

I gave the blue bag to Pat who put it on the floor with a shudder. I got out of the darkened van, wincing as I realised how much colder it had become. The water was halfway up the concrete jetty now, smelling of darkness and night, and chilling the air. It was a bit lighter by the windows, and I felt along the workbench, finally finding a rag and wiping my hands. I had no idea what was on the rag, I might have been making things a lot worse.

Some of the bigger ships had lights on now, the odd porthole glowing faintly in the misty dusk, but HH57 was dark, except for two small lights on the side. Maybe no-one had seen the lights come on in the van, and we'd just have to sit tight now, waiting for Horatio or Trevor to come looking for us.

Pat got out of the van and stood beside me, staring out into the dusk.

'What d'you think?' she whispered.

I shrugged. 'Not sure. There's no movement at the moment.'

'If he's not in the van,' Pat said. 'Do you think he's somewhere else? I mean, in here?'

'Mr Moffat? Oh, God. I don't know. Surely not?'

'Well they didn't throw the murder weapon away, maybe they aren't as tidy as we thought?'

'I think we should mark the van in some way,' I said. 'In case they dump it.'

'Mark it with what?'

I started to root around on the work-bench, feeling for some sharp implement.

'This?' I held up a long screwdriver. Pat took it from me and turned it over a few times.

'You mean,' she said, 'put our names, or something, so if they put the van in the sea, or burn it up, people will know.'

'Yes. I think so.'

'You think' – Pat sounded small, and very far away – 'You think we might not be around to tell the tale?'

I said nothing. What could I have said?

I reached out and we hugged each other tight. Finally, Pat said, 'right, let's get on. Where's best to do it?'

'I'm not sure. Somewhere they won't spot it straight off?'

We opened the back doors and I lifted the rubber matting from the flat area of the van.

Pat knelt on the doubled-over mat and started. She scratched as deep as she could, P+I into the metal. I felt it with my fingertips rather than saw it.

'Good. Somewhere else too?'

Pat pulled the matting flat and closed the back doors and walked round the van.

'Here,' she said, crouching down. 'In the wheel arch.'

I looked out of the windows as she was getting the screwdriver into position, grinding the head into the metal with a sickening shriek.

'Hang on a minute,' Pat said from near the floor. 'P&I.'

I looked at her.

'PI,' she said. 'Private investigators.'

I shrugged.

She stood up. 'That's what we are.'

'I'm not sure about that. I've employed a PI, once, for Sir Dougall. I think you have to have a licence and be a former soldier or from the police, something like that.'

Pat looked slightly dismayed. 'We'll get a licence then.'

'Why, why would we do that?'

Pat crouched down by the wheel again. 'I need a new job. And so do you.'

'You don't need a job,' I said. 'You're the postwoman. You're the heart of the village.'

Pat jabbed at the tyre with the screwdriver. 'My job's at risk.'

'At risk of what?' I said, rubbing my arms, the cold really getting into my bones.

'At risk. That's what they say when they're going to make you redundant. Because there aren't enough people living in the village, so there isn't enough post to deliver, see.'

'Oh, Pat,' I said. 'I'm so sorry, I had no idea. But I still don't think we're cut out to be private investigators. I think we're just two middle-aged women blundering about in the dark.'

'I'm going to let this tyre down,' Pat said.

'That'll cheer me up. Promise me you'll think about it.'

'Yes, yes. I'll think about it, but please, hurry.'

'Alright,' Pat said. 'I'll do one more, for maximum inconvenience.'

'Have to be quick,' I said. 'HH57 is coming this way.'

CHAPTER THIRTY

Pat straightened up and came to stand beside me.

The green boat, with the wheelhouse now glowing faintly, was pushing away from the side of the bigger ship.

We strained to peer out of the darkened shed, tense and breathless. The boat turned downstream, slowly, slowly and then straightened, moving towards the jetty outside our prison.

One of us let out a little whimper, and I'm quite prepared to admit it was me.

'Quick!' Pat said. 'Under the tarpaulin'

We fumbled to get it over our heads, both of us crouching in front of the bonnet of the van, hidden from the doorway by the vehicle, and the dusk.

The engine sound of HH57 was much louder now. I felt I could hear it through my ears, but also in the beating of my heart. My arms were tingling and I felt short of breath. I used the sound to cover my words.

'Pat,' I said. 'I think I'm having a heart attack.'

'You what?' I could feel her turning to face me, but I couldn't see a thing. I felt my breathing get more shallow, and my arms felt tingly and heavy.

'You're not having a heart attack,' she said. 'You're having a panic attack. That's what that is.'

'Is it?'

'Well, I'm having one myself, so I should think so.'

'Oh, Pat – '

'Shh.'

We waited, straining every muscle. She must have been right because my arms were recovering and the sensation of mounting madness and fear had completely receded. Just saying it out loud appeared to have cured it completely, leaving me clear and calm. Clammy too.

We heard footsteps come up the gravel towards the shed.

Pat leaned in to whisper, a tiny thread of sound. 'I'm not going down without a fight.'

I nodded and grabbed her hand.

We heard a key in the padlock; someone was making plenty of noise, and why shouldn't they, who did they think was around to hear them?

Finally we heard the click of the padlock opening and the door being dragged open. The cold wet air curled in under the body of the van and it was welcome on my hot skin. Whoever had opened the door flicked on a feeble overhead light and that crept in under the bottom of the tarpaulin. If he stayed at the entrance to the shed and looked in the rear of the van we'd be safe. Even if he looked inside the front doors we might remain hidden in the gloom. If he attempted to walk right round the van, he'd certainly see us, trapped between the front bumper and the workbench, shrouded in tarpaulin.

I heard the back doors of the van open. The van rocked slightly as he put his weight on the floor. He retreated and slammed the doors again.

He moved to the driver's side – the side nearest me, opening the door. I braced myself again for the movement of the van as he got in. I gathered a big handful of the end of the tarpaulin in my hands. If he got any closer, I planned to leap up, keeping the tarpaulin over my head, shouting. He might be off-balance for a minute, and that might be enough. I could see Pat doing the same on her side. I was taking deep breaths now, sucking in the cold air and forcing it down into my body, calling on all the power I had, regretting bitterly all the days I hadn't gone to the gym.

The man was rummaging about in the front of the van. He was looking for the murder weapon. I looked at Pat, not that I could really see her under the thick cover, but I knew she'd be thinking the same thing.

'What the – '

The man's voice was loud in the darkness, loud and very Cornish.

If he'd been in the van before, he couldn't fail to notice that it was different. There were bits of pasty all over the front seat – we'd used the bag for the chisel, and my half-eaten pasty was on the dashboard where Pat had left it.

The front door opened and slammed shut, I could see the man's feet coming past the side of the car, coming closer, close.

'Aaahhh,' I shouted as loud as I could, rearing up with a wall of tarpaulin between me and him. I lurched to where I thought he'd be but he stepped backwards and I fell forwards onto the concrete. Pat stepped over me, kicking me in the kidney as she went, and as I looked up I could see her chasing – actually chasing – the man. Well, boy, really. She caught him at the doorway and spun him round.

'Danny Trevarro! You bloody monkey. What're you doing mixed up in this?'

She slapped him, really hard, and his head rocked back.

'Oww. Mrs Greep, don't hurt me,' he said, cowering.

I got up. My left knee was really sore and I hobbled over to them.

'Greep?' I said to Pat.

'A very old Devonshire name,' she said.

'Trevor's very proud of it.'

The boy struggled in her grasp and we took a shoulder each and shook him.

'Who the hell are you?' I asked him. He looked even more panicked.

'Hang on,' I said, turning back to the window. 'Is there anyone on that ship, watching us?'

He shook his head. 'No, I'm the caretaker. I'm meant to be on there now, only they made me come back over and find the...the – ' He gestured towards the van. 'And I was supposed to get rid of the van, but look, there's two flat tyres.'

' – The murder weapon,' Pat said to him, not releasing her grip on his shoulder.

He nodded. He looked worse now, the side of his face livid where Pat had slapped him, and his whole body twisted with worry and stress. 'You're not going anywhere,' Pat said.

I opened both back doors of the van and made him sit down inside, though Pat needed a bit of persuasion to let him go. I went outside and fetched the padlock and closed the door. At least we wouldn't be locked in again.

'Right,' I said, taking up a position next to Pat who was standing in front of the miserable Danny, her arms folded.

'You'd better sing like a canary,' Pat said. I gave her a look.

'What?' she said.

'What does that even mean?' Danny said.

'How did you get mixed up in this?' I said.

'You know two people have been killed, right?'

He nodded, and to my horror, started to weep quietly, his face blooming with blotches.

'I'm going to be next, I know it,' he said.

Pat and I said nothing. We just looked at him.

Finally Pat relented. 'Get a grip!' she said, nudging his foot with her own. 'We'll help you. But you gotta tell us the truth.'

He swiped his hand across his face. 'I can't. I can't tell.'

'OK, then,' I said. 'We'll be off.'

'They'll kill me!' he shrieked.

'You shoulda thought of that,' Pat said. 'You were a good boy, always were, I don't know how you got mixed up in this.'

'How do you know him?' I asked her.

'His mother is married to the sister of my cousin-in-law.'

'Right,' I said. None the wiser. I turned back to Danny who'd crumbled.

'I thought it was a lark, you know, bit of extra money, no-one was getting hurt. I just wanted some new waterproofs and some new kit for the boat.'

'What were you doing?' I said.

'I was the 'creeper' – that was all I had to do. It was never meant to come to this!'

'What the hell is a creeper?' I turned to Pat, who kicked his foot again, a bit less affectionately this time.

'It's a smuggling thing,' he said, mumbling. 'The sinker hides something Then later on, see, a 'creeper' comes along and gets it up, if 'tis in the water, and goes off with it. And they never see each other, so they can't...you know – '

' – they can't incriminate each other,' I said. 'Or murder each other.'

Danny Trevarro shivered at that.

'Where did it all go wrong?' Pat said.

'I was meant to go out with a package on Friday.' His voice was a bit stronger now.

Pat and I looked at each other. We knew exactly what he was meant to drop off then.

'In HH57?' I asked, pointing out at where the craft bobbed by the jetty.

'No, no, that's not always here. I got a little boat I go crabbing in, or fishing, or lobsters, sometimes. Just a few pots, see, and then there's no fuss, no-one notices. So I goes to the place where I get the package and no-one comes. No package.'

'Where is that?' Pat asked. 'Where do you collect the package?' She sounded really stern. I looked at her in amazement. She was really made for this.

He looked up at us and I'd like to think we presented a scary rampart to him, but we probably just appeared mad.

'Camerton. Camerton beach. The bins only get emptied once a month in the winter, see, so I lift the lid of the bin and there's the package inside. Well, up 'til now.'

'Go on,' Pat said. 'What did you do then?'

'Well, I went out in the boat anyway, making it look like normal. Then when I got back into harbour, the boat, HH57 was there. Tied up right where I usually tie up. And they called me on the boat, said they had a bit of engine trouble, so, in case anyone was listening.'

'Wait,' I said. My knee was really throbbing where I'd hit the floor. I found a bucket and a slightly frayed garden chair, and Pat and I made ourselves comfortable, still safely between Danny and the door.

'Go on.'

'They told me the package hadn't arrived, well, I knew that didn't I? I mean, I just been looking for it, hopping around in that storm, on the beach.'

We nodded.

'Then they said, they had another job for me. And I said I didn't want another job. I was so scared, 'cos I knew I wasn't meant to have seen them. I been doing this for months, and never seen the other people, so I knew as soon as I saw them, I was in big trouble.'

Pat nodded. 'You got that right, Danny, you are in big trouble.'

'So I tried, I really tried to get out of it. I told them, I had two jobs already, thank you very much, working for them, and working for Falmouth Harbour, caretaking up here?' He gestured to the ships.

'What do you do?' I asked, really interested. 'Isn't it lonely?'

'No, it's great. You got to check pumps and stuff like that, and you get to wander round the whole empty ship, and you can have friends on board, parties if you want, but girls don't like it,' he said sadly, 'they think it's a bit creepy.'

'So you split your time between caretaking and smuggling.' Pat brought us back on track.

'Yeah. So when I told them what other job I do, they got really interested. Said a place to hide things where people could only approach by water was very much what they was looking for.'

'What did they need to hide, if the package hadn't arrived?' I asked him.

'I dunno,' Danny said, lowering his head and wiping his nose on his sleeve.

'Wake up!' Pat said. 'Aren't you forgetting someone?' She tilted her chin at the van.

'Mr Moffat.'

'Oh God,' Darren said, looking green. 'Is that his name?'

'Where is he?' I asked.

'On board,' Darren said. 'On the ship. That's why the other one is dead. The other caretaker.'

'The other body, from the beach.' Pat looked at me. 'But who is he, he's not a local?'

Danny nodded. 'No. He came in from the company that owns the ship. They have to train me, see, in all the systems, and he's got – he had – family over here, so he went off on leave for a few weeks. Then he came back, and he was clearing out his stuff and I didn't know! I didn't know he'd come back, he had a little dinghy on the other side of the ship, and I was helping that man, Smith, and one of the others bring the dead one on board. Carlos saw us – he went mad he did, and there was a fight.' He started to cry again.

'And Smith strangled him, with his bare hands. And then the other one hit him with the chisel. And it was so quick, it was like a gun. And there was blood all over the deck.'

I looked at Pat. We'd been in the room with Smith, both quite taken with his handsome face and white shirt. That shirt was probably brand new, I thought, feeling a bit nauseous. He probably had to take a set of clean clothes wherever he went.

Danny started to rock slightly, and I saw Pat visibly pull herself together.

'There, there,' she said. 'Come on now, better out than in.' And she sat in the back of the van with him and stroked his shoulder. 'Alright, you're a good boy, we know that.'

He lifted his tear-streaked face. 'And they made me help them, they did, and I thought they were gonna kill me too, but they put him in the boat and took him out into the bay and I told them just where to throw him in.'

'And he washed up, just as you planned,'

I said. 'You did the right thing, Danny, you did what you could.'

'No!' He started sobbing again. 'He wasn't meant to wash up for a couple of days, but we've had storms, see, and now they're gonna find out, and they'll come for me. They still need me to do a few things – get rid of the van, and the murder weapon, they they'll come for me. That one with the chisel.'

'We've got the chisel,' Pat said, looking at me proudly.

'They'll get another chisel,' Danny shouted. 'There in't a shortage of chisels!'

'Can you get away?' I said. 'Go somewhere?'

He nodded. 'I planned it. I was gonna do it tonight.'

'Then do it,' I said. 'How are you going to contact them? Are you supposed to tell them you got the murder weapon and hid the van?'

He shook his head. 'No, they just told me to do it. Then they want me to take the boat back round to Mevagissey, and wait for them there.'

'What's your plan?' I said.

'I was going to take the boat back, leave it there on the mooring, get a lift into town and get a train to Bristol.'

'Bristol? Do you know anyone there?' Pat looked concerned for him.

'Nope. But I reckon I can get a job, or lie low, or something.'

I sighed. 'It isn't a great plan,' I said. 'But it doesn't have to be. I think it will all be over by tomorrow night. Tuesday, maybe.'

'How can you be sure?' Danny asked me.

'The package,' I said. 'The one that didn't arrive for you to drop into the sea?'

He nodded.

'I've got it.'

In the end, we came up with another plan. It was Pat who remembered that Mr Moffat was still on the ship. Danny didn't know what they were planning to do with him, but he thought they wanted to take him further afield before dropping him somewhere. Dropping two bodies in the sea seemed to be one body too far. So the plan changed. We went over it several times, carefully.

'Are you sure?' I asked him, again.

He nodded. 'I think it can work. It is a better plan really. I never been to Bristol.'

'But you have to be sure.' Pat looked him sternly.

'Yes, yeah. I think I can do it.'

So we agreed, Danny would drive – was that the word? *Take* the trawler HH57 back to Mevagissey. Then he'd go, not to Bristol, but back here to the jungle-dark river with the ghostly white ships at anchor. He'd bring a small dinghy, and row out to the ship. He climb the side of the ship, then pull the dinghy and the ladder up after him. He'd keep all lights off, and stay off the deck. He'd be able to see anyone approaching by water.

'This way, you aren't so exposed as catching a bus, and a train,' I said, more for my benefit than his.

'And someone's keeping an eye on Mr Moffat,' Pat reminded him.

'Yes. I won't let anything happen, I promise.' Danny looked scared, but resolute. 'I'll probably have to go to prison. Won't I? It was only little things I wanted, I'm not a big criminal.'

'All the small things add up to the big thing,' I told him.

'Ooh,' Pat said. 'It's like Janice is in the room with us.'

Pat and I waved him off at the jetty and went back into the shed. We covered the van again and retrieved the chisel in the blue and white Penwithick plastic bag. I looked around for somewhere to put it. High above me was a beam crossing the ceiling. I stood on the upturned bucket and put it there. We both looked up from floor level. Invisible. I wiped my hands on my jeans and put the bucket away. Pat turned off the lights and we closed the padlock.

HH57 was almost out of sight round the bend now. The little dinghy which Darren had untied from the deck swung about, tethered to the jetty, dancing like a puppy.

Pat and I got back in her car and sat for a

minute.

'Let's get up the hill, find a signal and ring Trevor,' she said. 'We've been gone hours.'

'How scary was that?' I wondered, doing up my seat-belt.

Pat started the car. 'Scariest thing ever?'

I nodded.

At the top of the hill my phone picked up a signal and we phoned Trevor. He didn't pick up, so we left a message telling him we were on our way home.

It was dark by now and Pat drove carefully between the high banks. We passed the church where we'd found Tyrone – I was surprised, I hadn't realised how close all the pieces of this nasty puzzle actually were. Things looked different depending on which way you approached them, I thought.

'What about the other one?' I asked Pat. 'Danny drops the packages in the sea.'

She nodded.

'But who gets them out? He called them something.' I tried to remember.

'Sinkers and creepers. According to the old smuggling tales, anyway.'

'So Danny would get the package out of the bin, and put it in a lobster pot or something, and take it out to sea, and HH57 would collect it, later. And take it...where?'

'HH57' Pat said. 'That's a proper trawler, wouldn't have any trouble going right out to sea.

Could meet up with a bigger boat. Or go a long way away.'

'There's even more people involved now, then. Danny picks the package up, but who drops it off? Mr Moffat? How would he get out to Camerton Beach if he arrived by bus? And has he been delivering the packages all along, or has it been a different person each time?'

We were driving along the coast now, and Pat turned into a wide car park with a dark wooded hill behind it. Deep in the fold of the hill I could see the lights on in a house. A large house, it seemed to me.

'What's that?' I said, turning round to look behind us as we lurched over the rutted surface.

'Camerton Castle,' she said. 'This is Camerton Beach.'

I gasped, looking around me. 'This is where it happens?'

We looked out at the white line of the surf, the only thing visible in the blackness.

'Right.' I pushed my seat back a bit and wound the car window down. The air was cool and the smell of the sea rushed in. I could hear the hiss of the sucking waves on the shore, and further out, the restless pull of the tide, moving the massive depths back and forth across the earth. The sky was dark, the odd star breaking through the low scudding clouds.

Finally Pat spoke. 'You know you said organised crime was all about money, and we couldn't see where the money was?'

I nodded.

'Well, we were thinking it was a lot of money, and we'd notice it straight away. But Danny didn't have a lot of money, did he? He said, all he wanted was some new bits for his boat, some new waterproofs. Little trickles, see, nobody notices that. They just think someone's had a good catch, or maybe a bit of luck on the horses. As long as no-one makes too much of a splash.'

I nodded again. 'Yes.'

'And you told Danny, all the small things add up to the big thing.'

'Yes, rule number 1.'

I wound the window up, feeling the chill creeping into the car. I wondered if anyone was watching us, from the castle deep in the woods. Did we look suspicious, sitting in the dark with the engine idling?

Pat turned the car lights on and began to reverse slowly in a big curve, the headlights raking the bare borders of the car park.

'What now?' I asked.

'I think I know someone who's got a bit of extra cash. Someone who's got an excuse to potter about not caring what anyone else thinks.'

'Oh. You think they might be the other end of the chain?' I was suddenly really energised, the pain in my knee receding.

'Yep. I do.' Pat was speeding up now, her

face resolute. I looked back at the lights in the castle windows as we sped past, up the hill away from the beach.

'Who! Who is it?'

'You know who it is,' Pat said. 'You've met her.'

'Her? Are you sure?'

'No. I'm not sure. But Trevor said she chose the most expensive tiles. And he's there right now, at Winnie's, tarting up her bathroom.'

CHAPTER THIRTY-ONE

'Are you sure?' Pat said, for about the fiftieth time. We'd arrived back at Glebelands Guest House and I was making tea.

'Absolutely. We have to get Winnie out of her own house.'

'But I can't search her house and be here too,' Pat said, dunking a chocolate digestive.

'I know. But I'll be safe enough. We don't think she's a killer, do we?'

Pat shrugged, miserably. 'I don't know anything, anymore,' she said. 'She's in this up to her nasty straggly hair.'

I nodded. 'But she's only doing what Danny did – a tiny bit of the big picture. And we don't even know for sure. She might be completely innocent.'

Pat slammed her mug down on the table. 'Innocent my arse! She's had her hooks in Petey from the start, using her wiles.'

I tried to picture any of Winnie's wiles, and found I couldn't.

'Does Petey really love her?' I wondered.

'He's smitten. Got any more biscuits?'

'Let's do this first. Come on.'

We sat together at the dining room table so Pat could hear Winnie on the phone. It rang in her cottage with an old-fashioned, far away burring tone.

'Hello? Who is this?' What an odd greeting, from Winnie.

'Oh hi, Winnie,' I said. 'This is Isabel. Pat's friend.'

'Oh. What d'you want?'

Rude! Pat mouthed at me.

'Right, well, Winnie, I know you mentioned your new bathroom, and you were looking for inspiration,' Winnie had never mentioned looking for inspiration but I thought she might bite at this bait, 'and I thought, I wondered, if you'd like to come up to The Manse? I mean, I hardly know anyone in the village and I thought, we could have a glass of wine, and you could look at the bathrooms, and maybe the ones in the guest house too, and, you know, get some ideas.'

There was a long silence. Was Winnie calculating whether I knew that Trevor had already started work on her bathroom? Was she thinking she could get inside The Manse and have a look around? Was she, in short, thinking she was cleverer than me? That wouldn't have been difficult for the past few months, when my brain felt like a mouldy sponge. But I was back now, and I had a team.

Finally Winnie spoke, with her usual energy and enthusiasm. 'Yeah, I could do that, I suppose.'

Pat punched the air.

'Ooh,' I said, 'that's great, come up now, can

you? I don't want to spend another Sunday evening on my own, – oh, unless you've got plans?'

Pat rolled her eyes and mimed drinking a pint. Was that all Winnie and Petey ever did?

'Alright<' Winnie said. 'I'll come up.'

'Lovely' I almost shrieked, 'proper girls' night in!'

Pat mimed being violently sick and I had to ring off.

'Quick!' I said. 'She's coming. Get out, don't be seen.'

'Alright, alright, let me get my coat on.'

'No time,' I said, picking up her coat and pushing her down the hallway. 'Are you really alright with the next bit?' I asked at the front door.

Pat disappeared for a minute into her waterproof.

'Yep,' she said, when she re-emerged. 'I'm fine. I'll park the car at my house, walk to Winnie's, make sure she doesn't see me. If she leaves Trevor there, working, I'll get him to let me in. Then I'll search the house.'

I opened the front door and looked out, both ways. Clear.

'That's the bit I'm not sure about,' I said. 'What are you going to find? And what if you don't find anything incriminating, does that mean she's not involved?'

'Or does it mean she's cleverer than we think?' Pat said.

'And...look, I don't like to say this,' I started, 'But, just because we don't like her...'

'No,' Pat said. 'That doesn't mean she's guilty. It would just be a bonus.'

She got in the car and wound the window down.

'Will Trevor agree to this?' I wondered. 'Winnie is his customer, after all. There's bound to be a, some sort of code, isn't there?'

'All codes are off tonight,' Pat said, and reversed the car, flinging a handful of gravel into the lane and squealing off into the night.

After Pat left I went round the guest house putting some lights on randomly, then locked up and went next door to The Manse.

There was a nice bottle of white wine in the fridge, and I rinsed two good wine glasses and put them on the table, found an ancient jar of olives and opened them, sniffed them, and decided they were fine.

I ran upstairs and changed into clothes that hadn't been anywhere near a boathouse tarpaulin, gave myself a spritz of Chanel and fluffed up my hair. I looked – not great, but pretty normal, though I felt anything but.

About ten minutes after I'd said goodbye to Pat, Winnie knocked on the door.

'Hello,' I said. 'Lovely to see you.' Winnie followed me into the kitchen. She was wearing another of her droopy dresses and her hair rested sadly on her shoulders, and her face was dour.

'Glass of wine?' I said and started to pour.

'Not for me,' she said. 'I don't drink.

I nearly gasped aloud. 'Oh, dear,' I said. I looked longingly at the frosting glass and replaced it on the table. I knew very well Winnie drank, but she was choosing not to drink with me. A little bit of me felt hurt, but I squashed that. If she didn't want to have a drink with me, that might be for a better reason than refusing my hospitality. With massive regret I put the cork back in the bottle and returned it to the fridge. Now, suddenly the smell of the wine, the grapes, the sunshiney bouquet seemed to fill the kitchen, and I felt furious with Winnie.

'Let's have a look round, shall we?' I said, 'and I'll make some coffee later.'

I led the way out of the kitchen towards the utility room. 'There's a little cloakroom here,'

I opened the door and turned the light on. Winnie peered in, looking a bit brighter. 'Nice,' she said. 'Nice tiles.' She craned her neck and looked closely around the room, but I thought she was also paying quite a bit of attention to the passage outside which housed other doorways.

'Oh, but you've already been in here, haven't you, Winnie?' I said.

She looked blank.

'When Petey was looking after the house, and you came to keep him company.'

'No,' she lied.

I raised my eyebrows at her.

'I mean, I didn't know about this one, I went upstairs to a bathroom.' She recovered quickly, but she lacked the speed of thought to be a good liar.

'Let's go then.' I pushed her ahead of me, back towards the kitchen.

She moved with her customary slowness and I nearly screamed with frustration. Did she realise how close she was to the precious bag – if not the contents? It was right there, on the other side of the utility room door, but we were finally past it and in the kitchen again, moving towards the bottom of the stairs. Now I moved ahead of her and noticed her eyes, flickering and darting like bats, moving over the room.

'Upstairs!' I said triumphantly. 'Three lovely bathrooms up here.'

'Three?' She sneered. 'Some people, don't know they're born.'

'I suppose,' I said. 'But it is a big house, and Sir Dougall is very wealthy. So, why not. I mean, if we had that kind of money, hey?'

'Don't suppose he used a local tradesman, though,' she said. 'Don't suppose he supports the locals.'

'I don't know. I didn't take much notice. He does have lots of art, though, and you're an artist, aren't you?'

We'd reached the wide landing and I continued with my distraction techniques. 'Look at this lovely watercolour. What's your favourite medium? Do you work all year round, or just in the summer?'

The landing, though spacious, felt suddenly very small. Winnie was standing just a fraction too close, and I felt waves of anger coming off her. I moved slightly, gripping the bannister. I was being ridiculous, I know. She was only expressing quite understandable envy and resentment in this lovely, spacious house, with its absent owner.

'I don't sell much in the winter,' she said, miserably.

'You must be glad spring's on the way. Come and see the family bathroom.'

We looked into the lovely blue and white room, seashells on the windowsill and sand-coloured tile floor.

'Isn't it heavenly,' I said, and I meant it. Long

hot soaks in that massive tub had been the highlight of my day for the first few months I was here. The room was a sanctuary, and the care and beauty of its construction couldn't fail to lift the spirits. But when I looked back to Winnie, I was horrified to see her face was red and her eyes were swimming with tears.

'Oh, Winnie,' I said, putting my hand on her arm. She was the second person I'd reduced to tears today.

'Get off me.' She pulled back and swiped at her eyes with the hem of her ratty cardigan.

'I'm sorry. Would you rather sit downstairs? Perhaps you've had enough of bathrooms?'

'I'm just tired. Got a lot on my mind.'

'Of course. Yes. Look, I know we don't know each other well, but, if you need someone to talk to, I can keep a secret. I had to, working for Sir Dougall.'

'Talk to you?' Winnie said, sneering at me openly, 'why on earth would I talk to you?'

'Well. I just thought,'

'Three bathrooms, you said.' Winnie looked around her.

I felt very uncomfortable at the next door. I shouldn't be showing her into the master bedroom, but I was committed now.

'Lots of storage space,' I pointed out spitefully. Let her take a good look at all the wardrobes and cupboards she wouldn't be able to look inside.

'Whirlpool bath.' I gestured. 'Bidet. Twin sinks. Underfloor heating. All so, so lovely.'

She shrugged.

'What's your colour scheme?' I asked her.

'White. Bit of beige.'

'Oh. That's a surprise.'

She peered at me suspiciously. 'Why?'

'Well you're such a colourful person, aren't you, I mean, your dresses. So bright. I thought you'd go for something a bit more exotic.

She squinted at me but shrugged and followed reluctantly up to the attic floor, a little shower room with a sloping ceiling.

Just as we got there, there was a loud knock on the front door and we both jumped. That surprised me, because what did Winnie have to fear?

I decided to take a risk.

'You stay here,' I said, 'Have a good look around, I'll see who that is.'

She'd make straight for the master bedroom, I was sure, and I'd catch her in the act.

I opened the front door, finger on my lips, and Pat nodded.

'No!' I said loudly. 'I'm OK for logs, thanks.' Pat slipped into the house and I closed the door.

I pointed upstairs. I could hear the faint creak of floorboards as Winnie moved around the house.

'Well?'

'I found a big roll of money,' Pat whispered. 'I put it back where I found it, but it was £5,475.'

'Where?'

'In the tea caddy.'

'Tea caddy? Who has a tea caddy nowadays?'

Pat nodded. 'Trevor's still there, working as though nothing's wrong.'

I gestured for her to sit down where she was and wait, and I tiptoed to the bottom of the stairs. A door had opened softly on the floor above. Winnie had obviously been into the master bedroom and was now trying the other bedrooms on that floor.

I stepped lightly on every third stair and reached the landing soundlessly. Winnie was in the bedroom on the left, the door was ajar and I could see her standing in front of the open wardrobe. I flung the door open and said in my most reasonable tone, 'there's no bathroom in there, Winnie.'

She whirled round. 'I'm not doing any harm!' she said. 'I'm just naturally curious.'

'Nosy, more like,' I said. 'Come downstairs now, please.' I held the door open for her, and closed it behind her. She trudged down the stairs ahead of me, limp and defeated.

'Sit there please,' I said, pulling out a kitchen chair. 'Pat!'

Winnie looked up in surprise as Pat came into the room.

'Winnie's been having a nice look round,' I said as Pat sat opposite Winnie at the table.

'Has she?' Pat said. 'Looking at the bathrooms?'

'Not just the bathrooms,' I said. 'Was it, Winnie?'

She looked at me, her doughy face scrunched up around her glittering eyes.

'That's not the problem, though, Winnie, it is?' I said. 'I'm more interested in what you said upstairs.'

Winnie looked blank; all trace of the former tears were gone.

'You said,' I tapped my lip with my finger, thoughtfully, 'you said, 'I'm not doing any harm'.'

Winnie shifted slightly and wrapped her cardigan more tightly around her. She was really quite slight, with a bony, spare frame. Her vast ugly clothes made it look as though she took up more space than she really needed.

I turned to Pat. 'That's what Danny said, isn't it?' I asked her. 'He said, 'I'm not doing any harm. Just a small thing for a small amount of money'.'

'Who's Danny?' Winnie said.

'Oh you don't know him, not in person,' I said. 'But he cleans up after you.'

Pat and Winnie both looked blank now.

'When you leave your package in the litter bin at Camerton Beach. Danny picks it up.'

Winnie sprang up. 'What's she on about?' She turned to Pat. 'Let me out.'

Pat pushed her back into her chair.

'You can leave, Winnie,' I said. 'But I need to tell you what we know.'

'What you know,' Winnie sneered. 'You don't know anything. You're a sad old woman who couldn't even leave the house for weeks. You've got a weird haircut, and you had a Pot Noodle for your Christmas dinner.'

Pat gasped. 'Who told you that!'

'I am not old,' I said with as much dignity as I could manage. 'I'm just older than I've ever been. And so are you. And, I have risen above the Pot Noodle.' Pat reached over and touched my arm in support.

'I admit the Pot Noodle was a low point, but I have moved on. And frankly, Winnie, a person with hair like yours is not in a position to point the finger.'

Winnie's hand flew to her tangled curls in amazement.

'Actually,' Pat said, 'while we're on the topic

of Pot Noodles, I am a bit peckish.'

I nodded. 'Let's order something from the pub.'

Winnie pushed her chair back again but didn't get up. 'You can't keep me here, this is kidnapping. You can't keep me here, even if you do feed me.'

'We're not ordering anything for you,' Pat said, heading for the phone.

'Right,' I said. 'Let's get started. You've been doing a job for a handsome man. Mr Smith.'

Winnie's lip curled. 'You don't even know his real name,' she said.

'That's helpful,' I said. 'I mean, I didn't really think he was called Smith, but that's helpful to have it confirmed.'

She looked furious.

'So, you've been getting a package – maybe over your garden wall? I'm not sure about that. But I am sure you've been taking it to Camerton Beach and leaving it there. And you haven't seen who leaves the package for you, or who collects it, but you've been getting some money, and now you've spent that money on a new bathroom.'

I stopped to gauge the effect of my words. They were hitting home. Winnie's eyes were glittering and she stared at me intently, her sallow face pale and still. Pat came back to the table.

'Be about ten minutes. Horatio's bringing it up.'

I nodded without taking my eyes off Winnie's face.

'Mr Smith,' I said. 'So handsome, isn't he? So elegant, so beautifully dressed. But he kills people. He's killed two people this week alone, and I've seen them, close up. Strangled with his bare hands, and then finished off with a chisel to the side of the head. And then he disposes of the bodies.'

Pat nodded. 'He does,' she murmurs. 'Although, I can't figure out how he keeps his suits so nice.'

Winnie looked bilious now. 'Why are you telling me this? I've only met him once, this week. This is nothing to do with me.'

'But it has everything to do with you,' I said. 'Where is this week's package? Did you keep it, are you double-crossing him?'

'What! No! That's what I told him. No package came this week, that's why he came to my house, I never seen him before, honest. But I couldn't deliver something that never arrived, could I? It wasn't there, and I didn't know what to do. But you can't say I stole it.'

Pat looked at me in triumph. 'You're so good, Isabel,' she said. 'Good and bad, at the same time.'

Winnie looked from Pat to me. 'What? What are you talking about?'

'You've given us enough to be going on with,' I said.

To give her some credit, Winnie held out a lot longer than Danny, but now she put her head down on the table and began to sob.

Pat prodded her. 'Here, people got to eat off that table.'

I passed Winnie the kitchen roll.

'Come on,' I said, 'we've got to think, now. You're in danger.'

'Oh, help me!' Winnie sobbed, mopping her face. 'He's going to get me, he's going to kill me.'

'Probably,' Pat said, rather too cheerfully.

Winnie started wailing in earnest and we almost didn't hear the front door. Whoever it was rapped again. We froze.

'That could be Horatio,' Pat said. 'With the supper.'

'Or it could be Nick. Or Smith. Oh, do shut up, Winnie.'

'Yeah,' Pat said. 'Shut up, Winnie.'

Half an hour later, things seemed much brighter and even Winnie was quiet. We were all sitting round the table mopping up fish stew with big hunks of bread. Winnie had managed a few mouthfuls, but we didn't press her. Of course we'd ordered enough for her, but we weren't too bothered if she went hungry.

I pushed back from the table. 'Coffee, anyone? We've got plans to make.'

'There's a cheesecake,' Pat said, rooting around in the bag Horatio had brought up from the pub.

'A whole one?'

'Looks like it.'

I sat back down.

'What are you going to do?' Winnie said. She had some colour back in her face now.

'What are YOU going to do?' I said. 'What's your exit strategy?'

She shook her head. 'I just thought it would go on for a little while, and then stop.'

'You know what your trouble is,' Pat said. 'You didn't think it through, did you?'

'Oh don't try and bully me,' Winnie said. 'You've never liked me.'

Pat nodded.

'But that man, Smith,' Winnie said, 'he knows I didn't steal the package. He knows that man didn't drop it off, that's why he killed him. So if anyone's going to get killed for it, it'll probably be you.'

I stared at her, knowing she was right.

Pat leaned forward and took the piece of cheesecake off Winnie's plate and took it over to the bin.

'No more nice things for you, little Missy,' she said. 'And no more dealings with my cousin. And can I just say, I'm very sorry I ever welcomed you into my home. And I gave you a recipe for bread pudding and that was my grandmother's, that was. Not that you've ever cooked it. And no-one would eat it, coming out of your kitchen.'

I tutted at Winnie. 'I gave you a bit of time to root around upstairs. Did you find the package?'

She glared at me. 'You know I didn't. Got it well hid, haven't you? Gonna make a bit of money yourself?'

'This is all very well,' I said. 'We can go on sniping at each other for days – well, hours. But what ARE you going to do, Winnie? Why don't you go to the police, admit everything. It will go much better for you in the end, when they're caught.'

'I don't trust the police,' Winnie said. Pat looked over at me. Neither did we, but I wasn't going to say that to Winnie.

'I'll have to hide for a bit,' Winnie said.

I nodded. 'It won't be for long. They're going to close their operation – with their main supplier dead, they'll have to move on.'

Winnie looked around the lovely kitchen. 'I

just wanted something nice,' she said. 'A bathroom with no leaks, and no mould.'

Pat started to protest, but I knew exactly what Winnie meant. Sometimes things were so dark, even the smallest flicker of light was enough to keep you pressing on.

'You don't know,' Winnie said. 'You're both so lucky.'

'Winnie.' I tried really hard to be patient. 'You've made a really common mistake. I hope one day you realise that. You look at other people, other people's lives and you think they've got it sorted, they've got the house, the partner, the life they want. But no-one really has it all. Look at this house. Sir Dougall's house. All the money he wants, but did you ever see him down here, playing on the beach with his boys? Making a sandcastle? No. You didn't, because he was never here, was he? So stop being envious of other people. You had something lots of people never find, you had true love from a decent man. You had your art, something you were good at and which gave you pleasure. You had a community. You had Pat and Trevor in your lives.'

'Oh,' Pat said, dabbing her face with a tea-towel. 'I'm filling up. And you never even mentioned the bread pudding recipe.'

'I was getting to that.'

'We'll help you,' I said. 'We don't want anyone else to die.'

'Even you.' Pat glowered at her.

'We'll take you to a safe place. You'll be able to hide there, and you'll be able to meet the other person, the one who collected your parcels. He's in hiding too. But you can't tell anyone where you are.'

Winnie nodded. 'Alright. I've had enough of this village, anyway. I don't like the damp sea air, it gets in your joints in the winter.'

'That's good,' I said. 'You'll be able to make a fresh start. Maybe get a new haircut.'

Winnie lowered her head like a bull. 'Like yours?' she said. 'Look like a clown?'

'That's the girl!' I said to Pat. 'That's the old Winnie, back on top!'

CHAPTER THIRTY-TWO

'I don't know why we're even helping her,' Pat said as we stripped the pantry of tinned goods.

Cans, packets and bottles, we heaped what little food we could find into a Bag for Life – which I hoped was a good omen. The supplies were to enable Winnie and Danny to survive for a couple of nights – maybe longer – on the strange ghostly ship in the river.

'I wonder if it's cold, on that ship?' I said.

'Don't care,' Pat said. 'Let them freeze.'

'Pat, that's just not you. Go on, go upstairs and see what you can find.'

Pat went off, muttering under her breath, and I stood for a moment in the quiet of the pantry.

We'd realised we'd need a boat to get Winnie aboard the ship, and even then it would only work if Danny was back from Mevagissey and recognised us and let the ladder down. I didn't know how to row, and doubted Winnie would be much of a help either. We wanted to keep Horatio in the dark – we were hiding criminals, after all – so we had to throw ourselves on

Uncle Nat's mercy, and Pat had rung him up. Of course he had a rowing boat, but it was 'down the pond'. So we'd have to go to the farm first, retrieve the rowing boat, get it on some kind of vehicle, transport it to the river and put Winnie aboard the big ship. It was all overwhelming and I leaned my hot face against the cool plaster of the pantry wall and took deep breaths. Winnie was moving about in the kitchen behind me but I was pretty sure she wouldn't attempt to go anywhere. Like Danny, she seemed to have suddenly woken from a dream of steady but modest income, a victimless crime which would go undetected. Like Danny she now seemed deflated, defeated. She needed us. I straightened up, and remembered Janice's list, *Prepare for the worst, then you'll be ready for anything.*

Pat was in the kitchen, persuading Winnie to put a hoodie and an anorak over the top of her cardigan. Between us we half dragged Winnie to the car, and piled in. When we got to Uncle Nat's, a small miracle had occurred. Nat was waiting by the side of a truck with a flat back and a battered green cab. On the bed of the truck, behind a low metal panel, was a wooden rowing boat, propped up like a beached shark. Petey was securing it with ropes, while Nat looked on.

When Winnie saw Petey she got out of the car and rushed over, sobbing again. Petey gave her a hug and patted her back, but I could see his face and he looked crushed. A wave of sadness rushed over me, almost bringing me to my knees.

'You alright, maidy?' Uncle Nat said, coming over to us.

I nodded. 'Just tired.'

'I don't know why you want to go rowing, on a night like this,' Nat said, 'but you carry on, all of you.' And he lurched off over the dark yard, his bulk silhouetted for a moment in the orange doorway, before he disappeared.

Petey pushed Winnie into the truck and got in behind the wheel. He wound the window down. 'Only one more seat.'

'I'll go,' I told Pat. 'You stay here with Uncle Nat. Here,' and I took off my watch and gave her my mobile phone. I wasn't sure how wet we'd get, putting the boat in the water and getting it out again. I had no idea how to do what I thought we ought to do.

'Do be careful,' she said. 'Petey – look after yourself. And Isabel.' Petey nodded.

'Not you,' Pat said to Winnie. 'Don't care if no-one looks after you.' And she trudged off towards the farmhouse, following Uncle Nat.

The truck groaned beneath us as we crossed the gravel of the yard, and Winnie started gulping in hiccups as her tears subsided.

'You should have stuck with what you had,' Petey told her. 'Silly mare.'

We retraced the route to the river and the captive ships. It seemed much longer ago that I'd been there with Pat, and I leaned my head back and tried to compose myself as the darkness whipped by the side of the high cab. Finally Petey slowed, and I looked up at the arch of trees above us, the lane descending into the blackness of the riverbank.

Petey turned the truck around and backed towards the river slowly, craning out of the window and letting in the chill night air.

Finally we were close enough. Winnie and I got out and stood to one side while he operated something in the cab, and the bed of the truck lifted. The rowing boat was now hanging above the muddy bank, and Petey released a rope and slowly lowered it down. The three of us heaving together got it further out, where the mud and water were more equally mixed.

'Will it float?' I whispered to Petey.

'It has been known to float,' he said. 'I'm not saying how recent.'

Winnie started to whimper. 'I don't want to drown.'

'You aren't going to drown,' I said. 'Unless you don't shut up.'

Petey held tightly to the rope and pushed against the boat with his foot. It swung out further into the river, and bucked against his hold like an angry calf, but it floated.

'Come on,' I said to Winnie. 'Get in.'

She took her time about it but was finally sitting, hunched over on the flat plank which formed the seat of the boat. Petey handed me the rope and got in himself.

'Let us go,' he said, lifting the oars and fitting them to the boat.

'No, I have to come,' I said.

'Too many,' Petey argued.

'Danny won't let you in, he knows me.'

'He knows me, little tyke,' Petey said using an oar to paddle himself in place.

'Not about this, I'm getting in.' And I waited until the boat swung round again and put one leg over the side, my other foot lifting out of the mud with a sucking sigh.

I settled myself next to Winnie and rubbed

her back comfortingly. 'Not long now, Winnie.'

Petey pushed against the riverbank again and took one long stroke and we were flung out into the river, the boat rocking crazily and the meaty, dark-green smell of the river filling the air. I thought longingly of the farmhouse, Pat and her uncle sitting round the table, and the gas fire popping, the smell of an overheating dog. I could hardly see the riverbank now, we seemed to float between the river and the dark starless sky. I could feel that Petey had stopped rowing, and then I felt a gentle bump and reached out to touch the rough skin of the sleeping ship. There was a faint outline of light, high up above us. Was there a light on inside? Was that the rectangular door Danny had used earlier today?

I banged on the side of the ship and almost laughed aloud. It sounded puny and ridiculous. There was no way Danny would hear that. Petey was panting and struggling to keep us level as the river tried to wrap us in its curves and sweep us out to sea.

'Help me!' I said to Winnie. 'Bang now, together.'

She leaned across me and we banged, all four fists together, and we set up a dim clang in the metal hull.

I called upwards, 'Danny, can you hear us? Danny, this is Isabel. From this afternoon?'

We banged again. 'Danny, I've got someone who has to hide with you.'

Petey was wheezing now with the effort. I worried about him. Winnie was slumped on the seat looking like a pile of discarded and mismatched clothes.

I gave up trying to be discreet. 'Danny!' I shouted at the top of my voice. 'Danny!'

Suddenly I was blinded by a bright light. Petey cursed and the rowing boat banged against the side of the ship, and even Winnie was jolted into a faint mewling. Petey and I shaded our eyes and looked up. I couldn't see anything, just the bright orange rectangle high in the hull.

'Danny, this is Isabel, from this afternoon. I've got someone who needs to hide with you.'

The light went out and it seemed all the darker without it. I shivered with fear suddenly. What if it wasn't Danny up there? What if Smith had already found him and we were walking into a trap? A clanking behind us made us all crane our heads round, which wasn't good for the stability of the boat. We'd been facing down river, but Danny – or whoever – had opened a much lower door, in the side of the ship, behind us. Petey struggled against the oars and pulled us back against the river, back along the side of the ship to the nearer door. A torch beam came out and played over our faces. The beam lingered over Winnie, who hid her face, and then returned to me. I smiled and waved, stupidly. If it wasn't Danny, if it was Smith, we'd just have to let the current carry us away. Eventually the torch was drawn in and the holder shone it on his own face. It was Danny, horrific in the torchlight, but alive, and in command of the ship.

He pushed a bundle of rope and wood out of the doorway and Pete pushed us off with one oar to avoid it hitting us. It resolved itself into a ladder and once we were close enough Petey and I grabbed it and held the boat as still as we could manage.

'Winnie,' I shouted, 'come on, get up the ladder.'

'No. No, I can't go up there.' She looked up at the hatch, about ten feet above us, and hunched down even smaller on her bench.

'Come on, lovely.' Petey said. 'We want you safe and sound, don't we?'

Winnie looked doubtful, but she didn't shift.

'I'm going up, Winnie,' I said. 'How hard can it be?'

I grabbed the damp end of the ladder. The shallow wooden treads rested against the curved hull and there was nothing to grab onto except the tread above. With my foot on the first rung the shift of my weight sent the rowing boat tilting again and Petey cursed, leaning into the oars. There was nothing for it, I had to step up, off the row boat and onto the ladder. Now I just hung there, flat against the ship, only the strength of my arms keeping me from the black-hearted river.

'Winnie,' I shouted back. 'If you don't get up there, they'll find you and they'll kill you. They've killed already and they're not going to stop.'

I stepped higher. One step. Keeping my feet sideways on the treads, trying to keep flat and not let the ladder swing out, I managed another step. From somewhere, in a previous life it seemed, I could hear a Pilates teacher talking about the importance of a strong core, and I regretted all those evenings I hadn't left work early enough to catch a class. I clenched everything I had, and with my shoulders and arms burning I managed another step. Now I was near enough for Danny to reach his hands down. Not near enough for him to grab me, but it helped to know someone was there.

'Come on, Miss,' he called, and I looked up to see his head and shoulders against the night sky, his hands reaching down.

One more step and he was close enough to take my wrist and use his strength to pull me the rest of the way. I lay gasping on the cold metal deck, not even caring now about Winnie.

I turned my head to see Danny back in the doorway, leaning out and murmuring. *Winnie must be coming up*, I thought, and fell back into an exhausted stupor.

Finally she was on the deck beside me, still crying. Danny stepped over her and extended his hand to help me stand.

'She's not going to go on like that, is she?' he said.

'Probably.' I looked around me. We were obviously on a car deck, a vast open space with lines painted on the floor and luminous safety notices providing dots of light in the distance.

I looked out of the open hatch to see Petey, still rowing against the river. I hoped it would be easier now there was only his bantam weight in the boat.

'Shall we just leave her here?' Danny said.

'Have you got somewhere she can sleep?'

'Five cabins. No sheets, but some blankets. Even got a bit of milk for tea.'

'Oh, I brought some supplies, down there. I'll go back down.'

'No,' Danny said. 'We'll lower a bit of rope, I'll get some.'

And he turned away, into the darkness.

'Winnie,' I bent down and shook her. 'Winnie, come on. Danny's got a place you can sleep, you'll be safe here.'

Winnie got slowly to her feet, pushing her hair back from her face.

'D'you think I'm gonna thank you?' she said. 'I got nothing to thank you for. You get lost and stop interfering in my life.'

Well. I sighed. Alright. If that's how she wanted it.

Danny was coming back with a coil of rope and I turned towards the hatch to give instructions to Petey. I could see, suddenly, in Danny's face, that the plan had changed. I could see it in his face before I felt it between my shoulder-blades, as Winnie pushed me and Danny took a step towards me – just a moment too late – and I also took a step forwards, towards the open hatch which was much, much closer than I remembered. I stepped out, as simply as going from one room to the other, but the room I entered now belonged to the river, and the night.

CHAPTER THIRTY-THREE

There was a split second when I thought I was going to land on Petey and kill us both, but I didn't, I fell feet first into the river. Down and down I went, blackness and cold all around. There was a moment when it felt almost comfortable, then I bobbed up to the surface and took in a lungful of muddy water mixed with night air. It was impossible to see anything, or hear anything, and the strong hand of the river was pushing me.

I tried to gather my thoughts and find the river bank, but hanging there in the water, only my face lifted upwards to the air, I felt almost as though I was where I ought to be. Then an image of Pat and Uncle Nat waiting in the kitchen intruded, and I thought I heard Petey calling my name, and I could hear Danny shouting something. I kicked the river, hard, and started to fight. Then the entire world crashed into me, crushing my face against the side of the wooden boat, while Petey grabbed what remained of my hair and shouted at me.

I lifted my arm onto the side of the boat, but my hand was too cold to grip. My legs were drifting under the boat, drawn by the current. It would have been so easy to let go, drifting under and out to sea, and I don't know what happened, but I clung on, with Petey struggling to row and hold my hand at the same time, and then I felt something pushing up at my feet from below, my legs crumpling into the mud, and Peter dragging me half in, half out of the river, staggering back into my element, onto dry land.

'What?' I managed to say to Petey, who was pulling the boat up the bank.

I could hear his voice, but I couldn't understand what he was saying.

'Get them clothes off.' He was unbuttoning his jacket and loosening his belt. The sight was so ridiculous I started giggling.

'Petey! I think Winnie can see us, she'll be furious.'

'Dead to me,' Petey said. 'She's dead to me. She tried to kill you.' Petey was stripped down to his grey thermal underwear now.

'Did she?' I stood quietly as Petey undressed me. He was shivering, but I was not. That was strange.

'Did you hit your head? How many fingers am I holding up?'

I squinted. 'Three? Why are we taking our clothes off?'

Petey was redressing me in his discarded shirt, which was warm, and dry.

'Come on, Isabel. Take those jeans off.'

It was painful to peel them down my legs, but

I managed. I stopped when I got to my feet. 'Oh look. One of my boots has gone.'

Petey bent down to undo the other boot. He braced me on his shoulders and I stepped out of the sodden jeans. He passed me his trousers and held me up as I fumbled into them. There were only two legs in the trousers, and only two legs on my body, but I felt like an octopus with nerve damage, struggling to find the limits of myself and the shape of the surrounding world.

'I think I've gone a bit peculiar, Petey,' I said.

'You got cold, in the river,' he said. 'That'll do it.'

'Oh, yes. I was in the river.'

He turned me to look. We were downstream of the ship, I could barely even make it out, just a blob of slightly lighter grey in the darkness. We were standing on a grassy bank under some trees, the gurgle of the river the only sound.

'We got to go back in the boat,' Petey said. 'We got to get back upstream, to the truck.'

I nodded, though I don't know if he saw me. He picked up the sodden clothes and the one boot and put them in the bottom of the boat and helped me in. I was beginning to feel cold now, and wrapped his flannel shirt and padded jacket more tightly around me.

'Are you OK, Petey? You must be cold.'

'Not long now, we'll be in the truck.'

I looked at the river curiously, hardly aware of Petey rowing behind me. Now that I was dressed and dry, the river looked foreign to me, the enemy. Had I really reclined in its embrace? I shuddered. We were drawing level with the ship and I looked up to see Danny in a rectangle of orange light. He waved at me and I managed to lift my arm – as heavy as an anchor chain – and give him a wave in return. I wondered vaguely about Winnie, then she slipped from my mind. Leaning forward, I let my head dangle heavily and let the thoughts flow over me. The boat was lurching, but I didn't care. Then Petey grabbed me.

'Ow. Hurting.' I tried to rub my arm but Petey was forcing me up the river bank.

'Come on. Get over to the truck,' he said, pushing me. My bare feet were cold and gritty and I winced, but when he opened the door of the truck and boosted me up on the high seat it felt like coming home. I lay across the front seat, shivering, my feet drawn up, while Petey got the rowing boat back onto the truck. In a moment of clarity I realised why he wasn't just leaving it on the bank, but then I felt myself falling, and I drifted until Petey got back in the truck and started the engine. Immediately a blast of scorching, dusty air hit me from the vents and I started to revive.

'I fell in the river,' I said to Petey. 'I fell in the river, and I got out.'

'Well,' he said, pulling away from the bank into the dark lane, 'you've got the basics right there.'

I shivered and shook all the way back to the farm. I found the bag of tinned goods we'd meant to give to Danny, and I felt guilty that he'd have to share his meagre rations with Winnie.

Back at the farmhouse the kitchen door

was closed, but there were plenty of lights on. Pat's car was still in the yard, but there was no sign of Trevor's van. I wondered why he was going on with Winnie's bathroom – he must know now there was scant chance he'd ever be paid.

Petey parked as close to the back door as he could, and I picked my way across the cold gravel in my bare feet.

Inside the kitchen, Pat and Uncle Nat fell silent as we entered; me in Petey's clothes, him in his long combinations and work boots.

'Alright then?' Petey said. 'Got the kettle on?'

Pat took me upstairs to Uncle Nat's bathroom and put the shower on. She rooted around in the bathroom cupboard and found a bottle of ancient shampoo and pointed to a pile of towels on the wide windowsill and went out.

Downstairs I could hear Uncle Nat asking questions, and Petey not really answering them. I got in the shower.

About twenty minutes later I felt very much better. I was warm, for one thing, and I'd dug a lump of mud out of one ear, and given my hair at least three washes. Uncle Nat's bathroom didn't run to conditioner or body lotion, but it was as luxurious as a spa holiday to me at that moment.

I wrapped my hair in a towel, wrapped myself in several more, and opened the door. Pat had left a set of folded pyjamas outside, very clean but slightly threadbare, blue and white stripes, and a pair of thick woollen socks.

After I put them on, I went downstairs.

'Got your clothes in the wash,' Pat said. 'Not sure if they'll recover.'

I shrugged. 'Not sure I'll recover!'

Pat regarded me seriously. 'You could have died, Isabel. Petey said he thought you had.'

I shrugged again. 'Here I am.'

'Come on in here!' Uncle Nat shouted from the sitting room. I hadn't been in there before and I sank gratefully into a fat brocade sofa, opposite the roaring log-burner. I rubbed my hands together.

'Warming up, are you?' Uncle Nat was sitting in a massive rocking chair near the granite fireplace.

'Where's Petey?'

'Gone to talk to Trevor,' Pat said, handing me a mug of tea.

'Is Trevor still at Winnie's?'

Pat nodded. 'We thought it was best to act natural, as far as we could.'

'Hmm.' I blew on the tea and took a couple of big gulps. 'I wonder if that river water is safe,' I mused.

'Did you swallow much?' Uncle Nat looked interested.

'I'm not sure.'

He nodded. 'Probably got some cow muck

in it, and some fertiliser, off the fields. Nothing'll do you too much harm.'

I frowned at the tea.

'Look, you're lucky to be alive,' Pat said, sinking down beside me on the sofa. 'Petey said it was touch and go.'

'Yes, I'm not going to worry about a bit of river water,' I said.

'What were you doing in the river anyway?' Uncle Nat asked.

Pat hesitated. 'We can't tell you,' she said.

'Can't we?' I asked her.

'No, no. You probably can't,' Nat said. 'I cannot keep a secret, that's quite true. First person who came along tomorrow, I'd be spilling the beans, I can't deny that.' He folded his hands across a check shirt as big as a marquee, and gave me a grin.

'It was an accident. That's all I'll say.' I waved off Pat's protests. Petey had obviously told her exactly what happened.

'Come out in the kitchen,' Pat said. I groaned, it was so warm, and so comfy where I was, but I battled my way out of the cushions and followed her out.

'You need some ice on your face,' she said, opening the freezer and passing me a packet of peas.

'Do I?' I put my hands up to my face. She was right, one side was puffy and sore. 'I hardly noticed that. It must have been when I slammed into the boat.' I wrapped the peas in a damp tea-towel and went to sit by the kitchen fire.

'Danny and Winnie are safe there, are they?' Pat sat down opposite, in Nat's huge chair.

'I think so. For now. I think you'd have to be really clever to get in there, without someone letting you in. You'd need a massive can opener.'

Pat nodded. 'When is this all going to be over?'

'Tomorrow, Tuesday maybe?'

'Are you sure?'

'Absolutely. After the last guest checks out, I'll call a cab, get the package – no, wait, leave the package where it is – just go to the police.'

'But not the local police,' Pat said.

'No. Not locally, because of Trenoweth. We don't trust him.'

Pat nodded. 'So, you'll get a taxi to the station, then get a train somewhere – don't tell me where – and then go to the police.'

I thought about it. 'I suppose I might go to London.'

'Oh, don't go back there, Isabel.'

'I know some police in London. And the head of security at Spence Industries, he's an ex-policeman. He could advise me.'

'I'd feel much safer if you were here,' Pat said.

'Safer? I can't look after anyone,' I protested, pointing at my pyjamas and the huge thick socks hanging off my feet.

Pat nodded. 'You nearly died. I just want some reassurance,' she said.

'I can't give you that. But I'm here, sitting at this table.' I rapped on it with the hand which wasn't holding the frozen peas to my face. 'And if I hadn't really, really wanted to be here, I'd be floating out to sea about now, like a mermaid with a very aggressive haircut.'

CHAPTER THIRTY-FOUR

I woke up on Monday morning in my attic bedroom in The Manse, with almost no memory of going to bed, though I knew I'd had a long hot bath with masses of glossy Chanel bubbles, in the master bathroom. Might as well indulge while I could.

I'd remembered the night though and the day before. Every time I tried to turn over, my left knee hurt me, and made me flop about awkwardly. And my face was sore and the muscles in my shoulders were tender and hot. I dressed carefully, and for the first time in months, I put on proper make-up. I had to. One side of my face was purple and swollen. I enjoyed the moment though, sitting at the dressing table, looking at myself. I looked different, and not just because the foundation wasn't quite up to disguising the swollen and scraped side of my face. The savage haircut left my cheekbones exposed and I looked thinner, bleaker. Definitely older. But with after adding blusher and mascara, I felt

I was becoming more myself. Finally, I paused with my bright fuchsia Dior lipstick in my hand. Now, there was no going back.

I arrived at the guest house – only paces away, feeling that something momentous had happened. I was ready for battle.

Most of the rooms were ready – I left them that way each day, but I still went through them all.

Room 2 needed attention. I stripped the big bed quickly and got right down to the bare mattress. I unzipped the connecting strip and raised the little bars that joined the base, and pushed both halves of the bed apart, making twin beds. Then I remade the beds with single bedding, struggling to get the single duvets out of the linen closet and into the duvet covers, and stuffed the big heap of clean double-bedding back in the cupboard. I could use that later.

I was absolutely sure some of the guests due to arrive today were fakes. But who had booked them in? Smith, Trenoweth or Nick? They had all come to search the house, that much was surely certain, but what was the risk to each other, and to me?

I put my phone on to charge in the kitchen. Now that I'd got it back in my pocket and not hidden in a locked room, I was as inseparable from it as I'd ever been, but there was more to do. I stood over it, tethered to the worktop, and steadily deleted names and numbers, hundreds of them, until I was left with my semi-estranged brother and his wife; then Tanya and a couple of other old friends; Dougall Spence (London office, home, New York office, Beijing office) and the phone number marked 'help.' I reached for Janice's phone book, dog-eared and grimy at the corners, with a picture of a very young Prince Charles and Princess Diana on the cover, and entered numbers for Uncle Nat at Lower Lestoon Farm, Janice's daughter, and the Smuggler's Arms. I already had Pat's number and I rang it now.

'Isabel – ' Pat sounded out of breath. 'Are you alright?'

'Thanks. Janice rang yesterday, and she's had a lot of bookings over the website.'

'That's good,' Pat said. 'Oh, wait. No. Isabel, you've got to get out of there.'

'I can't. Besides, two of the guests have been booked in for ages – the Chapmans – they're coming down for their niece's wedding. So I have to look after them.'

'I'll come in tonight. Have you got a spare room? Trevor and me, we'll come and stay the night.'

'No, honestly, Pat, it will be OK. I don't want to disrupt your entire life. If the other guests are from Smith, they'll want to search the house, but I think they'll be discreet.'

'But you don't know that, Isabel.'

'No. Right.' I looked out of the kitchen window. The house next door was still and quiet, the curtains drawn. The parking area was deserted and the sky above the house was looking cheery and spring-like. What bad thing could possibly happen in a place like this?'

'Isabel.' Pat was being firm. 'Ring Horatio. Tell him to be on stand-by.'

'Stand-by? Is there such a thing?'

'He could come and stay in The Manse, wouldn't that make you feel safer?'

I would feel safer, but he wouldn't.

'No, that's OK, Pat. But, could you come in tomorrow, on your rounds?'

'I surely will! And Horatio will pop in too, and maybe Trevor and Petey. We'll be there, Isabel, I promise.'

'Thanks. I'm sure by this time tomorrow we'll all be having a laugh about the whole thing.'

The house felt a bit cold, so I gave it a blast of central heating. I laid up all the dining tables and sat in the front room, trying not to stare at the door. I picked a book off the shelf, but had no appetite for Miss Marple, and put it back. I decided to do something I'd been putting off for ages.

I tried to eat some lunch but I wasn't really hungry. I looked at the rules from the second envelope. They kept me on the right track so far, but I wasn't sure about rule 6: *Try to look as though you're enjoying it.* It wasn't a bad rule, in general, but maybe a bit ambitious for now. I set up the kitchen with all the things I'd need to prepare the breakfasts tomorrow morning and made sure I had enough of everything in the fridge. I felt restless. Without really thinking about it, I picked up my phone and rang Sir Dougall.

He answered on the third ring.

'Isabel – where the hell have you been?'

'You know where you've been – I'm in your house. Well, next door at the moment.'

'If I'd known you'd still be there three months later I'd have never given you the key.'

I couldn't think of anything to say. I didn't think he was really cross with me, but you couldn't always tell. And if he was? Well, he had every right.

'So how are you feeling, girlie? Up to coming back?' No. He wasn't angry.

'I'm not sure. I mean, I'm feeling better, much better. But I'm not sure about coming back.'

'You aren't, then. I know that. Because you've really got to want this job – so if you aren't sure, you don't want it.'

'But I don't know what I DO want.'

'I reckon that puts you with about nine-tenths of the population.'

I sighed. 'I'm sorry.'

'Oh, cut the crap.'

I laughed. 'I've missed you. I've missed talking to you.'

'Well not as much as I've missed you. I had to give your job to that idiot boy, James, and he was a stupid as you told me he was.'

James was the younger brother of the current Lady Spence. Sir Dougall had given him a job in the company, and he'd gradually upset and alienated so many people he ended up assisting me. Or at least that's what he told people. Sir Dougall and I knew the truth. I gave him a series of meaningless errands which kept him out of my hair, and gave him something to brag about with his equally clueless trust-fund friends.

'Well, at least he's keen.'

'I need more than that. Come back, I'll double your salary.'

I gasped. That was a considerable sum of money,

'Thanks! But – '

' – No thanks.'

'I think so. Yes, I'm sure. I will come back though, help you find someone, if that's any use to you? I need to come back to London at some point, sort out my flat, pack up my things.'

I could hear him snort. 'Better than nothing, I suppose. When can you get here?'

'Oh. Well. I'm running the guest house next door at the moment.'

With that he started the gasping wheeze

that passed for a laugh.

'What! Cooking sausages for tourists? Isabel, after all you've done?'

While he laughed, I looked out of the window at the sea, which was pale grey under a white sky.

'I don't think of it like that, I suppose,' I said. 'I think of it as giving people what they want, what they need, to have a nice time. And I think that's honest work, actually. It is an honourable occupation.'

'And working for me isn't?'

'I didn't mean that, exactly. Maybe a bit.'

'If it works for you, Isabel, then it works for you.'

'Janice will be back in a couple of weeks, I'll know more then.'

'Who the hell is Janice?'

'Your neighbour. The woman who owns the guest house and has lived here, next to The Manse, for seventeen years.'

'Well I never spent much time there, it was for the kids really.'

'You might have more kids – with the current Lady Spence?'

He started wheezing again. 'Not likely.'

'Oh dear. I hope everything's alright?'

'Fine, just fine. Nothing I can talk about on the phone. And what about you, have you ditched that loser?'

'Ivan was not a loser. He offered to leave

his wife. At the end.'

'Didn't think he had it in him.'

'Neither did I. In fact, I think I was counting on him not having it in him.'

More wheezing came down the phone from Sir Dougall's London home. I felt so fond of him, suddenly. Not working for him would be like losing a part of myself. He'd always been there for me, even when he was driving me to distraction.

'So,' he finally stopped gasping. 'You don't know what you're gonna do, you haven't got a rich boyfriend, you haven't got a job once whatsername comes back to fry her own sausages, and now you're gonna tell me you are happier than you've been in years.'

I paused.

'Hmm? Isabel?'

'As ever, Sir Dougall, you are totally correct.'

CHAPTER THIRTY-FIVE

The first person to arrive was Mr Lark. He pulled up in an old Ford estate, battered and slightly neglected looking, and unloaded an ancient canvas and leather travel bag. I met him at the front door. He was in his seventies, I judged, but still tall and he stooped slightly, like someone who has spent a lifetime avoiding low beams. He had a gentle smile and a firm handshake and I liked him immediately. I showed him up to his room and he was very happy with everything. I left him to unpack, told him how to order his breakfast for tomorrow morning and went back downstairs. I mentally crossed him off my list. Mr Lark and the Chapmans were in the clear, so that left Loomes and Lewis, plus the young man named Marks and his girlfriend.

I had a brainwave. At least two of those people must be connected to Nick, so I rang Horatio.

'I've had an idea,' I said, from the utility room.

'Why are you whispering?'

'I don't want to alarm anyone.'

'You're alarming me.'

'Horatio. Listen. The guest house is nearly full tonight. I've got a couple who've been booked in for ages, plus a lovely older gentleman who has just arrived. But I've also got two more rooms – a pair of guys called Loomes and Lewis, plus a couple, the man is called Marks, don't know about the woman. But I'm thinking, if one pair are from Smith and the other pair from Nick, – or maybe they're in it together – they'll have to make contact with *someone* at some point.'

'Ah. I see where you're going with this.'

'Right. So, can you do something?'

'I can. I'm going to go and paint the harbour.'

'What? Now? This is no time for watercolours, Horatio.'

'Oh yes it is, Miss Isabel, it is exactly the right time to set up an easel and a stool on the harbour wall, facing Coastguard Cottage, and sit there until dusk falls.'

Brilliant. 'Brilliant, Horatio,' I said. 'What about after dark?'

'Upstairs room of the Smuggler's. Chips and beer, sitting in the window seat. What could be nicer? I'll ring Aunty Pat, tell her. They can meet me there and we can take it in turns.'

'Horatio. I can't thank you enough. Call

me, or text me if you see anything. I'll text you with descriptions when the others turn up.'

'Don't rely on it, Isabel. Remember? The phone signal down there isn't good. I can run a bit up the hill and get a signal there, but it won't be instant.'

'No. Alright. We'll manage. Won't we?'

'Sure to, Isabel.'

I put my phone back in my jeans pocket. It wasn't going to leave my body now for the next twenty-four hours. I also had the keys to The Manse on a cord round my neck. I went to the front door and looked up and down the lane. No-one in sight. I rushed out of the front door and across to The Manse and let myself in. I locked the front door behind me, and even bolted it, struggling with the ancient mechanism. No-one had locked that for decades, I thought. I'd find some oil somewhere and give it a bit of care.

I went up to the attic, picking up my old make-up bag and the black jacket I'd been wearing when I arrived. I stopped at the master bedroom and found another pair of flat shoes – Chanel this time, black quilted leather with the discreet camellia and monogram on the toes.

Out of the house, locking and double-checking and back into the guest house, just in time to see Mr Lark coming down the stairs.

'Everything all right for you, Mr Lark?'

'Lovely, my dear. What a beautiful spot.

Perfect for me.'

'Janice – the lady who owns this place – she said you were an ornithologist. That's quite funny, isn't it?'

'An ornithologist called Lark. Yes, that would be funny,' he said. 'But I'm actually an ophthalmologist, though I have recently retired.'

'Oh.'

'Not nearly as interesting,' he said, a bit mournfully.

'No. Well, I don't mean that. I'm sure it is interesting.'

'You're very sweet, dear.'

'So, what brings you to Gorran Porth, Mr Lark?'

'Well, I've just retired, as I say, so I'm thinking about buying a little holiday place. And I'm having a super time, I must say, just driving around and looking at seaside villages, and deciding what to do with myself.'

'That does sound nice.'

'Would you recommend Gorran Porth? I suppose you must, since you live here?'

'I...I probably would recommend it. There are prettier villages, and richer ones, certainly. But there's a lovely little beach, lots of walks. And the people, the people are a bit special.' If you disregarded Winnie, Danny, and all the out-of-town criminals, I supposed.

Mr Lark was zipping up his raincoat.

'I thought I'd take a short walk now, before

it gets dark. I'm just going to get my boots out of the car.'

'Don't let me hold you up, Mr Lark. Please. Enjoy your walk and I'll see you at breakfast tomorrow morning.'

I waved him off from the front door, and he disappeared round the side of the house. I heard his car open, then as I went back into the kitchen I could see him striding off down the lane. He'd certainly kept himself in good shape; all those years in a darkened room had not sapped his vitality, it crackled off him.

A car was coming along the lane, and it slowed down as it came level with him. The window went down and I could see Mr Lark pointing back over his shoulder to the house. He gave the occupants a wave as it moved off, and the car pulled in on the shared gravel area and I knew the next pair of guests were here.

In the moment before they got out of the car and came to the front door, I slipped on the black jacket I was carrying, and swapped the borrowed trainers for the Chanel ballet flats. I managed a quick refresh of hot pink lipstick and just had time to primp my hair before I got the front door for the next guests.

I felt a bit more confident now, I knew I would look purposeful and in control, all in black, good haircut, lipstick, and smelling of Chanel. None of those things would have saved Mr Moffat, I knew, but they might save me.

I opened the door to a young couple.

'Mr Marks,' I said. 'I'm Isabel.' I shook his hand firmly. 'Do come in. And you must be?'

I put my hand out to the younger woman.

'Louise. We nearly drove right past, a nice man gave us directions.'

'Welcome to Glebelands Guest House. Can I ask you both to sign the register please?'

I watched them really closely as they both signed in, Richard Marks and Louise Bailey, but they showed no hesitation. They wore matching Belstaff jackets, and they both looked sleek and well groomed. Richard had that super-confident look that comes with the ability to earn lots of money and I had him pegged as something in finance. Louise had a lovely sweet face, cheerful and smiling and she looked like everyone's favourite primary-school teacher. If a primary-school teacher also had time to be a triathlete.

'I've put you in Room 4, let's go up. Can you manage your bags?'

Of course they could manage their bags, they only had a small duffle bag and what appeared to be a laptop bag, but Janice had told me to always ask.

I led them upstairs and along the landing to the back bedroom.

'You don't have a full sea view, I'm sorry to say, but you do have – ' I gestured into the room.

'Oh, that's lovely, thanks.' Richard said. 'Isn't that lovely, darling.'

They were in their mid-thirties, I'd guess. Not in the first flush of young love, but they looked comfortable and happy together. I looked at their hands, where there were no wedding rings displayed.

'And what brings you to Gorran Porth?' I said.

'Well, Richard's going to be – probably – going to be working down here,' Louise said.

'Oh? That's nice. New job?'

'No, same old job, but new area,' Richard explained.

'So, you'll be house-hunting then,' I said.

'That's right. Living the dream, moving to Cornwall.' Louise beamed over at Richard.

'You must have done that too,' Richard said. 'You're not from here?'

'No! No. London born and bred, but I moved here at the end of last year.'

'You love it?' Louise asked. 'It must be so peaceful, after London.'

'Peaceful. Yes,' I lied. 'Everyone says so.' I gave them my very best beaming smile. 'Breakfast 8.30 in the morning, until 10. Well, ten-ish if you want a lie-in. There's a card on the bed, fill in what you want and leave it outside tonight. Now I'll leave you to take a good look around the area. See you tomorrow.'

On my way past Room 6, I unlocked the door, and propped it slightly open with the doorstop I used when I was cleaning. I wasn't sure yet who might want to look in there, but I wanted to make life easy for them.

I felt in need of tea and toast now, and that's why I was in the kitchen when the next car arrived. It was the smartest one so far, a black Range Rover, shiny and well kept. A criminal's car? They'd call it 'wheels', wouldn't they. I remained where I was, eating another mouthful of toast and sipping my tea while I waited for them to get to the front door. Two men got out of the Range Rover and looked around, unspeaking. They were medium height and average build, and forgettably dressed in jeans. One of them had a polo-shirt under a fleece, the other had a collared shirt under a jumper. You really couldn't have found two less memorable types. I looked at them long and hard. Could I risk taking a photo? I opened the pantry door to hide behind, and watched through a thin slice of window. I tilted the phone around the side of the door and got a few shots. I'd text them to Horatio later, though he really wouldn't need it, strangers were thin on the ground in Gorran Porth, at this time of year.

They were at the front door now so I wiped my mouth and went to meet them.

'Hello, Mr Loomes and Mr Lewis,' I said, shaking hands with them. Firm, dry handshakes. Eyes darting around like ferrets, up and down the hall, up and down me then back to my face.

'Do follow me, you'll be in the twin-bedded room, that's Room 2. Can you manage your luggage? Of course you can. And what brings you to Gorran Porth?'

We were at the door of their room and I was a bit out of breath. I smiled brightly and gestured into the room. 'Partial sea view.'

They nodded and moved efficiently into the room, putting an overnight bag by the side of each bed. They didn't speak, just looked at me slightly blankly.

'Right. Breakfast is 8.30am until 10. Please fill out the card and leave it outside your door, or on the hall table. By 9pm tonight. Have a pleasant stay.'

Room 3, my temporary bedroom, was next to this room and I felt slightly disturbed at the thought of sleeping there tonight. They looked to me as though they'd be standing with a glass pressed against the wall, the minute they heard me go in. I wondered what to do. I probably wouldn't sleep a wink anyway. Maybe I'd just sit up all night, in the dining room. No. What if I fell asleep there and one of the guests saw me? Janice would be livid.

I went back to the kitchen and made another piece of toast. There was something in the parking area, a bit of litter blowing about. How annoying. A gentle breeze set the white paper rolling slightly this way and that. I went out through the back door and took it back into the kitchen. It was a scrunched-up piece of note-paper, with holes on the top where it had been torn from a spiral of wire. It was white. With blue print. And the print said, Penwithick Pasties.

I spread it out on the countertop and photographed it with my phone. There was writing on it but I didn't have time to investigate before I heard a commotion on the stairs.

'Miss!'

I went out to see.

'Isabel,' I said. 'Mr Loomes. Or are you Mr Lewis? What can I do for you?'

'Geoff. Geoff Loomes. I can't seem to figure out the shower. Could you come and give me some advice?'

'Sure. It isn't difficult, but sometimes they look too complicated for their own good, don't they?' I went into the tiny bathroom but Loomes stayed in the doorway, giving me room to work. Lewis was not in the room. Hmm. I leaned into the shower enclosure. 'Here. This one for on and off, and this one for hot and cold. See?'

'I feel such a fool,' he said, not attempting to soften the moment with a smile.

'Yes. Well, not to worry. I'll leave you to it.'

As I went back downstairs there was a dark shape at the front door. I stopped, one foot on the last stair, one held up. *Ridiculous,* I thought, stepping down. *You aren't Bambi, get on with it.*

I opened the front door. 'Mr and Mrs Chapman?'

And in they came, and we went through the 'breakfast/lovely spot/so peaceful' conversation again, though I knew why they were here, they were going to their niece's wedding tomorrow and they'd been booked in for ages. They were, from my point of view, in the clear. I took them up to the room, where we all basked for a moment in the clear blue view. I looked down at the harbour wall and spotted a hunched figure with an easel.

'Oh, someone's painting a picture,' Mrs Chapman said, squinting slightly into the distance. 'I wonder if he's got a gallery.'

'He's a notable local artist,' I told them. 'Best not to disturb him at his work.'

'Ooh, I wouldn't intrude.' Mrs Chapman nodded.

'Well, breakfast is any time to suit you, though before 10am would be great. See you in the morning.'

I left them hanging up their wedding outfits and went back to the kitchen. Someone had been in there. Someone had been really helpful and tidied the piece of litter completely away.

I went into the front room and sat in

the window seat, surrounded on three sides by bay windows and with the open room ahead of me. No way I could be surprised here. Keeping my phone down below window level I sent the photo of Loomes and Lewis to Horatio. Then I sent the photo of the page from the Penwithick Pasties order book to Tanya, just for good measure. With the message – *keep safe for a week or two.*

One by one, all the guests left the house. Mr Lark was still out walking, I supposed, but it was getting dark. The Chapmans were driving to Wadebridge to meet up with other family who were there for the wedding. The two other pairs went off down the hill, about ten minutes apart.

I waited until they were out of sight, then rushed to The Manse and grabbed some clean clothes and hurried back to the guest house. I fetched my toothbrush and a few toiletries, and stashed them in the downstairs cloakroom, behind the utility room. I found a spare duvet and pillow in the linen cupboard and put them in the utility room too, inside the tumble dryer. That brought back in a rush the memory of my other hiding place next door so when the front doorbell rang, I jumped about a foot in the air. I peered round the dining room door to look down the hallway. Pat. Pat and Trevor. I opened the door with relief.

'Come in. I'll put the kettle on.'

'We're on our way home, but we wanted to check,' Pat said.

'I'm really pleased to see you. I've got a full house. They're all checked in, but they've gone out.'

I waited until they were both sitting down in the dining room and I'd closed the door.

'Tell us you're going to be safe, Isabel,' Pat said.

'I think so. I guess. Tomorrow I'll take the bag to a police station – not Trenoweth's – and see what happens. Trenoweth might be in on it, but not everyone can be. Surely? All I care about is this being over, so I can get on with life.'

Pat and Trevor nodded. They looked tired and watchful. Of course, with Winnie in trouble, the crime had come close to their family, their community.

'Horatio's watching Nick's cottage,' I told them. 'In case any of the guests try to contact him. He's going to the pub when it gets dark.'

'We'd better go to the pub,' Trevor said. 'Hadn't we? Keep him company?'

'What about Isabel?' Pat turned to him. 'Who's going to keep her company?

'I'll be fine.'

'No. You go, Trevor, and I'll stay here with Isabel. Just until bedtime.'

I felt my chin wobble. 'That would be lovely.'

'Now come on, Isabel. We'll manage, won't we?' Trevor patted my hand.

'Yes. We'll be fine. Is there any news from

the hospital? Tyrone?'

They shook their heads. 'Not good news,' Trevor said, although I could see Pat was trying to shut him up. 'They got him in one of those induced comas.'

'Right. That's a good sign, though, isn't it? They're giving him time to heal.'

'Exactly,' Pat said, glaring at Trevor. 'That's exactly it.'

'How are you off for food?' Pat said.

'I've got eggs, bacon, sausages, toast...what did you fancy?'

'I could bring something up from the pub,' Trevor suggested.

'Ooh. Lovely. They'll have a nice curry tonight, won't they?' Pat rubbed her hands together.

'What about you, Isabel?'

'I don't think I could manage much.'

'Alright, a small portion for you. How about some of that nice soup they do?'

'Fine. Soup for me. And something sweet after. Surprise me.'

'Right you are. I'd better get down there now. Getting dark, Horatio will be in from the Harbour Wall.'

'Take care, love,' Pat said, and I waited behind while she walked him to the front door.

The house phone rang. Horatio.

'I've moved into the Smuggler's. I'm ringing from the phone upstairs, my mobile signal isn't good down here, so I rang to tell you that.'

'I've sent you some photos.'

'Not to worry. I'll get them later, I'll go out for a walk and they'll come through when I get up the hill a bit.'

'Are there any strangers in there?'

'Yeah, one older guy, tall, looks important, one young couple and two blokes.'

'Full house. Apart from the two people I know are real, because they booked a long time ago. Before...Mr Moffat.'

Which was four days ago. What a lot had changed.

'Horatio? Trevor's on his way down to you, to keep you company. Only he's going to bring some food up to us.'

'Alright, I'll keep watching.'

Pat and I went into the front room and stretched out on a sofa each. It was a spacious room, and they were big sofas and I can't imagine Janice ever lay flat on one, her feet up on the arm and her head flung back to look at the ceiling.

'Are you scared?' Pat asked.

'Not really. I feel quite calm. I get moments, though.'

'You've done right by him, by Mr Moffat,' Pat said.

'We all have. And he did right by me. I've met you, and Trevor, and Horatio and Uncle Nat. Loads of other people too.'

'And we could be private investigators

too,' Pat said.

'Well I certainly have to be something. I've resigned from my job,' I told her.

I stood up and looked in the mirror above the mantelpiece.

'How did you feel about being fifty, Pat?

'Better than the alternative, isn't it? You don't need to worry, you've kept yourself in good shape,' Pat said, entirely without malice.

'For all the good it's done me. All those facials, all those manicures.' I put my hands on my temples and pulled the skin taut. Better.

'Did you have a big party?' I asked her.

'You bet I did. Upstairs in the Smuggler's Arms. Everyone was there. It was the summer, so we ended up in the sea. It was a gorgeous night, and we didn't go home 'til the dawn. Hang on, did you have your birthday since you've been here?'

'Yes. January 4th. I was still spending twenty hours a day in bed at that point. It passed me by. When I was getting...weird, in London, everyone thought it was a mid-life crisis. But I don't think it was.'

'You must have been under a lot of stress at work. And then, having an affair with a married man. That couldn't end well, could it?'

'No. I suppose not.'

'And how do you feel now?'

'I'd quite like today to be over. I'd like to wake up tomorrow and see the sky over the harbour, all pink and soft. And I'd like to cook breakfast for pleasant people, and then send them off for enjoyable days, and make their beds and then put my walking boots on and go up over the moor, past the farm, down the track to the beach.'

Pat nodded. 'And no dead bodies.'

'Absolutely no dead bodies.'

'What do you think is going to happen – tonight or tomorrow?'

'Someone's going to look for the bag, Mr Moffat's missing bag, and then we'll know who is a bad guy.' Even as I said it I knew it sounded serious.

'We already know who is a bad guy. Probably.'

'We think we do. We think Smith is bad because he took the body away.'

Pat nodded. 'And because Danny actually saw him there when someone was murdered.'

I winced. 'And we think Nick is bad because he had some contact with Mr Moffat.'

'But Mr Moffat was the victim,' Pat said. 'And we don't know that he knew him well.'

'But Mr Moffat was doing something wrong. In that luggage. Very wrong.'

Pat nodded, looking worried. 'What about Trenoweth?'

I sighed. 'I thought better of him. I mean, he's new in the area, and a bit patronising, but I still thought he'd be interested in solving a crime.'

'How do you know he's new?'

I went out to the kitchen and fetched the police business card from the cutlery drawer.

'Here. The printed bit of the card is for Trenoweth's sidekick, but Trenoweth's name is written on in biro. You wouldn't do that unless you didn't have a business card of your own.'

Pat looked at it for a bit, turning it over as if to find the answer. 'What will you do, if someone asks you direct – about Mr Moffat's luggage?'

I lay back down on the sofa opposite Pat and stared at the ceiling.

'I have no idea. What would Janice do?'

'Janice? She'd be no good, not at that kind of thing. Although she did once have a groper.'

'A groper? A guest who groped her?'

Pat nodded. 'She told me, she got a rolled up newspaper and hit him on the head with it. That cured him. But as for smuggling and murder, I don't think that's up her street. You might as well ask what would Miss Marple do.'

I sat up on one elbow. 'Well, what would Miss Marple do?'

Before Pat could answer, the house phone rang again and I raced out to the kitchen to answer it. It was Horatio.

'Trevor's on his way up, with the food. I haven't picked up your messages, I haven't been able to get out to get a signal, but they're all still in the pub. And Nick. All sitting separately, and not speaking to each other. The two guys are drinking beer, but they're driving Demelza mad, making two half pints last an hour. The young couple are eating a big meal, but not drinking and Nick's reading a book and drinking a pint of cider. And the old bloke is sitting with Petey and keeping him well topped up.'

'I can picture it, Horatio. I hope you're alright? Managing to eat and drink too?'

'Don't you worry about me, Isabel, I'm on this. I'm thinking I might follow them out.'

'But we know where they're going. They're coming up here to the guest house.'

'Ah. Right.' I could hear the comforting sounds of the pub in Horatio's background.

'I suppose, though,' I said, 'one of the parties might still need to speak to Nick.'

'That's it, that's what I was thinking. So I'll follow Nick. That's what I'll do.'

'Be careful, Horatio,' I said. 'He's not really a writer, I'm sure of that.'

'No. I'll take care. Better go, people will start to wonder what I'm up to.'

'See you in the morning?'

'Yep, see you tomorrow.'

As I replaced the phone I heard the front door opening. My heart started to race, but it was only Trevor, with the food. We went into the dining room and sat at the smallest table. Trevor unpacked the collection of containers and Pat and I started to eat.

'There's a terrible sea-fog,' he said. 'The harbour's full of boats that have come in for safety, and round at Portwennick they've got some big boats sheltering in the bay, according to Demelza's brother. He's just come back from there, said 'twas dangerous driving.'

I reached over and flicked up the corner of the dining room curtain.

'I hate that,' I said. 'I hate this kind of weather.'

'This will be the last one for a while,' Trevor said. 'Weather's on the turn.'

'Is it?'

'You'll see.'

Pat and I finished our supper and then I made more tea – coffee for Trevor – and found some biscuits and we went back into the front room.

Pat's eyes were starting to droop and I felt guilty. She had an early start.

'Trevor,' I said, 'you should take Pat home.'

'No!' they both said.

'Yes. Honestly, I'll be alright here. No-one's going to hurt me. They'll search the house, but very quietly I should think, then they'll regroup. And by then I'll know who it is. I'll get a taxi to the station in St Austell, and I'll get a train and go to a police station in another town, and I'll tell them everything, I'll even take Mr Moffat's bag, to prove it. Then someone will come down here and sort it out.'

'I don't know,' Trevor said, though I could see he was torn. Pat was weary.

'And let's not forget,' I told him, 'The Chapmans and Mr Lark are proper guests, and Janice would be livid if I didn't look after them properly.' I shuddered to think of the entry on Trip Advisor: *the guest house was fine, except for the dead body.*

CHAPTER THIRTY-SIX

I had the jitters in a big way after they'd left, so I tried to keep busy. I went upstairs and tidied the bedroom I used – Room 3, which shared the bathroom on the landing with Room 6. Once all my own things – which were few – were in the chest of drawers, I turned on a bed-side light and locked the bedroom door from the outside. The Chapmans and Mr Lark had both left their breakfast cards outside their doors, so I collected those. No signs from the other two rooms, I'd have to wait for them to go to bed. I didn't mind that, I wasn't planning on a deep sleep tonight.

I paused at the top of the landing. I had keys for all the rooms. I could search them all if I wanted. Damn. I should have thought of that while Trevor and Pat were in the house to keep watch. Now if I did it I ran the risk of some-one coming back while I was in their room. I dithered on the top of the stairs for a bit and I was saved by headlights coming along the lane, and the crunch of gravel under tyres as a car pulled in. That would be the Chapmans, they were the only ones who had gone out in a car.

I ducked back into Room 3, I didn't want to make conversation with them.

They came up the stairs chatting quietly and I listened carefully as they let themselves into their room and went inside.

Then I did something I'd never done before. I had my master key in my hand, so I let myself into the door to the attic stairs. Janice lived up here, in a compact flat, complete with bathroom, but no kitchen. She had asked me if wanted to use it when she went off to her sister's, but I preferred the anonymity of a guest bedroom. We'd agreed that if I had the chance to let Room 3 to a paying customer, I would, but Janice knew that was unlikely before the start of the season. I'd have to make a decision soon. Easter was two weeks away, and everything changed at Easter, or so everyone in Gorran Porth had told me.

The attic window faced down the lane into the village and with the light off, from this vantage point, I had a perfect view. Or it would have been a perfect view if there wasn't a thick roll of sea-mist wrapped round the house. I could see the diffused lights from a few houses, but there was no comforting flash from the lighthouse, and even the vast blackness of the sea was blanked out. It felt like being at the bottom of a deep valley, as though there was another set of walls close around the house. I opened the window slightly, trying not to make a noise. That was better, I could at least hear. There was a fluffy blanket on the end of the sofa, so I grabbed that, and sat on the back of the armchair in the window. That gave me enough height to see, and was so uncomfortable I couldn't fall asleep.

About half an hour in, I was struggling to stay awake. In Janice's bathroom I closed the door and turned the light on. There were no windows, so no-one could know I was here. I rooted through the basket of toiletries and found a nail file and some hand cream and took them back to my lookout to give myself a bit of a manicure. That distracted me for a bit longer but I was hampered by the darkness. Suddenly, two floor below the front door clicked closed. Carefully. I hadn't heard any steps approaching the house and I tensed, adrenaline rushing back.

Whoever was in the house was silent, so that suggested Mr Lark, he was the only person alone. I listened; if he was coming up the stairs he was doing it very carefully. Finally I heard the sound of a door closing on the floor below me and I breathed again.

Shielding the light with my hand I checked my phone. No messages, so perhaps Horatio still couldn't get a signal.

I strained to listen. Was that footsteps? It

was. One pair though, so it was neither of the couples returning for the night. Though Loomes and Lewis weren't actually a couple, though, so they might leave the pub separately. The footsteps didn't cross gravel, and gradually they faded away, so they weren't approaching the guest house. Who was out walking at this time of night, and on Glebelands Lane which contained only two properties? Now I had something else to worry about and I wished I could see sideways, to The Manse.

Pulling the blanket a bit tighter I sat back down and tried to focus. Something was eluding me, I knew, but I had that stupid foggy feeling you get when you really need a good night's sleep. I thought back to the times when I'd felt like this for weeks, months even. I'd lived under that pressure for years, and although my time in Cornwall hadn't yet come to an end, all it had really taken was three months, to sift through all that mess, and get my life sorted out. Three months of time and space and some cooked breakfasts and exposure to Pat's inexhaustible supply of snacks.

More footsteps, and murmuring voices. I leaned closer to the window. The mist was actually coming into the room now, but I welcomed the chill, it was reviving me.

I could hear a woman's voice – Louise, but not Richard answering her, it was either Loomes or Lewis. Both couples together? I hadn't imagined that scenario. They all came in together, still chatting, but they quieted as they went upstairs, and all I could hear were whispered goodnights as they went into their separate rooms. I looked at my phone again. It was 10.30pm, early for a London night out, but way past my bedtime now. Everyone was in the house, preparing for bed, so perhaps I could rest too?

I closed the window carefully and sat down in the armchair. I'd give them half an hour, collect the breakfast cards and turn off my bedroom light, then I'd go downstairs and try to sleep in the utility room until dawn.

None of that happened.

I fell into a deep sleep and woke up with a stiff neck, freezing cold and panicked. It took a moment to realise where I was, and why I was asleep sitting up. I looked at my phone which was face down on the chair beside me. It was now 3.18am. A text had come in at 11pm from Horatio. '*They all left the pub together.*'

I tiptoed down from the attic. Down on the ground floor there was a night light plugged in below the hall table, there for the safety of any late returning or early rising guests. I checked the front door. It was on the latch. I thought I'd taken it off the latch when Pat and Trevor left. Possibly one of the guests had gone out to their car for something? Or had one of them done it when they returned from the pub? Either way, the house had been open to anyone from the time I'd been asleep until now. I locked the door, the mechanism moving smoothly and quietly.

The breakfast orders were on the hall table and I stood in the gloom for a moment, thinking ahead to morning. Would I be standing at the stove, wearing my 'Gorran Porth Rocks' commemorative apron and serving up a full English with a bright smile, or would I be looking like Mr Moffat by dawn?

I passed through the dining room and the kitchen, slowly, quietly, hardly breathing. I was thirsty and wanted cool orange juice from the fridge, but was afraid to open the door, the light would be seen by anyone watching from outside. Instead, I took a cup off the dining room table and ran the tap very slowly until I'd got enough to drink.

At the back door I tried the handle. Locked. Fine. That was fine. So I was feeling slightly more relieved as I used the downstairs bathroom and went into the utility room. I spread some clean towels flat on the tiled floor. It would be cold, but better than sleeping upstairs. I got down on the floor, pulled the duvet high up over my head, and punched the single pillow into a more supportive shape. There was enough room to turn round, crammed in between the two large washers on one side, and the dryer and the spare freezer on the other side.

The room smelled comforting and clean. My feet were against the door. There was no lock – who needs to lock a utility room – but I'd be woken immediately if anyone came in. I set my phone alarm for 6am and tried to sleep.

CHAPTER THIRTY-SEVEN

It was a cold and uncomfortable few hours, but I must have dropped off just before 6.am because the alarm woke me. I couldn't really stretch out, but I tried at least to mentally prepare for the day ahead. I thought about Pat who had been at work for hours. And Malcolm, loading his fresh warm pasties in their wooden trays, sending his drivers out across the countryside to deliver delight. I wondered about poor Tyrone, was he still in a coma? Above me the house was sleeping quietly and I summoned the strength from somewhere to get up. I gathered up a few clothes and toiletries and went to the downstairs bathroom. I made myself presentable and applied a bright pink lipstick and a spray of expensive perfume, fluffing up my short hair in the mirror.

It was far too early to start breakfast, but I felt it gave me an advantage, being up and about. I went through the downstairs of the house opening curtains, plumping cushions, straightening rugs. I checked the front door –

still locked. The mist still pressed around the house, and although it was fairly light, I knew we wouldn't see the sun all day. I was almost glad to be trapped in the house with a potential killer, this mist was horrible to walk in; I remembered jumping out of my skin once when I passed a cow looking over the bank of a field. I hadn't seen it until I was about six feet away, and I couldn't see its dun-coloured body in the mist, just the massive head with the deep purple eyes, watching me with amusement.

Some scrambled eggs and half a pot of tea later and I started to hear movement in the house. The Chapmans would be laying out their wedding clothes, shoes they didn't wear often. I could hear muffled voices, but had no idea whose.

I put the sausages on, and filled the toasters and kettles, ready.

The first people down were Loomes and Lewis, which annoyed me though I didn't understand why. They seemed to have developed personalities since they'd checked in, and the personalities were perky in the extreme. They asked a million and one questions: didn't I just love living in Cornwall, were the eggs free range, was the tea Cornish – they'd heard there was a tea plantation in Cornwall. They dawdled over big bowls of cereal and no, they wouldn't want their cooked breakfast right now, they'd sit and chat for a bit. *Great.* Then the Chapmans arrived and they were easy to please and they started chatting with Loomes and Lewis, and that took the pressure off me. I grabbed another mug of tea for myself, and opened the kitchen window a bit. I put two perfectly cooked breakfasts in front of the Chapmans and with that Mr Lark arrived, rubbing his hands with pleasure when he saw the Chapmans' plates.

'Good morning, one and all!' he said and he was answered with a chorus of greetings.

He helped himself to orange juice and cereals.

I offered Loomes and Lewis their cooked breakfasts and they declined again.

'We love Cornwall,' the Chapmans were saying to Mr Lark, 'but we couldn't live here, we like all the amenities of a city.'

'Ah, well, wouldn't suit everyone, I suppose,' he said. 'I've given my heart to Cornwall, I can't wait to move here.'

Loomes said that perhaps he was ready for his breakfast now, but Lewis wasn't.

I heard the front door open. That could only be Richard and Louise, going out. I went out of the dining room to see what was going on, and they called out,

'Just stretching our legs!' and went off down the lane. I couldn't imagine what they'd see in this mist, but the ghostly atmosphere and sheer denseness of it was probably worth a look.

I had told them breakfast could be until 10am. I left the front door on the latch for Pat. I was starting to relax and even enjoy myself, it had been ages since I'd felt like this – busy, but flying through the tasks and hitting my mark every time. I loved it. It wasn't high finance or international mergers but it *was* the most important meal of the day.

Back in the dining room the Chapmans were on to their last pieces of toast and declining a fresh pot of coffee.

'You've given us a great start to the day, Isabel,' Mrs Chapman said. 'We must be getting off though, we're picking up the groom's great-aunt and I've been warned she's a bit...difficult.'

'There's a lot of it about,' Mr Chapman said with a sidelong look at his wife.

'Don't take any notice of him, dear,' Mrs Chapman said. 'He'll enjoy it when he gets there, all that free drink, and plenty of food. I can't wait. Lovely to see all the family again.'

Off they went.

Loomes had finished his cooked breakfast, and wanted more coffee and toast. Lewis had decided he was ready to eat now, but told me not to hurry, he didn't have anywhere to be.

Then Richard came back in, he said Louise wasn't ready for her breakfast, but could he have his?

This was all fine, I told myself as I moved sausages, bacon, mushrooms, tomatoes and baked beans around the various areas of the kitchen. I had both grills on the go and the windows were getting steamy from all the toast and pots of tea and coffee. I felt things slipping slightly out of my control. I wished I'd just got everyone into the room at the same time. Now I didn't know where everyone was, I still hadn't figured out what was bothering me about last night, and I was sure that at least one of the pairs of guests were criminals.

I planned to get Lewis and Richard's breakfasts ready at the same time, while Loomes finished up. Mr Lark was still sipping coffee and making polite conversation though it was stalling a bit without the chatty Chapmans.

'Oh are you off?' I said to Loomes, who was on his feet as I came back into the room.

'Just going out for a bit of air.'

I watched him from the dining room doorway and he did indeed go outside. Then the Chapmans came downstairs with their bags and I took their key back from them, thanked them and sent them on their way. They were staying at the wedding venue that night, so I could start on their room as soon as breakfast was over. Now, only sweet Mr Lark to worry about. I wondered if I should text Pat and Horatio. I put my hand in my back pocket to feel my phone. Not there. Of course, on the side in the downstairs bathroom where I'd got ready this morning. OK, nothing to worry about. I'd nip back there after checking everyone in the dining room.

When I got back there, Mr Lark was still sipping away – that man loved his coffee – and Richard and Lewis were waiting. I plated up their breakfasts as quickly as I could and plonked the food in front of them.

'Is Louise alright?' I asked Richard. 'Is she going to want a cooked breakfast?'

'Um. No, she'll probably be alright with cereals and toast. Don't worry.'

'Well, if she's down in a bit, I'll have something for her, I'm sure. More coffee, Mr Lark?'

'I'm alright for now, my dear, thank you,' he said with a twinkly smile.

'Right. I'll just have a little tidy up and leave you to it,' I said, racing back through the kitchen to the downstairs bathroom. The phone wasn't there. I checked the utility room, shaking out the duvet and towels which had made up my bed. Nothing. I kicked the pile of clothes I'd changed out of this morning, grabbing my jeans by the legs and hoping against hope to hear an expensive clatter on the floor. Nothing. I felt a cold sweat wash over me.

I went back into the kitchen, tidying, wiping, cleaning things up while my mind skittered about. I realised that both couples had split up, one of each pair was either outside, or inside. What did that mean? Were they all in it? Or did that mean that one of each pair cancelled out the other?

I went back into the dining room, trying to sound composed and rational.

Mr Lark was looking at a mobile phone. I thought for a terrible moment it was mine, but it was a different model. It seemed incongruous in his old hands, and I noticed he was reading a text, adjusting his glasses on his nose to see the small words.

'Right. I'd better get going,' he said. Thank you for a delightful breakfast, Isabel.'

'My pleasure, Mr Lark. I hope you'll find something lovely today.'

Lewis and Richard looked up from their breakfast. 'Mr Lark is house-hunting, isn't that fun!' I said, aware that I was sounding slightly hysterical.

Mr Lark moved slowly out of the dining room.

'I'm just going to sit down and make a few phone calls,' he said, gesturing to the front room.

'Fine, that's fine. Would you like some more coffee? I could bring it in there.'

'How thoughtful. That would be lovely.'

So I went off to make another pot of coffee, topping up Lewis and Richard on the way. There was something very odd about the way they were interacting. They weren't speaking, but they seemed to be eating and drinking in complete harmony. Each mouthful was almost synchronised.

I heard the front door open and close.

Loomes, or Louise? And if the latter, did she want her breakfast? I didn't go out to see, just made up a little tray with coffee, milk and a mug, and took it out into the dining room.

'If that's Louise,' I told Richard, 'I'll get something on for her in a minute.'

'Right,' Richard said, though he didn't look particularly bothered about his girlfriend's breakfast plans.

I carried the tray into the front room, and put it down on the coffee table.

As I straightened up, the door closed firmly behind me, and I saw that Smith had been standing behind it.

I looked from him to Mr Lark who was smiling benignly.

'Isabel, I think you've met Mr Smith?' he said. 'Smith, I've been drinking coffee all morning, would you like this cup?'

'Very thoughtful, Mr Lark,' Smith said. 'Don't mind if I do.'

'Sit down, Isabel,' Mr Lark said, gesturing at the sofa.

I sat down. So that' was what had been bothering me since yesterday. Horatio had been watching both the couples – and I'd trusted the Chapmans – but no-one wondered what Mr Lark had been doing all evening. He'd gone off for a walk after he arrived, but where had he been between then, and going to the pub in the evening?

Smith poured his coffee and sat down on the sofa opposite. Mr Lark was sitting in a wooden chair which was normally under the little writing desk in the corner. He'd moved it nearer the centre of the room and he sat upright, relaxed. Even slightly languid. He reminded me of an old-fashioned movie star. I couldn't take my eyes off him.

'Now, Isabel. You have something which belongs to me,' he said. 'It belongs to me, and not to you. And if you keep something which doesn't belong to you, then that's...well, I think we'd call that stealing, wouldn't we?' He appealed to Smith, who nodded.

'You have an honest face, Isabel.' He went on, 'I can't think you'd be comfortable with stealing. I think you want to tell us where our property is, so that we can collect it, and then we can go away and you can carry on preparing your really rather lovely breakfasts. How does that seem?'

Before I could answer, I could hear muted sounds in the dining room. There was a clatter of crockery and the sound of something heavier hitting the ground. Furniture? Or a body. And which one? Would someone come in at any moment to rescue me, or was my hero already dead?

There was complete silence in the house once more. All three of us sat, heads cocked slightly, but there was no movement. I wondered why Smith didn't rush out to take a look.

'Ah, the dear boy has slightly jumped the gun,' Mr Lark said. 'He's always been headstrong. Hasn't he?' Smith nodded again.

'So. Isabel. How shall we proceed? Will you tell us where our property is? Or shall we burn down your guest house, and cut off your head?'

I gasped. 'You're a criminal!' I said. 'You're just a common criminal.'

'Isabel, that's a bit elitist, don't you think? A trifle old-fashioned?'

Behind him, I saw a flicker of movement outside the front window. A shape, but I couldn't make out what it was. If Richard was Lark's man, that meant Louise was his too. But if it was Lewis, that meant Loomes was outside? So where was Louise? And who had my phone? I was getting cross now – this had gone on long enough. I might not be able to defeat Smith and Lark, but I wasn't going to make things easy for them.

'I don't know what you mean. If that man, Mr Moffat, had something with him, you'd have found it when you took him away.'

Smith looked uncomfortable.

'That was the plan,' Lark said, with a hard stare at the younger man. 'Yes, that was certainly the plan. But as you know, Isabel, Mr Moffat did not have his luggage with him when he...died.'

'When you killed him,' I said to Smith.

'We know that Mr Moffat hid his luggage,

Isabel, and we are pretty sure you know where it is.'

'Why would I know where it is?' I asked. 'I don't live here, this isn't my business. I just cook the breakfasts.'

'I think you did just cook the breakfasts, Isabel,' Lark said. 'But I think you've rather gone beyond that, haven't you? I think you've been a very quick learner, and I wonder if you feel there might be something in it for you?'

'Ooh,' I said, sitting forward. 'Is there! Is there something in it for me?'

'There may well be,' Mr Lark said. 'You may well live long enough to tell us where the luggage is. That's what's in it for you, Isabel.'

Smith smirked at me.

'We could go and look,' I said. 'Let's start at the top of the house and work our way down.'

'We've already done that, Isabel.'

I tried not to show how horrified I was.

'Your sense of personal security is pleasingly old-fashioned,' Mr Lark said. 'One of the joys of life in a remote Cornish village, wouldn't you say?'

'Hang on,' I said. 'If Mr Moffat had the luggage, doesn't it still technically belong to Mr Moffat?'

'No, Isabel. The luggage and its contents belong to me.'

'What is it? Is it really worth killing for?'

'Mr Smith?' Lark said, 'Is it worth killing

for?' Smith put his finger to his chin in a parody of thinking.

'If you say so, Mr Lark,' he said with a nasty chuckle.

I couldn't disguise my disgust at that.

'Now, Isabel,' Mr Lark said, 'don't be such a sourpuss, you weren't always so disapproving of handsome Mr Smith, were you?'

I could feel myself flushing. This was all uncomfortable and frightening stuff, but I comforted myself with the thought that time was marching on. Soon Pat or Horatio would knock at the front door and when I didn't answer, they'd come round to the window and peer in. Or they'd go right past this window and look in at the dining room and see...I couldn't imagine what they'd see, but they'd surely raise the alarm.

'I suppose you have my mobile phone,' I said. 'Not content with stealing from a dead man.'

'Do we have Isabel's mobile phone, Smith?' Lark asked him.

'We do, Mr Lark, as instructed.'

Lark smiled at me.

'You are really good looking,' I said to Smith. 'But people must figure it out quite quickly, don't they? How ugly you really are?'

Smith shrugged. He was a pro, he wasn't going to be fazed by me giving him playground insults.

'Isabel,' Lark said, standing up. 'What we'd like to do now is go next door, and take a look in that very spacious house. I bet there are lots of nooks and crannies in there, and you've been keeping the curtains drawn so we couldn't see in, haven't you?'

My heart sank at that. This was the lowest point. I knew Nick had been watching me, watching the house, so that clinched it, he *was* one of Lark's men. I felt stupid, and lost. The whole thing felt hopeless now.

'Alright,' I said. 'Let's go next door.'

'Give us the key,' Lark said. 'On the ribbon around your neck.'

I fished it out from under my apron and t-shirt and handed it to Smith, who had crossed the room quickly.

He grabbed the key in one hand and my upper arm in the other. He hauled me upright and I stood on his foot heavily and said, 'Ouch. You are hurting me. Stop it.'

I might at least slow them down.

CHAPTER THIRTY-EIGHT

I made Smith drag me to the front door, and out into the chilly mist which wrapped itself close around us. Lark closed the front door behind us, but it didn't sound as though he unlatched it, so I hoped whoever came up the hill next would be able to get in. Unless, was there danger still in the house? Whoever had been the winner of the fight in the dining room was still in there. I dug my heels in slightly and Smith had to put his weight behind his hand on my arm, my heels leaving deep ruts in the gravel. One of the dainty Chanel ballet flats came off my foot and I screeched as my bare sole hit the damp driveway.

'Ow! This is inhuman,' I shouted – hoping someone was listening. 'What kind of a monster murders someone without shoes on!' I yelled at Smith.

He bundled me inside the house which Lark had opened. It was quiet and dark with all the curtains still closed.

They forced me into the kitchen and Smith put me in a chair and went to stand by the back door.

'Where is the luggage?' Lark said. 'Quick as you can, Isabel, I have a lunch appointment in Plymouth.'

'I have no idea where it is,' I said. I turned my head slightly to see the cooker clock. The time was 9.40am. Slightly late for Pat to call. I hoped she was OK. The mist was heavy and local drivers took no heed of adverse weather. Worrying about her for a moment took my mind off my situation until Lark dragged me back.

'Now, Isabel,' he said. 'You may have mislaid your mobile phone, but I have kept hold of mine.' He showed me.

'And I've just received notification from my associates in the area. We kept the pasty van – did you ever wonder about that? You found the disposable item, but we kept the van.'

'Tyrone is a person, not a disposable item,' I shouted at the top of my voice. 'And he's alive, and he's going to be fine!'

Lark made a 'maybe/maybe not' gesture with his hand.

'We have the van. And we have your lovely friends, the postal worker and the special constable, and they are in the van. And the van is at the top of a cliff. And the tide is in. Quite high in fact. So, let's open Isabel's lost luggage locker, shall we?'

'I need to see a photo.'

'A what?'

'I need to see a photo, of them, in the van. Your associate can take a photo and text it to you, and if I see it, I'll try to help you. I'm not promising anything mind you, but I do know this house pretty well.'

With that, and to my complete amazement, Lark reached out and slapped me in the face. It hurt, really hurt badly, but the shock was worse. He was so quick, and he betrayed nothing in his face as he came towards me.

Tears started to pour down my cheek, already raw from yesterday, and my eye was seeing sparks. I put my hand up to my cheekbone. Smith looked completely impassive, though I saw him looking at his watch.

'Photo,' I said, to Lark.

'No, Isabel, I won't be sending you a photo of your friends. You'll help me, because that's what people do. They help me to get what I want.'

'No, Lark,' I said, 'you haven't got my friends in the pasty van, and that's why you won't be sending me a photo of them.'

He was about to answer me, I knew it, when we heard a sound on the gravel. A single crunch, not footsteps, unless the person was out there now, balancing on one foot. Lark turned to Smith who crouched down and lifted a tiny corner of the kitchen blind. Even I could see through my one good eye, that the mist was keeping our secrets.

Smith turned back to Lark with a shrug, but I could see they were worried, and Lark looked at the clock.

'Shall I tell you,' I said, 'how I know you haven't got my friends?'

'Showing off, Isabel?' Lark said.

'I know where the pasty van was, and my clever friend let two of the tyres down, and Smith here doesn't look as though he could change a wheel in a hurry, even if you had two spares. And, you can't get a picture, because there's no signal.'

Lark breathed in, very slowly.

'We were pushed for time,' he said, quietly. 'But we will not wait any longer.'

He came over to where I was sitting and put one hand on my head.

I started to sob out loud. This was it, wasn't it? I didn't want to beg or bargain, I hardly had the breath for it anyway, but I knew this was where he took out the sharp implement to stab me in the head.

'That's a very nice haircut, Isabel,' he said. 'Very...striking.'

Then his hands went down over my face and settled round my neck and started to squeeze.

I put my hands up on his wrists and tried to struggle but he was pushing down with such force I couldn't rise up from the chair. The kitchen seemed to get darker, and I could see Smith watching with mild interest over Lark's shoulder, and I tried to point to Smith and say 'look' at what was happening behind him, but then there was nothing.

The next thing I knew I was looking at the kitchen ceiling, though it took a while to work that out, as I hadn't seen it from that angle before. I turned my head painfully, and there next to me on the floor lying face down was Mr Lark. I sat up with difficulty. Mr Lark was watching me silently, his hands taped together behind his back and Smith was on the floor too and his hands were being secured by Trenoweth's sidekick. I lay back down with a sigh.

'Isabel?' Another voice approached, and it was Nick, stepping over Smith and Lark to crouch next to me. 'Can you see me?'

'Of course I can see you,' I said. Or at least, that was my intention but only a hoarse croak came out.

'Don't talk,' he said unnecessarily.

Trenoweth came into the kitchen with a paramedic in a green jumpsuit behind him, and some uniformed police.

I scowled at Trenoweth.

'Sorry,' he said with a shrug. 'I think you shouldn't be in here,' he said to Nick, who ignored him. 'No press at this stage.'

Two uniformed police, one on either side, got Lark up into a standing position and hustled him out.

A bit later they came back for Smith. While that was happening the paramedic was helping me to sit up, putting something that looked like a plastic clothes-peg on my finger and pulling the neck of my t-shirt down to put sticky pads on my chest. I was still wearing my apron and I started to pluck at the knot, flapping around and dislodging some of the medical kit.

'Isabel,' Nick shouted from across the room. 'You're in enough trouble as it is, just sit there quietly for a bit.'

I glared at him but the nice paramedic undid the apron and got it over my head.

'Thank you,' I mouthed.

'Your blood oxygen level is fine,' he said. 'And your heart rate is coming down.'

I nodded.

He put his cool hand on my neck and I winced.

'You'll need to go to hospital, have all that checked out.'

'Not yet,' I whispered. I pointed at Trenoweth and Nick and back to myself and made a 'talk' motion with my hand.

They both sighed, and Nick left the room.

The paramedic helped me to sit up at the kitchen table.

'Incidentally, Miss Blunt,' Trenoweth said,

'where *is* the luggage? Do you actually have it?'

'Not yet,' I whispered again. 'Show me some ID.'

Trenoweth laughed. 'Yes. Sorry. I really am a policeman. I'm sorry I appeared to not believe you at the beach but I'd had a phone call.'

I nodded.

He went on. 'I'd been warned, Wainwright – you know him as Lark – he was on his way to Cornwall. We didn't know if we could flush him out, but we did. Or, you did.'

I nodded and made a 'keep going' gesture.

'All we really needed to do was get him to Gorran Porth and catch him doing something – anything. A speeding fine would have been enough. Him trying to murder you was a complete bonus, really.'

'Great!' I mouthed, giving him two sarcastic thumbs up.

'Well. Yeah. Sorry about that. Reynolds was outside the back door and I was outside the front, but you'd left all the curtains closed, so it was only when Smith lifted the blind we could see where you were. We thought they might have guns, see.'

'They're lo-tech,' I whispered. 'Fortunately for me.'

'They're capable of very high-tech unpleasantness,' Nick said, coming back into the kitchen.

'Could you all sit down please?' said the

paramedic. You're making Miss Blunt crick her neck and I think she could do without that.'

They sat down obediently and the paramedic busied himself in the corner with paperwork and putting things back in his massive green rucksack.

'Who are you?' I whispered at Nick. 'Press?'

He shrugged and said nothing.

I pointed at Trenoweth. 'You said press.'

Trenoweth shrugged.

'I'm a writer, like I told you,' Nick said. 'And I came here to work on my book. My novel,' he insisted as I glared at him. 'OK, I'm also a journalist, and yes, someone rang me.'

'From Mevagissey,' I croaked.

And, look, Isabel – ' he leaned in – 'It is *still* going on, so we have to be really careful.'

I nodded.

'I made contact with the local police, as a courtesy, and so Trenoweth knew I was here. And that's when I made a big mistake.'

I looked from Trenoweth to Nick and back again. 'Well?' I gestured.

'I knew the delivery was coming into town on the bus, so I tried to make conversation with him, just being friendly, when he got off the bus. And to my amazement, he started to panic.'

I turned to Trenoweth.

'Mr Moffatt wasn't the usual delivery person,' Trenoweth said.

Nick took his mobile phone out and put

it under Trenoweth's chin to record. Trenoweth was having none of it and flicked it away.

'This upright member of the press,' Trenoweth jerked his thumb at Nick, 'got involved.'

Nick shook his head. 'No. I did not. You're not pinning this on me. He asked me, Moffatt asked me where he could stay that night. He was white with fear and I asked him if he was OK, and he told me he needed a place to stay.'

Nick put his phone back in the top pocket of his shirt, and I was sure he was still recording. He went on. 'So, I wanted him in the pub, obviously, where I could keep an eye on him. But he didn't like it. He wanted to go further away, up the hill.'

I pointed to myself and they both nodded. 'Why me?'

Trenoweth shrugged again. 'Who knows? Better views? Buy himself some time?'

'So I was hanging around as much as I could,' Nick said. 'And it was a bit of luck I saw him on the harbour wall that night, and I got talking to him, managed to get a bit of his story.'

I nodded. I wanted to say, 'yes, you're very good at that, aren't you?' but I honestly didn't have the strength.

'He didn't admit to being involved with anything, but he'd been told to do something, and he didn't want to do it, and it wasn't anything to do with him. And he needed to think it over. I begged him to come and stay with me, let me help him, but I must have said too much, seemed a bit...keen.'

Trenoweth took up the tale. 'He must have been scared, because he missed the drop. The goods weren't delivered so the person who picked them up and moved them on didn't find them. So what did Mr Moffat do with them? He broke into this house, and hid the goods.'

'And got murdered,' I whispered. 'Don't forget that.'

'Right,' Nick said. 'And they came back, looking for the bag.'

'And you looked for it too,' I said.

'Yeah. You rushed me, I almost got caught in the house.'

'But you didn't find it,' I said.

'No. But you did. And you hid it, and that's what delayed Smith and Lark – sorry, Wainwright – long enough for us to get here.'

'What about Pat and Horatio! Are they alright?'

'They're fine. Actually, they're in the snug at the Smuggler's Arms, drinking Irish coffee with Detective Officer Loomes.'

'Loomes is police?' I gripped my throat as though that would make it less painful to speak. 'What about Lewis, and Richard?'

'Well, not so straightforward. Lewis is being patched up next door, but he didn't hold on to Richard.'

'He got away?'

'No, we've got him, now. He tried to delay Postwoman Pat, kept her talking, but your friend – who doesn't strike me as the suspicious type – got the wind up her and 'accidentally' rammed Richard with her postal trollies. Your friend ran off shouting for her nephew, the one whose car has been blocking me in all weekend, and the nephew found Richard limping down Back Lane and apprehended him.'

'And fortunately, I was already on the scene,' said Trenoweth, 'but they've still come out of it like heroes, don't you worry.'

I pointed to the utility room. I was suddenly very tired and wanted to lie down.

Nick disappeared and came back in a few minutes later with the black bag. He put it on the kitchen table and took out the dishwasher tablets and washing powder. I pointed to the fridge but that wasn't specific so I went over and opened the door myself, passing Nick the jar of Nutella.

'You're very thorough, Isabel,' he said.

I nodded.

'Can we hook it out?' Trenoweth said, peering over my shoulder?

'I've got something that might help,' the paramedic said, and they went for it with a long silver instrument which had some medical purpose I didn't want to think about.

Finally the small brass key was in Nick's palm.

'The study,' I said.

I had to grab both their sleeves as they rushed off.

'Wait.' I opened the freezer and took out the soup carton. I found a pan and lifted the lid of the AGA, ripped off the cardboard carton and put the frozen block of soup in the pan.

'Bureau keys,' I said.

'Of course,' Trenoweth said. 'Where else are you going to hide them.'

Gradually the block of soup softened and collapsed and they used the paramedic's instrument again to hook the warm keys out of the mulligatawny. I took them off the hook, rinsed them, tossing them from hand to hand, and went to the study door. Nick reached past me to unlock it and we all went inside.

I unlocked the bureau, and knelt on the rug, reaching back into the bureau to pull out the wrapped packs of passports and handing them to Nick. Trenoweth went back to fetch the black bag and they repacked them, zipping the bag closed.

'I am going to need to take a statement,' Trenoweth said with what he obviously thought was a smile.

'Hospital first,' Nick said. 'Statement later.'

I nodded.

'I'll take you,' Nick said. 'If that's OK?'

I nodded again. At last, something was going right.

Outside, the lane was crowded with vehicles. There was a police car at either end of the lane, completely blocking it and isolating the two houses. There was a dark van in front of the big house, and another ordinary car behind it. Plus an ambulance. For me, I guessed.

I looked around to see where Lark and Smith were.

'They've gone, on their way up to London,' Nick assured me.

'Phone!' I croaked. 'My phone.'

'You'll get it back, eventually,' Nick said.

'Now!' I squeaked.

Trenoweth shouted for Reynolds who came trotting up, red-faced, excited. They huddled together, talking in low voices.

Nick and I skirted round the parked vehicles and Nick held open the door of a plain red car which was parked at the top of the hill which led down to the village.

'In you get, Wonder Woman,' he said.

'Where are we going?'

'Hospital. Truro.'

'Pub first,' I insisted. So instead of pulling up out of the village and onto the fast road, we cruised down the hill and arrived at the pub and Nick just stopped in the road, blocking it. Outside the pub was crowded with gawkers, and we pushed our way past whispering faces and went upstairs to where a table was set with papers and documents and Horatio and Pat were sitting with some uniformed officers. They both jumped up when they saw me. Pat gave me a big hug and I burst into tears.

'What have you done!' Pat shouted at Nick.

I pulled back and showed her my neck, and pointed to Nick.

'She can't really speak,' he said, helpfully. 'Someone tried to kill her.'

'I can see that,' Pat said, 'and why didn't you do something about it!'

I shook her shoulders to get her to shut up. 'Are you alright?' I whispered. 'And Horatio?'

Pat nodded.

'We're alright, although I nearly needed to change my shorts in a hurry I can tell you that, but I stopped him – did you hear – I stopped that thug, rammed him with my trollies. He's sitting over there with a bag of ice on his little gentleman. I made him cry. Big baby.'

I nodded, smiling through my tears.

'And Horatio isn't in the dog house any more. He's only a blinking hero.'

I smiled some more, feeling my whole face smarting now, but I didn't care.

'You get on now, Isabel,' Pat said. 'Go and get the doctor to look at you, and we'll have a fine old celebration when you get back.'

Nick led me away, and I waved to Pat from the top of the stairs. We retraced our steps though the crowd downstairs, waving to Demelza, and out into the cool air. I stopped outside, taking in the harbour view, the glimpse of Coastguard Cottage and the hair salon. The corner store and the bus stop. The little things which made up my world.

We got back in the car and Nick pulled out slowly into the road. Opposite, as we paused to let the bus go through, was the simple wooden finger post which marked the South West Coastal Path. Mevagissey. I grabbed Nick's arm and pointed to it.

'Mevagissey,' I tried to say.

'I know,' he said. 'And yes, that's going to figure quite largely in my piece.'

I punched his arm. 'Go there. Now!'

'What? Why? We need to get you to hospital.'

'Go there now,' I said again, hurting my voice with the force of my will. 'That's where Louise will be.'

'No, she'll be lying low.'

'Walking!' I said, pointing at the finger post. 'She's walking to Mevagissey and then she'll get in a boat and get away.' My eyes were streaming from the effort of speaking.

With a ripping sound of rubber on road, Nick took off.

CHAPTER THIRTY-NINE

I braced myself against the car door and tried not to look at the scenery rushing past in the narrow lanes. Nick was fumbling to get his phone out of his pocket and he passed it to me but I couldn't speak at all by now. I tried to scroll through the list of names but they seemed to be written in code and I couldn't decide which one was Trenoweth. We were on the outskirts of Mevagissey now and Nick was slowing down, looking around him anxiously. He stopped in the narrow road behind the houses which fronted the harbour, and I jumped out. I heard him shout after me, but I could also hear car horns behind him and I knew he'd have to move the car. I ran down a dark cobbled alley and out into the harbour which glittered like a bowl of lights under the white sky. The outer harbour was walled off with the mist, but I could clearly see the bulk of the aquarium, and I set off at a run towards it.

There were small groups of people around

as there had been yesterday, all going about their business and ignoring the little drama which I was trapped in. I wondered how long it would take Louise to walk here. I didn't think she could be here already, but I'd lost track of time. She might have started walking when I thought she'd gone out before breakfast. I hadn't seen her after that. And hadn't I been unconscious on the kitchen floor for a while? How long had I been blacked out and unaware? I reached the aquarium and sagged against the wall, my throat hurting as I struggled to get enough air into my lungs. I could see HH57 moving slightly in the silky calm waters of the outer harbour, and I said a little thank-you to Danny. Good, if I could just keep between that boat and Louise, I could stop her going anywhere. At least until Nick or more police arrived, at which time I could lie down on the floor in a tiny ball, and cry.

I straightened up and moved past the front doors of the aquarium and positioned myself in front of a big pile of plastic buckets and lobster posts. They had a slightly fishy smell but I didn't mind, I was between the Louise's escape and the land, there was no way she could get past me now. The only disadvantage to this position was that Nick couldn't see me, he'd have to be coming right round the aquarium to find me. I looked back over my shoulder, craning my neck to see if I could see him. Of course, this morning he hadn't been wearing his long red coat.

He'd been wearing – what? Jeans, definitely, and something dark blue on the top. I thought about all the times I'd spotted the red coat, and wondered about all the times I hadn't spotted him, without the coat.

I gave up looking out for him. He'd have to just find me. I kept as motionless as I could, while looking for any sign of movement coming my way. There was nothing. I looked down at HH57. It was still and quiet, the wheelhouse door locked and all the hatches on deck closed. Unless Louise had managed to get in and relock it, refasten it, she wasn't in there. I began to feel a bit unsure. What if I just got cold and tired here, and Nick got impatient and furious looking for me, and nothing ever happened? I was as quiet as I could be, I didn't want any passers-by stopping me and asking if I was alright, so I took a deep breath and tried to calm down. And then, in the space between one breath and the next, I heard it. Very close behind me, in the pile of lobster pots and netting and coiled ropes and plastic bins, I heard the tiny sound of a mobile phone vibrating.

I tried to shout, but nothing came out. I whirled around and started to fling lobster pots aside. They were much heavier than they looked, and they thumped against me as I grabbed them. My arms ached and my breath was rasping but there she was, Louise, coming towards me with a murderous rage in her face.

'Mummy, look at the lady!' I could hear a little child on the harbour wall. Normal life was going on all around us, but I was gripping one of Louise's hands, and pushing back on the other shoulder with my free hand. I was bracing with one leg and kicking at her shins with the other, trying to cry for help. Surely Nick could see this now? Louise was very strong and much younger than me, and she only had to drop a few feet off the wall and onto the boat and she'd be free. She'd reckoned without one thing though. I was absolutely furious.

She was making headway, there was no way I could keep her pinned against the aquarium so I suddenly released the hold I had on her and leapt out of the way. She went sprawling forward and I grabbed the nearest lobster pot. As she righted herself and turned back towards me, I swung it with all my weight at her face.

I could hear gasps and shrieks around me. The little child started crying in earnest and I knew just how it felt. Louise was staggering now, the lobster pot on the ground in front of her, her face bloody and her gaze unfocussed.

The little group of onlookers parted, and Nick ran into view, closely followed by Lewis, with a huge white dressing on his temple.

'Morning, Isabel,' he said brightly. 'Nice to see you again.'

I couldn't speak, just gave him a little wave and a smile, feeling slightly ridiculous now.

Lewis and the other man grabbed Louise by the shoulders and led her away. Nick picked up the lobster pot and placed it back on the pile by the aquarium wall.

'Nicely done,' he said. 'Thanks. Ready for the hospital now?'

CHAPTER FORTY

When I woke up it was dark. I was in a hospital and I'd been given a small room to myself which seemed unusual. The room was dim and quiet though I could hear activity further off. My throat was still sore, but a small woman in a white coat had already shone very bright lights down it, and told me there was no permanent damage and a few days' rest would really help. On the windowsill was a huge bunch of flowers. I swung my legs over the side of the bed. I didn't think flowers were allowed in hospitals nowadays, so a person of some influence must have been involved in that too. I looked at the card: 'From the desk of Sir Dougall Spence.'

The floor was cold, so I got back into bed and pulled the thin blankets up over my head.

When I woke up the next time it was full daylight and a nurse was standing at the bottom of my bed, holding a cup of tea. I took it from her, and she gave me a padded envelope too. Inside was my phone. I turned it on and found missed call alerts and texts, some from Pat and Horatio, but most from Tanya.

There was a knock at the door and I was pleased to hear my voice sounding a bit more normal.

'Come in.'

Trenoweth stuck his head round the door. 'Decent?' he asked.

I looked down at myself. I was wearing a hospital gown, so it was decent as long as I stayed in bed.

Trenoweth nodded at the nurse as she left, and he looked for a moment like a reasonably cheerful and sociable person.

'How are you feeling?' he said from the end of the bed.

'Are you on guard duty?'

'What? No, perfectly safe here. Just need a quick statement, that's all. But you might not feel up to talking very much.'

I nodded. 'I'll give it a try.'

He pulled out a chair from a stack of three, and moved it closer to my bedside.

'We just need to know, how did you find Louise?'

'I knew she was connected to that boat.' I told him about my trip to Mevagissey, and the two men watching the boat. 'I only realised after, they must have been waiting for a woman, not just some random person.'

Trenoweth nodded.

'So they thought I was Louise? Because they didn't actually know her?'

Trenoweth nodded again.

'Who were they, the two men? They didn't look quite right on the harbour. They stood out.'

Trenoweth looked almost cheerful. 'Oh, they would have stood out, yes. You almost had an encounter with one of the most powerful leaders in British organised crime. And his personal banker.'

I leaned back against the pillows.

Trenoweth scooted the chair back slightly. 'You aren't going to be sick, are you? You look a bit green. Shall I call someone?'

I shook my head. 'Where is Louise now?'

'Don't you worry about her. She's under lock and key, though she did need a bit of medical treatment. Nasty bruise on the shin. Broken nose.'

'I'm not sorry.'

'You shouldn't be. She had it coming.'

I nodded. 'I think she might have gotten away with it. Eventually I would have moved and she only had to slip down onto the boat. It was bad luck someone ringing her at just that point.'

'Not bad luck, exactly.'

'No?'

'Well, I've had to do a bit of digging, and there were times when I didn't quite know what to believe...but the phone call was connected to you.'

'Me?'

'Yes. It seems you found a piece of paper with a phone number written on it?'

'Oh, the Penwithick Pasties notepaper.'

'That's the one. And you sent it to a friend of yours – to keep it safe.'

'Tanya!'

'That's the one. And your message sent her into a panic and she couldn't raise you on the phone.'

'Because Smith had my phone.'

Trenoweth nodded. 'And so your friend Tanya took it into her head to ring the phone number written on the scrap of paper.'

I gaped at him. Speechless. He nodded again, looking as cheerful as I'd ever seen him.

'Yes, Isabel. That was Louise's phone number. Written down for her to rendezvous with Richard. They'd never met before the day they turned up at the guest house.'

'So Tanya saved the day.'

Trenoweth looked a bit pained. 'I'd like to think meticulous police work saved the day. And that's what I'll always maintain, outside this room. But yes, Tanya had a hand in it. And Postwoman Pat. And Horatio. And you, Isabel.'

'I had more than a hand in it,' I said.

'Yes, alright. You were in it right up to your lavishly bruised neck.'

'What about Nick?'

'Well, he's got a great story, but I'd be very careful about letting him use anything to do with you. No photos, no personal details. Just, you know. For your own personal safety.'

I lay back against the scratchy pillows and pulled the blanket a bit higher. There was so much to think about. Janice would be coming back to the guest house soon. There might be press coverage of the dead man, I'd have to explain that. Then I really wanted to speak to Tanya, and I imagined myself walking into her bright basement kitchen in Primrose Hill, greeting the boys, sitting round the big table with a glass of wine. I tried to think about my own flat, empty for months now, and found I couldn't quite call it to mind. I thought about my office. My inbox would be overflowing. No, of course it wouldn't. Someone would be dealing with my work – what had been my work.

Trenoweth was looking at the flowers and reading the card.

'Nice,' he said. 'So can I send a uniform in to get your statement?'

I nodded. 'What about Danny.' I asked him. 'Is he still on the ship?'

Trenoweth slapped his forehead. 'Is that where he is?'

'Haven't you been watching him?'

Trenoweth sat back down. 'Of course we have, of course. But you can see what it's like here. We couldn't throw too many people at it, strangers don't exactly blend in. We knew he was involved, in a small way, and we hoped he was still alive.'

'He's scared. He thought he was going to be next.'

'Well, he would have been, probably.'

'He's got Mr Moffatt with him.'

Trenoweth didn't say anything, but he took out his mobile phone.

'Why did Mr Moffatt come with the passports, and then not deliver them?'

Trenoweth shrugged. 'We won't know until someone talks. The usual person dropped out – we haven't found him. So they must have put pressure on what they thought was a weak link.'

'He wasn't, though. He wasn't the weak link. Any of them could have done it – Smith, Louise, Richard, even Mr Lark, why did they use Mr Moffatt?'

'Probably had something on him. Or wanted something on him. Then they'd have had him for life, see. That's how they work. But he was dispensable in the end.'

'And he brought them all down,' I said. 'Small, insignificant Mr Moffatt, he destroyed them all.'

Trenoweth smiled, his weary face looking cherubic for a moment.

'Wait,' I said. 'There's more. Winnie.'

Trenoweth groaned. 'Right. Where are

they? Do you know?'

I nodded and explained. 'You can try getting them out, but if they don't trust you, you'll need to take me along with you.'

'Right.' Trenoweth closed his notebook and stood up. 'Isabel. Is there anything I can do for you? Anything you need?'

I stared out of the window at the high clouds moving inland from the sea. I thought about the tide slurping into the harbour at Gorran Porth right about now. It wouldn't always be winter, would it? One day those curling waves would be warm enough for paddling. I looked back to Trenoweth.

'There is one thing,' I said. 'But you won't be able to help.'

'Try me' he said, trying his hardest to look friendly and helpful.

'I really need a pedicure.'

Trenoweth left, closing the door softly behind him.

CHAPTER FORTY-ONE

There they were, ten little coral nuggets of shiny delight. I was luxuriating on the Eames chair on the landing of The Manse. I'd snuggled under a blanket, but I kept pushing my feet out just to remind myself. I wasn't doing anything, just staring out at the pale blue sky and ragged clouds which cast dappled light on the pale wall. I felt peaceful and exhausted, and very content, so that when the door-bell rang – serious and inescapable – below, I felt mild irritation. I knew it wasn't Pat, she was up to something but wouldn't tell me what. I'd finished with Trenoweth for now, and he'd assured me, again, that all the major players in the gang were under lock and key. Tiptoeing down the stairs I took irrational pleasure in the cared-for look of my own feet, again.

I opened the door to Nick. His hands were behind his back.

'I wondered,' he said innocently, 'if you fancied something hot and spicy?' and he brought his hands forward to show me a lovely pair of Pot Noodles.

Waving him in, I locked the front door behind him.

He was in the kitchen, looking around in interest.

'Can hardly believe it,' he said, pulling out a chair.

I got wine out of the fridge and put glasses in front of him. He poured.

'I thought you'd gone,' I said. 'You disappeared pretty quickly.'

He sipped and looked a bit awkward. 'I was doing a deal.'

'What kind of deal?'

'For the story. This is going to be sensational. Seaside resort, smuggling, murder, mystery woman.'

I narrowed my eyes at him. 'Who is the mystery woman?' I said, with a bit of chill in my tone.

'Well, Louise of course.' He smiled at me and I could see how he'd built a career on getting people to tell him things. But not me.

'Keep it that way,' I said, trying not to sound as though I was begging.

'Look.' He leaned forward, serious. 'I admit, I thought you were involved. It seemed so odd, you turning up. I even wondered what had actually happened to Janice. I just couldn't see where you could fit in here.'

'You should probably know,' I told him, 'we were convinced you were involved, because you were seen talking to Mr Moffat. Twice.'

He nodded. 'I'm not proud of that. I put the story first, before the people.'

'Tell me about the deal.' I decided to let him off the hook.

'Big article, huge. Very prestigious publication. It'll be very good for me. And very good for you too – '

I held up a hand in protest and he went on ' – alright, very good for Gorran Porth then, good for business. In the summer.'

'Can you publish it before the trial? Trenoweth said...'

'This is a bit beyond Trenoweth's pay grade. It'll go to trial very quickly, because of all the people currently using all the previously trafficked passports.'

'Oh yes. How many times did they do it? Make the drops and get them out to sea?'

'Six. That I know of.'

'And how did they find the people – Winnie and Danny?'

Nick shrugged. 'I'm hoping you'll find out, and tell me.'

'No,' I said. 'Nothing to do with me. These are real people, with families and friends.'

'OK.' He gave up gracefully, smoothly.

'It seems a bit...complicated though,' I said. 'All those moving parts.'

Nick nodded. 'But everyone doing one small thing, keeps the trouble away from those at the top.'

'All the small things,' I said, 'add up to the big thing.'

'Huh,' he said. 'I've heard that somewhere before. Is it a local saying?'

Over his shoulder I could see the list from the second envelope, stuck on the fridge with magnets, where I'd left it.

'Must be,' I said, pouring more wine. The last two points in Janice's list now seemed to hover in the air, though only I could see them.

Try to look as though you're enjoying yourself Janice had scrawled at the bottom of the page. And then, in shakier writing, as though she was hurrying out of the room –

Or, better still, really enjoy yourself.

I watched him over the rim of my glass.

'You know I'm leaving tonight,' he said. 'And I won't be back.' He picked up one of the Pot Noodles and shook it like a maraca.

'You should probably take them with you,' I told him, 'for the journey.'

He put it down on the table. 'But then,' he said, 'we'd have to get something hot and spicy elsewhere.'

'I'm sure I've got something around here somewhere,' I said, and I reached out my hand. 'Come on, I'll show you where I found the bag, in the playroom.'

He brought the wine and the glasses and followed me out of the kitchen.

'Of all the rooms in the house,' he said, 'the playroom is my favourite.'

CHAPTER FORTY-TWO

As soon as I opened the door to the Smuggler's Arms I was enveloped in an embrace from Demelza before she ran back behind the bar to ease the cork out of a bottle of something which looked a bit like champagne. She poured me a glass and I licked the foam off the back of my hand.

'Upstairs!' she said, pointing, and everyone else in the bar was waving and smiling at me and shouting, 'Happy birthday, Isabel.'

By the time I got to the top of the stairs I was laughing and crying and I'd spilt a bit of champagne down my t-shirt. Pat was at the top of the stairs, Pat with her hair down and her eyes sparkling, clapping her hands with glee.

'Isabel! Do you hate surprises? Don't say you do! I wanted you to have a proper big birthday party!'

We hugged, and then I was hugging everyone: Trevor and Petey and Horatio and Uncle Nat. Marc was there, with Mavis, and Malcolm who I hardly recognised without his white trilby and hairnet. He had a fine head of hair.

I went round the whole room being introduced to the partners and friends of the people I knew. I told the edited, cleaned-up version of my story so many times it started to feel unreal.

Someone put a CD on the music system – sounds of the 90s – and people were dancing. There was a large table with bowls of salad and coleslaw and hunks of bread and cheese and in the middle, a massive fanned display of pasties. Penwithick, I presumed. Loomes and Lewis were there, and Trenoweth. Horatio was looking flushed and excited and I gave him the biggest hug.

'I've got something to tell you,' he said.

'I know! You're going to get an award.'

'Not that. No. Although, that is nice. No, I'm going to apply to art college. Well, a couple of colleges, in case I don't get into the first one. I'm going to become an artist.'

'That's fantastic news! Oh, that's great, Horatio.'

'What are you crying for now?'

'I'm just happy, happy for you.'

'Well, after...you know, after it all happened and they told me and Aunty Pat you were alive, I thought, life's short, isn't it? Short. And you don't know what's round the corner.'

'You don't. You really don't.'

I could see Trenoweth brooding in the corner. I went over and he made room on the bench next to him and we sat looking out at the room, in silence.

Eventually I spoke. 'Why did they steal Mr Moffat? After they'd killed him?'

He smiled, as much as he ever could. 'I knew you'd wonder that. I only figured it out when we found the second one, the one on the beach.'

'Carlos?'

'Yes, out of everyone he's the innocent party, him and Tyrone. And because the head-wounds were the same, it was obvious it was them. That was Richard's contribution. A long reach, like a boxer. And fast! God, you wouldn't stand a chance. But very predictable, couldn't change. So they couldn't afford to have bodies turning up with that injury, because he's got plenty of form, all over Europe.'

'But...he was already dead, wasn't he? Because there was no splatter.'

Trenoweth stared at me.

'Oh,' I said. 'Smith had to steal the body because people would have known they didn't actually kill Mr Moffat. He was already dead, just like Pat said.'

'Well, I don't care to know how Smith thinks,' Trenoweth said, 'but Mr Moffat died of natural causes. Possibly brought on by stress, or terror.'

I took a few sips of my drink. 'They were literally cleaning it up,' I said. 'You know what amazes me about that, anyone could have seen them putting Mr Moffat in a pasty van. I mean, that surely would have attracted attention?'

'But it didn't have Penwithick Pasties written on it,' Trenoweth pointed out. 'And they made sure that you and Horatio and Pat all trusted them, and felt safe with them. They were arrogant, and ruthless, yes, but they've been in business a long time, and they know how to get people to do their bidding – either willingly or unwillingly.'

'We were so stupid,' I said.

'You didn't break the law though, did you,' Trenoweth said. 'You just believed them for a morning, you didn't throw in your lot with them, like some others I can mention.'

'It's really going to change the village,' I said.

'Well. It might bring a bit of business for a week or two, when it comes to court, but for now it is all going very quiet, we've got a lot of clearing up our own. We've tracked down some pretty tasty suspects from the passports. People are sleeping soundly in their beds right now, and there's going to be a bang on the door very early one morning, soon.'

I shivered. Trenoweth's lean face looked devilish in the shadow of the dim the corner.

'And Gorran Porth can go back to being a quiet little town, and you can go back to running your guest house.'

I didn't have a guest house to run, but I didn't bother to correct him.

'What about you?' I asked him.

'I'm a Cornishman, I'm here to stay, now. We leave, but we always come back.'

We sat on in silence for a bit, people smiling over at us but leaving us cocooned against the party, each of us with our memories.

Eventually Loomes blundered up, insisting I had more champagne. I was going to regret this in the morning. I was so glad the guest house was empty. The night got hotter and louder and I whirled around the room, getting dizzy and laughing until my throat hurt again. Eventually some older people had to leave – Petey took Nat home. I hugged them both at the doorway, Petey a broken man.

'I'm so sorry,' I told him.

He shrugged. 'She'll get what's coming.'

Nat lumbered out into the night and Petey had to rush off in pursuit.

Pat linked her arm through mine and we watched them leaving in silence.

'Pat,' I said, when they were out of sight. 'Nick came round to see me last night.'

Pat's eyes were wide and sparkling. 'I knew it!' she said, 'soon as I saw you, I thought – 'she's had her baps buttered'.'

We collapsed into peals of laughter, bent over, clinging to each other, laughing with relief and the sheer joy of being alive. We recovered ourselves as Malcolm came up to say goodnight.

'Thank you for inviting me,' he said to Pat. 'I've had a lovely time.'

'Malcolm, we couldn't celebrate without you,' Pat said, putting her hand on his arm. 'I'm sorry your wife couldn't make it.'

'Ah, well.' He looked flushed. 'I wanted to talk to you about that. I know this is a social occasion, so perhaps I could come and see you, in the next few days?'

I looked at Pat. She looked away, twirling a curl of hair around one finger.

Malcolm went on. 'I know what you said, Pat, you aren't detectives, I know that, but I thought, well, you do sort things out, don't you, and honest, I don't know where to turn.'

Pat looked at me with a 'what are you going to say to that?' look on her face.

'We are NOT detectives,' I said, firmly. Malcolm's face glowed forlornly in the green exit light above the bar door. 'But we'll do what we can.'

Malcom left and Trevor came up behind us and the three of us stepped out onto the doorstep of the pub, the sound of the sea in the harbour overpowered by the sound of the party. The rest of the pub was closed now, the bar dim and silent behind us, but the throb of feet and music coming from the room above was comforting. I felt part of something, yet separate. My hot face welcomed the cool air and I took in deep breaths of the night.

'What's that smell?' I said. 'There's a blossomy sort of smell.'

Trevor and Pat sniffed the air, one on either side of me.

'Ah, that's the Clematis armandii,' Trevor said. 'Lovely old thing in the back garden of Dove Cottage. Used to be Uncle Nat's aunty lived there, but it's a holiday home now.'

'It's a lovely smell,' I said.

'I do always think,' Pat said, 'that's the smell of spring.'

I linked an arm though each of theirs.

'I've started to think,' I said, 'that's the smell of home.'

ACKNOWLEDGE-MENT

ABOUT THE AUTHOR

Suzy D Harris

Thank you for reading.

If you've enjoyed The Second Envelope, please leave a review and keep in touch for news of the next book in the series.

suzydharris.org

Printed in Great Britain
by Amazon